DARK VIDEO

A novel by Peter Church

Catalyst Press

Livermore, California

For further information,
write Catalyst Press,
2941 Kelly Street, Livermore CA 94551
or email info@catalystpress.org

In North America, this book is distributed by
Consortium Book Sales & Distribution, a division of Ingram.
Phone: 612/746-2600
cbsdinfo@ingramcontent.com
www.cbsd.com

In South Africa, Namibia, and Botswana,
this book is distributed by LAPA Publishers.
Phone: 012/401-0700
lapa@lapa.co.za
www.lapa.co.za

FIRST EDITION
10 9 8 7 6 5 4 3 2 1
Library of Congress Control Number: 2018964623

Cover design by Karen Vermeulen, Cape Town, South Africa

ISBN 9781946395214

Printed by Creda Printers, South Africa

FOREWORD

by Peter Church

As Y2K and its trepidation announced itself, the fears of machines exploding and cities being crippled by computer failure was soon replaced by an irresistible torrent of technological advancement that would agitate earth's billions of human inhabitants into a heightened frenzy of social networking.

It unleashed a new era that would forever change the business of art, music and literature, and disrupt and destroy countless businesses and industries as diverse as publishing, manufacturing and retail.

Skip forward to 2006, not long ago, but may as well be a million years past in tech developments. Back then, Netflix rented physical DVDs via the postal service, Microsoft was ready to bomb with Windows Vista, and the ability to move large amounts of data via flash drives was in its infancy. Smart phones? Huh? App Stores? Never heard of them. Nor Google Chrome, Solid State Drives, Amazon Kindle readers. And Uber, AirBnB, Twitter and Instagram hadn't even twinkled in the eyes of their maverick founders.

But Alistair Morgan, "golden boy" and university law student, is perfectly positioned to ride the new tech wave. Digital video sharing via YouTube is the hot new fad and FaceBook has emerged as a preferred platform for connecting with friends on the Net.

The backdrop is the city of Cape Town with its glorious scenery and compromised Third World potential, in a country where, despite a decade of "one man one vote" democracy, equality is a distant dream. In this carefree and privileged environment, dark forces lurk beneath the surface like a Great White shark cruising the blue waters of False Bay.

It is in this crucible of time and space that powerful criminal corporations can still, outside the prying eye of an effective internet authority, peddle illicit videos to wealthy individuals.

It is the time of Dark Video.

⊙

ALONG THE FOOTPATH

She never saw it coming.

First light, six o'clock on a Sunday morning, she ran with her head down. The boyfriend was on her mind. How long was it now? Two months? They'd met during the first week at varsity. No time to assess the market, but she'd gone for it anyway and was the envy of her friends; going out with a first team rugby player, six foot two, built and good looking. Introduced at a Rag Royalty function, with all the rugby players and the beauty queens in attendance. She'd even met his parents.

Left, right, left, right; she was in a good rhythm.

Despite his physical presence, he was quiet; dare she say it, dull. The night before, she'd excused herself early, bored with stories of the day's game, boys chugging beer, his ex-girlfriend's gang huddling in a group and eyeing her out, rugby groupies pretending to be interested. She'd fancied an evening out clubbing with her friends—but settled for an early night and a run with her friend Katie the next morning.

Except that Katie had car trouble. So she ran alone.

Even in running kit, Terri Phillips was attractive: a fresh faced nymph with peachy skin; straight blonde hair tied tightly against her face, pony bobbing from the back of a dark blue cap; tanned legs finished with fluffy socks in a pair of white tackies.

She bounced along the cement footpath on the misty slope of Table Mountain, past the university campus, in the direction of Newlands Forest. Eyes down, iPod pumping, wondering about her love life.

Smack! She ran straight into someone traveling in the opposite direction.

"Sorry, sorry."

She was still looking down, her head almost against the shoulder of the person she'd collided with. A man with a red jersey. She stepped aside, but his arm folded around her back and held her tightly.

"Hey," she said.

She tried to lift her hands to push him away; his hands slid down and grasped her wrists.

"Hey!"

The panic had not yet arrived. It was a friend, someone playing a trick on her. It had to be. The earpieces from the iPod fell from her head.

More hands came from behind now, covering her mouth and eyes. Too late to scream. The terror struck, a frenzy of warning signals erupting from her brain. She wrestled violently, twisting, a fly in a web, the sound of her own muffled yell venting the surge of her fear.

The man in front pushed her backwards, away from the road, toward the forest. She tensed her legs, trying to root herself to the spot, trying to sit down, but she suddenly felt them lifted up off the ground. She struggled desperately, nails clawing, frantically trying to free herself.

A scarf was tied around her head, covering her eyes, blinding her. A third person? She went limp; this was every woman's fear.

The trio carried her deeper into the forest where the early morning light struggled to break through. When she wriggled, the hands on her body intensified their grips until she ceased. She became still, paralyzed with fear; the footfalls on the undergrowth and her own hard breath the only sounds.

After what seemed like ages, her assailants came to a stop, lowered her to the ground, a bed of pine needles, arms still pinioning her.

She heard a voice for the first time, over her, soft but forceful. "Listen. Don't scream. If you do, I'll hurt you. Follow my instructions exactly and you'll be fine. Do you understand?"

Terri nodded. The voice was familiar; no one she recognized, but the type of person she might associate with. A reasonable voice. The hand came away from her mouth.

"What are you going to do to me?" she whispered.

"Don't talk. I won't hurt you. But no noise. Do you understand?"

Again Terri nodded. The remaining arms released her; she clutched her knees to her body.

"OK now do exactly what I say and, before you know it, we'll let you go."

She heard footsteps moving away from her, one person, but the presence of her other captors remained close. She could feel hot breath in her face.

"Take off your pants and pass them to me."

Terri went cold. The glimmer of trust that had been created evaporated in an instant.

"Remember: just do as I say."

"Is this a trick?"

A hand closed on her throat, tightly enough to answer the question.

"You're going to rape me," she said loudly and a slap stung her cheek.

"I said no talking! If you cooperate, we won't hurt you. Now do exactly what I say or there will be consequences."

She started to reply, but a hand cupped quickly over her mouth.

"No words, you hear! Nothing! You've got no choice. Now take off your pants and give them to me."

Terri was wearing a little white vest and short blue running pants. She wanted to tell the man that she wasn't wearing panties, but his hand blocked her mouth.

Why was this happening to her?

"I'm not going to ask you again. Fucking take them off."

Terri was paralyzed. She couldn't do it. She knew what would be next.

"If you don't, I'll just tear them off." The tone had regained its composure, but the threat was no less frightening.

Terri lifted her bottom off the ground and slowly slipped her running shorts down to her ankles. The hand detached from her mouth and whipped her shorts over her shoes. She whimpered, streams of tears running down her face, her hands quickly covering her groin.

"Mmm. Good girl. Now do the same with your vest."

"Please..." She could feel eyes on her body; she wanted an explanation. But the hand clamped firmly over her mouth. The whimper turned to sobs. A second hand grabbed firmly at her throat.

"Do it!"

She pulled the vest over her head, hands instantly returning to cover herself as it was yanked away. She was now naked, barring a sports bra, her socks and shoes.

"Now the bra."

She had no choice. She pulled the bra over her head and hands snatched it away from her. She instinctively covered herself again, an arm across her breasts, a hand between her legs.

"Now, put your hands behind your head."

"You're going to rape me," Terri whispered shakily.

"Oh I'd love to show you a good time, princess." She felt a hand run down her cheek. "But you'll be fine. Just do as I say."

She gasped as her arms were pulled roughly from behind, away from their protective zones. Even through her fear, she was aware of her exposed breasts, embarrassed by her nakedness.

"Hands behind your head! I'll keep my side of the bargain. You'll see."

She shook uncontrollably, elbows pointing forward, hands quivering behind her head; breath coming in short gasping sobs.

"Now, count to a hundred, sitting like you are, hands behind your head. Don't move. Don't call out. If you do, there'll be trouble. When you reach one hundred, you can take off the blindfold. Not before. You'll find your clothes nearby. Dress yourself and go back to wherever you came from. Don't try to look for us. You understand?"

She nodded consent, confused and disbelieving.

She heard the man behind her rise, then the man in front, the voice. Their footsteps trampled away across the dry undergrowth, each step a crackle, moving away, back toward the highway.

Terri counted slowly, ears tuned, each sound and scent amplified by her blindness, expecting the sudden reappearance of her tormentors. She shifted her seat on the bed of pine needles, resisting the temptation to get up and bolt for safety, resisting the temptation even to remove her hands from her head. What would be waiting for her when she took off the blindfold?

The footsteps disappeared gradually until complete silence enveloped her, the sound of her shallow breathing and her thumping heart was all that remained. It was surreal. She was alone, naked, blindfolded, counting to a hundred. Was this a joke?

When she reached the count, she removed the blindfold, a torn piece of checked material, and looked around nervously. Somewhere in the Newlands Forest on a blanket of pine needles, she sat, naked bar her socks and shoes. She covered her breasts again, hugging herself for warmth, her hands lodged in her armpits.

There was no one in sight. She rose tentatively to her feet. Red welts ringed her wrists; raised bangles of broken skin. Her white vest lay crumpled inside out on the ground, next to the iPod, still in its holder. She stumbled over to them, clutching; adjusted the vest and quickly pulled it over her head; picked up the iPod, scanned nervously back and forth, expecting her assailants to materialize at any second and the nightmare to resume.

Where were her pants? Her instinct told her to sprint down toward the road and safety, but her modesty declined. Find the pants! Besides, the footsteps had departed in that direction—perhaps they were waiting for her to ambush again. For a moment she appeared posed, her hands cupped over her crotch, shielding her nudity from the forest.

"What on earth?" She shook her head, raised a hand to her forehead.

Silence rung through the forest, the lack of movement strangely reassuring. All that remained of her attack and her attackers were rough indentations in the pine needles. She turned around, dusting off the dirt and pine needles that remained stuck to her naked bottom, started scouting around for the rest of her clothes. Her cap lay at the foot of a tree. She picked it up then, looking up, spotted her blue shorts suspended from a branch, several meters off the ground. How to get them? She jumped up, but they remained out of reach. A few half-hearted leaps before she abandoned the cause, examining her surroundings in search of a stick.

The silence was broken by a sound from higher up the mountain, a crunching of steps on the forest path, an imminent danger. Terri froze, body rigid, terror returning like a dark cloud blotting out the sun. She sank down to a huddle, legs folded, dreading a new onslaught, more terrified than before. She closed her eyes. If she couldn't see, it wouldn't happen. The footsteps came closer and then stopped. She braced herself.

"Are you OK?"

A new voice this time.

Terri remained rigid, head bowed, eyes tightly shut, fists clenched. To the new arrival, she looked as though she were meditating. Then he noticed she wore no pants. How embarrassing—was she peeing? Perhaps he should continue with his run?

But he didn't.

"Is everything OK?" he repeated. This voice was soft and nonthreatening, but she couldn't allow herself to look up. She felt a hand on her shoulder.

Terri opened her eyes and looked up, her face pale, eyes red. Relief instant, she started to sob.

"What happened to you?" The jogger knelt on his haunches and placed an arm gently around her shoulder. He touched her swollen wrist, his hands soft and cool.

"Have you been...raped?" The horror word.

Terri shook her head, hugging her knees tightly.

"Are you hurt?"

Again she shook her head.

"Can you get my pants?" Terri asked, pointing to a branch. His eyes followed her indication. He stood and walked toward the tree, scratching the back of his head. He was her age, maybe a couple of years older. Average height, probably a student, like her. He looked embarrassed.

He jumped up and tried to flick the pants off the branch but they were snagged on some smaller branches and he lacked the height to dislodge them. He turned around and shrugged his shoulders.

"I need to find a stick." He looked about, but no suitable tool existed. He glanced back at her, still seated, knees folded up under her chin, watching him, a traumatized child waiting for a parent to come to the rescue.

"If I give you a leg up, you should be able to reach them."

She stared at him, not moving.

"I'm naked." Through her sobs, she laughed at her predicament.

"I noticed. Look, not a time to be modest," he replied, trying to take control. "Come, I can give you my pants if you really want."

She pondered her dilemma, upper teeth on lower lip.

"I won't look, promise," he said, cupping his hand against his nearest eye, his discomfort lightening her embarrassment.

"Oh, what the hell." Terri stood up, making a token effort to shield her nudity. The jogger stooped down to his haunches and linked his hands as a foothold.

"No looking," she said, as she stepped her right foot in, locking her legs and holding the top of his head for balance. With his averted face pressed in to her thigh, he slowly raised himself to full height.

"You OK?" she asked, holding on to his head.

He grunted.

She accepted an upturned hand as support, glancing below and behind her in a sudden flash of modesty and imagining how bizarre it must look—a bare-bottomed girl, balancing precariously on the shoulders of a stranger, like a circus trapeze artist preparing for a stunt. Thank god, no one was watching.

He edged under the branch and she reached up to unhitch the shorts.

"Got it."

He crouched down for her to dismount and then turned away as she quickly pulled on her pants.

"My god," she said, turning to him. "What just happened to me?"

"I don't know. I was just running..."

The fear returned in an instant: "They may still be here!"

"Who?"

Her eyes darted in all directions.

"Look, just relax now. Tell me what happened?"

No answer.

"You're safe, OK. What's your name? I'm Alistair Morgan. Are you at UCT?"

UCT—University of Cape Town—familiar. A spark of composure returned. She looked at him. He, too, was vaguely familiar: good-looking, boyish features, friendly blue eyes. He wore a white T-shirt and black running shorts that looked shiny and new.

"We must get away, out of the forest. Maybe they'll come back." Terri's gaze shifted nervously. Confused, irrational.

"Uh, who are they?"

No reply. She advanced a few steps and scanned the surroundings.

"What're you looking for?"

She ran her hand across her chest and continued to glance around. "Nothing."

Where was her bra?

DARK VIDEO

She turned to him and gripped his wrist tightly. "Please stay with me. Promise you won't leave me."

"I won't leave you, I promise." He reached out to her and held her tightly against his chest; the shudder of her sobs sent a tremor through his body.

"Let's get you back home. Where do you stay? In res?"

With his arm protectively draped over her shoulder, he shepherded her toward the path, and back down to the road.

(▶)

Alistair Morgan escorted the frightened girl along the footpath adjacent to campus. They walked in silence for fifteen minutes across the empty UCT rugby fields, through the subway beneath Rhodes Drive and down Woolsack Drive toward the Kopano Men's Residence. Eventually Alistair spoke.

"Did they steal anything?"

Terri shook her head and showed him her iPod. She stopped, sat down on the pavement and put her hand to her face, tears running between her fingers. Alistair lowered himself on his haunches and placed a consoling arm over her shoulder.

"You make it right, boy," came a voice from across the road. They looked up to see a tall foreign student walking past in the other direction, another early riser; they ignored him.

"I feel so violated. As if someone has taken my most precious possession."

Alistair patted her on the back, not knowing what to say.

"Come now, Terri!" she scolded herself.

"Did you get a look at them?"

"No. It happened so fast. I was looking down and ran into someone. He was wearing a red tracksuit top, hoodie up, I think. That's all I saw. I didn't see their faces. But I'll remember the voice anywhere."

"The voice?"

"Yes. English speaking with a slight accent, a Cape Town accent. Our age. Must've been a student."

"Black or white?"

She shrugged.

"I think white."

"And any others?"

"Two or three. The man who spoke, then someone who grabbed me from behind. And a third man, I think. Yes. He blindfolded me and helped them drag me from the path."

"Jesus, that's crazy stuff. What were they doing?"

Terri didn't answer. She continued looking out in front of her, the experience too bizarre to contemplate. Here she was, sitting on the side of the road with a fellow student, unhurt, on a normal Sunday morning. She examined her swollen wrist; the red marks were already fading. Yet something strange and frightening had happened to her. Was it a practical joke? An act of revenge?

Alistair seemed to read her mind.

"Does someone want to make a fool of you?"

"Maybe." She laughed, wiping tears from her eyes.

"That's what it looks like to me. Friends of a jealous girlfriend?"

"Well, fuck them," she said defiantly. "Next time I will run with pepper spray. Fuck them!"

Alistair felt the words like a slap in the face, their harshness in contrast to the girl's gentle demeanor. Defiance. He was impressed.

Terri stood up and wiped her tears with the fabric of her vest. "Come on, let's go."

They continued down Woolsack, crossing the road and coming to Kopano, Alistair's residence. The low fence around it was hardly an imposing reflection of its common nickname, Belsen.

"We need to report what happened at the police station," said Alistair. "I'll drive you."

Terri stopped suddenly, leaving him to walk a pace or two before halting and looking back at her.

"I don't want to do that. They didn't do anything to me. They didn't hurt me. They didn't steal anything. I don't understand what they wanted. I just want to forget about it and get back to my room." She indicated Tugwell Residence, one of two dirty orange towers further down the road.

"I really don't think you have a choice here, Terri. You've got to report it. They were probably planning to rape you or even worse, and something must've scared them off. I know it's difficult. But if it happens to someone else, you'll feel responsible."

Alistair was studying law, a top third-year student at UCT, persuasive and principled.

"Come on, I'll go with you. My car's just around the corner."

⊙

The Rondebosch Police Station was quiet, a long wooden counter separating the law from the victims.

"We don't have a female officer to examine her," said the constable as he filled in the case docket. "I can call one in for her."

Terri crossed her legs.

"She doesn't need to be examined," said Alistair. "She wasn't raped."

The constable put down his pen and surveyed the complainants. He checked back through his notes.

"She was sexually violated, you said."

"But they didn't actually rape her. And they didn't...violate her either."

"So attempted rape, then?"

"No. Er, maybe. But I don't think so."

"OK, son, let's get this straight. They grabbed her, dragged her into the forest, made her remove her clothes and then left her."

"That's about right."

The constable looked skeptically from Alistair to Terri. "This sounds like normal student behavior," he muttered. He had manned the office the previous week during the Belsen Beer Race, the phones inundated with calls from irate residents complaining of public nudity and drunken behavior.

Terri started to cry again.

"Look," said Alistair. "Why don't you focus on taking the statement and giving us a case number?"

The constable returned to his script with a shake of the head. Alistair watched him closely as he continued his documentation.

$\odot$

"I can't thank you enough," said Terri, as Alistair turned his car into Rondebosch Main Road, escorting her back to her residence. He seemed as relieved as his passenger to be done with the police station, and he smiled as he drove.

"No sweat."

They pulled up at the lights. He looked across to her, glancing down briefly and noticing the darkness of her nipples pressed against the thin white material of her vest. A moment's silence before Terri shifted self-consciously in her seat, obscuring his view with her shoulder.

"Sorry," said Alistair, looking back at the road. But he couldn't help himself. "Do you always run like that?"

She reddened. "No, of course not. It's weird, I couldn't find my bra. I guess I wasn't exactly—with it." She started to laugh. He looked over to her again and laughed with her. The shake of her mirth jiggled her free breasts; he felt a stirring in his pants. An unexpected development.

"What's happening to me?" she said, laughing and crying at the same time. "It's a nightmare. Pinch me, wake me up."

He gave her a mock pinch on the leg and shifted in his seat, grateful for his loose-fitting shorts. The morning's events had suddenly shifted focus.

Terri leaned back in her seat. It smelled new.

"Nice car."

"You like? She's my baby." Alistair parked his new Audi A3 adjacent to the bus station outside Tugwell. Terri hopped out and walked around to the driver's window, shoulders hunched, arm across her chest.

"Please don't tell anyone about this." Her cap balanced strangely on her head.

He put his finger to his lips.

"Give me a shout if you need to talk. You know where Belsen is," he said, gesturing up the road. "I'm on Green second."

"Thank you."

"What a start to the day!"

"I just can't believe this happened to me." She held a hand up to her face.

"You shouldn't run on your own, I guess."

"I don't normally. I usually run with a friend. She didn't pitch this morning and I thought...well, I need the exercise. Anyway."

He watched her walk away; as she reached the Tugwell entrance, she turned around and looked back.

Alistair waved as he pulled away.

FIXING BUGS

The computer boffin battled bugs in the code; coffee mugs littered his desk, the ashtray overflowed with cigarette butts.

Four a.m. on a Sunday in Seattle, any twenty-five-year-old in his right mind would have been in bed with a throbbing head. Or, even better, still working on the headache.

But the Watchit help desk had called him at three o'clock the previous day—in the middle of a gaming session—to report that the new code, laid down on Friday, released Saturday morning, was crashing. It was his change. Luckily they'd phoned him directly. If he could solve it quickly no one else need know.

He'd tried a remote fix, logging in from his laptop and busting through a fortress of security and firewalls. But the noise from his pals' computer warring, and the unseasonable heat, and the tiny issue of the glitch that just wouldn't show itself, set him on the one hour drive to headquarters in Redmond.

In the humming sanity of an airconditioned computer room, he isolated the problem. But it didn't make sense.

The changes he'd made the week before were gone. It seemed as if someone had rolled back the software to an earlier version, one that excluded the latest security fixes.

So there he sat, surrounded by monitors and coffee cups, trying to work out how the hell quality control had overwritten his code and allowed some fucking hacker to deface the Help screen with a recipe for making Molotov cocktails. Not the kind you drink.

If he didn't solve the problem before escalation, his next few weeks would be snowed with post mortems, paper forests of reports, and flesh on flesh sessions with the supervisor. Ever since Watchit had started taking off, with volumes nearing five million downloads a day, they'd been flooded with creeps talking security and controls. The good old days in the back of the garage were a dream compared to this. Thank Christ he didn't work for YouTube.

The fix he'd created patched up the vulnerability, but he couldn't be sure something else hadn't been inserted. It was like looking for a flea on a camel's back. Better to bury it, no harm done, and avoid the scrutiny of the company's security officer. Wouldn't want them finding out about all his backdoor entries.

The screen monitoring incoming submissions beeped. He wheeled his chair across to the large screen that monitored incoming videos: 1,775 new postings since last release on Saturday evening. The censorship guys would be in at eight tomorrow to publish the new submissions. Everything had to be checked. The buzz words were "subversive" and "offensive." The video of the two women eating shit out of a cup had changed the game forever.

He rolled the cursor down the screen, curious as to the identity of the four a.m. sender, a fellow sufferer, beholden to the night. Or perhaps he was attached to his screen in the middle of the day on the other side of the world...

And that's when he saw it. A little black box that danced across the screen so quickly that he nearly missed it. If he'd blinked, he might have missed the flashing title: Dark Video. And when he looked for the new submission, it was gone. He shook his head to restart his brain.

"I must be imagining things."

The whirring of the machines and the air conditioning seemed to intensify. He felt as though he was aboard a giant spaceship.

"Coffee, I need coffee!" he said, as he dragged himself off to the kitchen.

THE TROJAN

Not far from Redmond—less than a shimmy to the left with a Google Earth cursor—Carlos De Palma, not his real name, was also awake, in his five million dollar Yarrow Point mansion.

He sat in his blue and white pajamas in front of a widescreen terminal, tapping his toes and waiting to confirm that the new Trojan Horse planted on www.watchit.com was operational. Ever since the Feds had shut down his Dark Video site, he'd been looking for an alternate input channel.

Watchit was vulnerable, ballistic growth in volumes, too many youngsters battling with complex security features; his hackers hadn't raised a sweat. After the OK had come from Redmond on Saturday morning, he'd emailed his agents to confirm the news: Dark Video was back in business.

Carlos caressed the keyboard with manicured fingers. He couldn't wait to see the videos bubbling under; it had been more than a month since his last channel was closed.

His screen flashed as the first submission appeared before him. "Nigeria stoning" read the title. He'd been expecting it. The grainy video came to light on his screen in jerky motions.

A furious crowd on the rampage, the backs of their heads bobbing, fists raised, violent movements; then a young woman stripped to her underwear, lying prone in the dirt, arms at her head, legs kicking in desperation, rocks and stones bouncing off her body. A full twenty minutes passes, the camera shaking, panning to wild faces and angry gestures, then back to the girl, more and more battered, before she eventually lies unmoving in the dirt, a collection of rocks and cement blocks surrounding her crumpled body.

Not bad. Too long, he'd have to edit it down—but not bad. Streets ahead of the low quality cellphone footage of the Kurdish stoning that had done the rounds some time back.

A noise startled him and he quickly muted the sound. No way his wife would be awake; she'd been up with the baby until midnight. He rubbed his face as he listened. Stubble already; he shaved twice a day but the growth was relentless. He could almost hear the hair growing on his body.

Nothing. Perhaps his senses were playing tricks on him again.

Carlos restarted the video and watched it frame by frame, cutting and pasting squares from the image and then magnifying them in a separate window.

It was real, he was sure. He'd already received the newspaper story and confirmation from the source. After ten years in the business, he had a feel for authenticity. But he'd double check tomorrow, let the tech boys inspect it.

He scanned his email box: sixteen out of seventeen agents replied and confirmed. All except Cape Town. He frowned and texted a reminder.

> Hey I know its Africa but r u guys with it??
> u get the msg?

It had taken a decade to build up the list of agents. Quality, not quantity. The Cape Town connection was one of his more recent acquisitions. Nothing marketable yet, but they'd shown promise; their next submission would hopefully make the grade.

He shook his head thinking about the shit floating about: bland reality bloating the bandwidth, poorly filmed, missing the point. Show the fear! It's what his clients demanded. And it's what he gave them.

Carlos kicked back his chair and stretched, looking through the window of his study into the black night. He couldn't see it, but he knew it was out there, a lush, verdant green lawn that sloped downwards, lined by rows of tall pines placed like sentries along the perimeter, to the water, and views of Carillon Point and Lake Washington. His wife loved Yarrow Point; a few hundred houses, a cultured social mix of well-to-do families. Tomorrow he'd walk the preserve, socialize with the old money, and cough up a generous donation. Hopefully, this one would secure him membership to the Yacht Club. When the neighbors asked, he told them he'd made his money in the dotcom boom. Not entirely untruthful. Even his wife believed it. And as long as she was happy...

He watched the Nigerian frenzy again, freezing on an image of the anguished woman, her face etched with the expression of a sacrificed animal.

"They're going to love this," he said out loud.

Carlos didn't keep a physical list of clients. Everything was committed to memory. He mentally scanned for possible clients, the keywords "snuff" and "violence." Then he would need to get phone numbers, locations and time zones.

"Let's start with Asia."

ALL THE TIME

Darkness in Washington, daylight in Cape Town.

The man in the black polo neck received a text message on his cellphone. He glanced at the screen, frowned, considered the time zone.

"You must relax," said the man opposite, behind a large yellowwood desk. He sat slightly side on, adjusting his glasses and looking down at a yellow manila file in his lap.

"I am relaxed, Dr. Adams," came the reply. The man sat erect in the chair, his hands clasped together in his lap. "Let's get on with it."

The psychiatrist looked up at his patient. "How long have you been in therapy?"

"Fifteen years."

"I see." Dr. Adams skimmed over the file, then looked up and stared carefully at the man in the polo neck. "You've changed therapists many times."

"Once a year. They ask the same questions. It gets boring. A change of scenery is pleasant." He smiled politely. The only window in the room looked straight onto the brick wall of an adjacent building.

"Do you still think about what happened?"

"Yes. Every day, I'd say."

Dr. Adams turned a page in the file, examining several photographs attached with paper clips to the cardboard. They showed a nude boy, his dark hair wet and matted, his body covered with welts and burns. He'd studied them closely. This patient wasn't his run of the mill Prozac mom.

"And do you think it affects your ability to function normally?"

"No."

"But you say you think about it every day."

"All the time." The man in the polo neck ran his hand through his hair. It was smooth and black, the same color as his jersey. He looked briefly at his hand and then placed it back in his lap.

"Do you find these sessions helpful?"

"No."

"But you never miss one."

"They're compulsory. After what happened, it was...a condition."

Dr. Adams turned another page. He ran his hand across his mouth. A color photograph showed a man lying on the floor. There was a knife in his temple. He looked up and smiled blandly.

"Of course," he said. "But I need to help you move on now."

"I have moved on, Doctor."

"But you still think about it?" He shuffled through some loose draw-ings. They showed a stick man with a knife in his head, red koki pen dripping from the wound.

"It is a choice," he answered.

Dr. Adams indicated with his palm for his patient to continue.

"I never want to forget the type of people that are out there." While he spoke, his fingers worked on his cellphone:

```
Got your message, Dark Video.
We have some new work to send you
```

GORILLAS

The digs in Lovers' Lane displayed no plaque announcing "Gorillas" as its name. But it had been known as such for three decades and now served as home to Devon Deacon, Johnny Jackson, and Richard Walker. Devon, the most respectable looking of the three, had secured the lease with old Miss Duckworth, and the long suffering spinster said they were the best tenants she'd ever had. They were all into their third lapsed year at university, credit wise; none much further than first year level from an academic results perspective. But the rent was always paid and for that she was grateful.

Their attire disclosed personality. Devon, the leader: a thin polo neck jersey, sleeves rolled up above the elbows uniformly on both sides, black stonewashed jeans and black shoes. Johnny, the bruiser: a faded white T-shirt, RHODESIA IS SUPER emblazoned across the front, short khaki pants and bare feet. Richard, the nerd: tight blue jeans with a belt, a short sleeve lounge shirt with glasses case in the pocket, brown and white docksiders matching neither his pants nor his shirt.

The three housemates sat in darkness in the living room, leaning forward, focused intently on a big-screen TV.

A knock on the front door. Devon killed the DVD; Johnny jumped up and padded quickly into the entrance hall.

"Who is it?" called Devon.

"It's just him," said Johnny returning to the lounge and gesturing with his thumb as Alistair Morgan followed behind. Alistair nodded his hellos and slumped into an easy chair.

The Gorillas' abode had once been gracious, an old landmark now neglected. The living room reeked of years of student life and spilled beer; ceilings yellowed, windows warped. Functionally, it exhibited the goods: a faux leather settee in navy blue, a couple of armchairs, some mismatched low tables, thick curtaining—a hodgepodge of aliens in a room with flaking paint. But if the furniture lacked class, no deficiency applied to the electronic equipment in the room: two big screen TVs, a DVD player, video machines, an impressive sound system with amplifier and several large speakers, a collection of sophisticated camera equipment lying on the carpet against the wall, two PC work stations, all connected 24/7 to the internet via an ADSL line.

"Rewind, rewind!" demanded Richard, uninterested in the new arrival. He wiped his mouth. A dim light filtered through the drawn curtains.

"So what's it look like?" asked Alistair, looking over to Devon.

Devon's eyes were alight. "Perfect. Do you have a case number?"

Alistair nodded.

"Take a look," said Devon, navigating with the DVD remote. "*Forest Frolic*. Scene one. Take one. Scenic impressions of a lush green forest. Lovely foliage. Peaceful. Beautiful setting. What have we here? Three young men and a lady. Spoiling my fine documentary."

Alistair leaned forward.

"Look at her shaking. She almost wet herself," said Richard, fiddling with the rim of his spectacles as if adjusting the focus.

The video continued with clarity, a paralyzed girl deposited on the ground, three men surrounding her, their faces not identifiable.

"You blocked the camera there," said Devon.

"I tried to get rid of my tracksuit," Alistair replied. "We must cut that piece. If she ever..."

"Relax. She'll never see it."

On the screen, a man in a red hoodie demanded and accepted pieces of clothing from the girl. The camera zoomed in on her naked body, shivering and shaking, eyes blindfolded; then in the background came the sound of departing footsteps.

"My master stroke was snagging her shorts in the tree," said Johnny. "It provides the best cinema."

The screen remained focused on the girl, hands behind her head, the camera flicking at her breasts, into the dark cleft between her legs. Beneath the image, a counter ticked the seconds away.

"A minute and a half," said Richard. "She counted slowly."

The girl removed her blindfold, stood up shakily, and retrieved her vest.

"This is my favorite bit." Johnny rubbed his hands together, watching intently as the camera hovered tightly around the girl's rear, swatches of pine needles attached to her buttocks. She reached vainly to free her pants from the tree. "Jump, baby, jump!"

Richard giggled nervously.

"And here's the Good Samaritan," said Devon, as Alistair jogged into picture. The girl shrank, clutching herself.

"Can you hear what he said to her?"

"Climb up on my shoulders, baby!" Johnny grabbed the remote from Devon and paused the screen, running each frame in slow motion as the girl mounted Alistair's shoulders. "That's the bit you missed."

Alistair whistled, transfixed by what he saw.

"Now check there," said Richard. "She's searching for her bra. She's too embarrassed to tell you." He giggled again.

"Here it is, baby, here it is," taunted Johnny, swinging a white sports bra in his hand. Alistair glanced sideways at Devon, but his gaze was locked on the screen.

The video faded as Terri and Alistair slipped out of camera.

Alistair remained in his chair, stroking the day old growth on his chin with the one hand and gently shaking his keys with the other. Devon looked over to him, awaiting his verdict.

"Very clever shooting," said Alistair. "You don't see a single shot of my face."

Devon smiled.

"Why thank you, Alistair. Not that it matters. I'll edit out the bits where your tracksuit shows."

Devon grabbed the remote from Johnny and zapped backwards.

"I want to show you guys something. These are the money shots. You think it's the tits and ass. That helps, obviously. But it isn't. It's the face. The expression. When realization sets in. Look here."

He froze on the frame with Terri taking off the blindfold, advanced forward frame by frame.

"See her expression. It's priceless. She's talking to us without saying a word."

He scrolled forward.

"Look. Here's where she hears Alistair. Before he even comes into picture. See. There. She's heard his footsteps, her whole body cringes, her eyes widen."

"OK, the expressions. Whatever," said Johnny. "Give me a go."

Johnny commandeered the remote and located the moment where Terri mounted Alistair's shoulder. The camera moved in, her pine-needled ass filling the screen.

"Now that's my money shot!"

"The girl, she's flippin' gorgeous," said Alistair. "Where did you find her?"

Devon and Richard shared a quick glance.

"Ask Johnny."

Johnny looked around smugly. "Her new boyfriend's ex pointed her out to me. Says she's a smug little bitch. I saw her dancing at the rugby club. A real little white underwear number."

"The ex-girlfriend doesn't know, I hope?"

"Of course not, Morgan. Do you think I've got shit for brains?"

Alistair looked down at Johnny's feet. "As a matter of fact..." He thought better of it and changed the topic, turning to Devon. "Have you spoken to Dark Video yet?"

"Yes. I phoned Carlos. He was still sleeping. I briefed him and based on what I said, he reckons it's worth ten thousand." Devon looked up and glanced around the room, as if expecting comment. "We get half upfront and the rest after he's checked the case number and validated authenticity. But he knows me now. Knows we won't screw him."

"Ten thousand dollars. A job well done." Alistair clapped his hands together, stood up, and walked to one of the computers, screensaver bouncing around the monitor.

"So Dark Video's back in business."

"Big time!" replied Richard, taking a seat at the other PC. He tapped on the keyboard and the three others joined him, standing behind and looking over his shoulder. He connected via Firefox to www.watchit. com. The Watchit home page appeared in a second, showing the latest amateur videos and innocuous shoots approved for viewing. The most recent had been posted four minutes earlier from someone called "hurricane" in Atlanta, "cool vid of marines chillin in iraq," read the caption. The next, from "Goldie" in Toronto, was titled "Skateboarders face plant." The thumbnail displayed a fully kitted skateboarder en route to his destiny against a brick wall. Several more submissions appeared below.

"Man, there's a lot of rubbish on this site," said Alistair. "Who makes all this crap?"

"Millions of self obsessed net junkies," replied Devon. "Welcome to Web 2.0, my friend."

"What a waste of bloody time. And they don't even get paid for their troubles."

"Maybe not on YouTube. But Watchit pays for the better clips. Up to five hundred dollars maybe."

"Serious? For this shit?"

"Not this stuff. The clips that end up in members only. Watchit may be smaller than YouTube, but it's edgier. They charge for the racier stuff that YouTube has to censor."

"But this is minor league compared to Dark Video," said Richard, joining in. "Watchit is just our entry point."

He pressed a sequence of control characters and moved the cursor back and forth across the screen.

"Where is it?" he moaned. "Where the....Aha!"

Suddenly a floating advert appeared on the screen: white writing on a black box. Richard navigated the mouse over the advert and clicked on it, but it darted away and disappeared. He waited and the box reappeared lower down on the screen. He swiped the cursor over the advert and clicked.

"You've got to be quick," he said. "Like going after a fly with a swatter. Got it!"

The advertising in the black box melted. The box began to expand until it filled the entire screen and the words "DARK VIDEO" blazed across the center of the screen.

Richard retreated from the keyboard, allowing Devon to lean over and enter data into the fields requesting client ID and password. He passed the keyboard back to Richard and "DARK VIDEO" lettering scrolled upwards to the top center of the screen. Two options appeared:

```
Submit Video...............
Review Video...............
```

Richard selected the "Review Video" option. Five thumbnails appeared on the screen showing the first frame of submitted clips. There were no origination details—sender's name or location—as existed on Watchit, only a simple description advertising each thumbnail.

```
"Man shot by police in Las Vegas"
"Stoning in Nigeria" ***NEW***
"Shark attack victim carried out the water"
"Hidden camera in frat house"
"Senator making love to stripper in car"

[NEXT] [PREVIOUS]
```

"The senator! The senator!" yelled Johnny.

Richard clicked on the thumbnail. A message appeared:

```
You are not authorized to view these videos.
Your current authorization is for submissions only.
Should you wish to become a client of Dark Video
then follow the instructions below.
```

The instructions read:
```
Deposit $500 into the account listed below and
```

submit your phone number. A representative
from Dark Video will contact you to discuss
the various options.

"Can't we get Carlos to open up the viewing mode for us?" Johnny
asked.

Devon shook his head. "Are you crazy? I've told you how much Carlos
charges his big clients: twenty thousand dollars or more to view one
video! Most are made to order and you'll never even see them posted.
These videos are for marketing—to attract new clients. Existing clients
go direct. They request a fantasy and Carlos puts the carrot out to his
agents."

"Carrot?" quizzed Alistair.

"We're his mules. He's after the top end, big spender sickos. All
submissions must be one hundred percent authenticated, case number,
newspaper articles. Proof. So the viewer is guaranteed he's viewing the
genuine article."

"But we could've faked it. Terri could be in on the scam. How'd he
know?" asked Alistair.

"He knows. He'd know if she was acting. His clients want to see
emotions, the whole trembling, quivering, crying bit. If he finds out we
conned him, we're history. I heard a story about—"

Johnny cut Devon off. "Ha! He's in America or wherever and we're in
Cape Town. Fat chance he'd catch us."

"Listen to this. I first made contact with Carlos a year or so ago. A few
weeks later, a big black guy walks up to me in the street in Claremont,
just like that, evil-looking bastard with a big seventies afro like he's from
the Jackson Five. T-shirt with a Warner Brothers logo—you know, like the
Laugh Out Loud T-shirts, but the caption says, 'If you see the police then
warn a brother.' Anyway the dude says he's my angel and Carlos sent him
to meet and greet. He's got a honey-sounding voice with a shrill pitch.
His voice and body don't match. He tells me a fairy story about how an
angel is a devil that has lost its horns, and..."

Johnny guffawed and pulled a packet of smokes from his pocket.
"Sounds like a big fairy."

"You're not going to smoke in here," whined Richard.

Devon continued unperturbed: "Warnabrother. Any problems, Carlos
says he'll be paying us a visit. They can't afford to mess about so I reckon
we can expect him soon. He'll check out our story. Carlos earns over a
hundred K from one standard video, if the quality's right. Subtract the

lousy ten thousand he pays us and there's plenty of budget remaining to validate the product. Low volume, high quality."

"Does he live here?" asked Johnny.

"Who? Warnabrother? No, he flits around the world on Dark Video business."

"A hit man? You serious?" Alistair this time.

"Sure I am."

"Shit, that's heavy. I never realized—"

"He's the stick, then," cut in Johnny. "There's the carrot and there's the stick."

"I guess you could say so," laughed Devon. "He's got soft, soft hands. He told me they get dry when he travels by plane. So he coats them in Vaseline and sleeps with gloves on to keep them moist."

"Fucking freak," said Johnny, drumming with his unlit cigarette.

"And he's always whistling," said Richard, as he continued flicking from screen to screen with deft slashes of the mouse. He'd heard it all before from Devon. "Whistling and humming. A big weirdo."

"Ja, you'd know." Johnny snorted, opening the curtains and walking out onto the balcony. He lit his smoke and turned back to face the room.

"Where does Carlos live?" asked Alistair.

Devon shrugged his shoulders. "He could be anywhere. It's irrelevant—the more anonymous, the better. His clients are heavy rollers: ambassadors, big shots in government, movie stars. We think he's American." He patted Richard on his shoulder.

"Carlos must be loaded," Alistair continued. He'd never thought much about the logistics behind Dark Video; he was always more interested in the thrill of the action, happy to let Devon take the lead and deal with the details. But this was their first big project for Carlos and his interest was piqued.

"Absolutely rolling! DV's got a monopoly at the top end. I know only one other outfit daring enough to play the market. They're small, called Mangle."

"Mangle?" enquired Johnny from the balcony. "What sort of a fucking name is that?"

Devon ducked his head. "Shhh! Christ sake, Johnny." Devon scanned the room, a brief encounter with each set of eyes. He lowered his voice. "Don't ever mention the name to Carlos. He goes ballistic. I asked Warnabrother about Mangle. I've never seen the color drain out the face of a black man. He interrogated me for ages. Surprised he didn't put bamboo shoots under my nails."

"Who are they? Where are they from?" asked Alistair.

"No one knows. I mean, who is Dark Video?" replied Devon.

"It's Carlos."

"Is it though? It could be anyone. The business is virtual, no physical bricks and mortar. What does 'Carlos' even mean? He's a voice on a telephone."

Johnny stubbed out his cigarette after a flurry of long drags. He re-entered the room, closed the curtains behind him, and restarted the video.

"I think Johnny's in love with Terri Phillips," joked Richard, sniggering.

"Hey, when last did you get laid, Ritchie?" Johnny's back was up.

"Well, at least when I did, it was with a human."

"Watch your fucking mouth, creepo!"

"Tsk. Tsk. Creepo! The weird words that come out of your mouth."

"I wouldn't talk, you homo."

"Hey, you guys. Cool it. I don't need your bickering!" Devon had had enough.

Alistair chuckled at Devon's restraint. "This is why I stay where I stay," he muttered.

"Well, why don't you fuck off back there, rich boy?"

Alistair shook his head, exchanged a glance with Devon.

Johnny skipped from one frame to the next. "Why wasn't I the Samaritan? I found her! That sweet little beaver rubbing on my neck," Johnny said.

On screen, Terri straddled Alistair's back to collect her shorts in the tree.

"Because you're an animal, Johnny, that's why," Alistair retorted without taking his eyes off the flickering screen. "She would've rather run back to her kidnappers than be saved by you."

"One of these days, Morgan, I'm telling you..."

Devon grabbed the remote from Johnny and paused the video, a reluctant wallpaper, a lingering still of Terri's inelegant dismount.

"Is she still going out with the rugby player?" asked Alistair. An image of dark nipples under her white running vest suddenly popped into his head.

"Yeah," said Johnny. "I saw them together yesterday. Lucky bastard. Wouldn't he love to check out this video?"

"Johnny, I don't need to remind you about the danger of loose lips, do I?" warned Devon.

"Oh yes," added Alistair. "Terri said she'd remember the voice of her assailant anywhere. Best you steer well clear of her..."

"Jesus! Why does everyone keep reminding me like I'm an idiot? I'm in no hurry for a prison term, I assure you."

Richard returned from the kitchen with a six pack of beer, passed the cans around. Alistair declined. The word "prison" felt like a kick in the balls.

"Chin chin," said Richard. Then, almost as an afterthought: "Carlos told Devon we'd get an extra fifty thousand if we raped her. Dollars."

Alistair's eyed widened. Devon shot Richard a dirty look.

"Yes, Morgan! If it wasn't for you," said Johnny. "All that effort! And then you let her go free without having any real fun."

Alistair shook his head. "Making fun of someone is one thing, you psycho. Harming them is another. You have to know where to draw the line."

"You don't think we harmed her?" Devon fixed an inquisitive gaze on Alistair. Alistair looked away, didn't answer.

"And fucking Morgan gets an equal split and did none of the work. We should've showed her a good time." Johnny rubbed his crotch.

"Shut up, Johnny," said Devon. "Rape is a fucking serious offense. I've already told Carlos it's not an option for us. We're not desperate."

"If we were caught..." Richard muttered.

"We're not going to get caught!" Devon interrupted.

Johnny whistled. "Fifty thousand! Think of all the time and planning. If there'd been another runner on the path, we'd have been screwed. A month of planning. Hard work for ten thousand dollars, split four fucking ways!"

"I wouldn't do it for ten times the amount," said Alistair.

"You're an asshole, Morgan," said Johnny. Devon raised his palm to calm things down.

"Anyway. She's diabolically hot! I plan to seduce her the legal way," announced Alistair.

Devon turned sharply on Alistair.

"Relax," Alistair reassured him. "I'll be cool. Remember my role here. She's bound to want to talk to me to deal with it."

"Not you, surely?"

"She'll be too embarrassed to speak to anyone else. Rather she confides in me than someone else. There's no connection."

Devon gave Alistair a long stare.

"What?" said Alistair, a thin smile touching the corner of his mouth.

"I know you too well, Alesandro. It's non-negotiable. Carlos would have a heart attack. If anyone makes contact with her, they'll answer to me." His expression tightened.

Johnny snorted. "As if Morgan would have any chance with her." No one responded. Their eyes were fixed to the flickering screen, Terri in just her vest, tight little ass, jumping vainly in the air. "She's fucking going out with Mr. Rugby. The next captain of the First Team."

"What if she comes to me?" asked Alistair.

"You make sure she doesn't!" said Devon. He flicked the remote and Terri's semi-naked body instantly disappeared from the television.

RED AND WHITE BIKINI

"Hey Maggie." Alistair Morgan darted through the Belsen entrance hall, shirtless, towel around his waist.

"Hello Allie," the receptionist replied. "You want your messages, angel?"

Alistair hit the brakes and turned around. Maggie handed over several sheets of square paper. He scanned the first and crumpled it, flashed a smile at his corpulent admirer.

"Girl problems, angel?" Maggie enquired, shifting her large rump on the hard wooden chair.

"Always." He smiled again, noting her discomfort. "One day I'll buy you a nice soft armchair to sit in, dear Maggie."

"Oh that would be fabulous," she cooed. "I can't sit on this chair for much longer. It's breaking me."

The retort was obvious but Alistair didn't let his charm veneer slip. He looked past her to the clock on the wall. A little after ten, the morning languished—his messages could wait for him to find some sun.

Five minutes later, he reclined next to the Belsen swimming pool. It was officially university property, but Belsen residents claimed moral ownership by virtue of its proximity next door.

Alistair seldom made it to his Monday morning lectures any more; there was always a pretty girl who made good notes. Or a not so pretty one, if need be. He hadn't been completely idle, though. Earlier he had hosed down the A3, a silver number with dropped suspension, his pride and joy. It had been a Christmas present from his father, John Morgan, CEO of Morganstar Communications, non-executive director on no less than seven listed boards. He had been eager to spend double the amount on his only son, but Alistair had certain impressions to uphold. "Too flash and you scare off the younger girls," he'd told Silverman, his neighbor on Green second.

He sprawled on a large, aquamarine towel, eyes hidden behind rimless Police sunglasses, unashamed of his tight blue Speedo masquerading as a banana hammock. A Speedo at the pool was mandatory for an even suntan.

He rolled onto his stomach, cast a lazy eye across the water to a blonde in a red and white bikini. On both sides, a grass embankment sloped down to the concrete edge of the swimming pool; opposite him and behind the girl, a long concrete viewing stand occupied the length of the pool.

He formed a mock screen with his fingers, framed the girl in a make-shift lens. He'd seen her some place before. Or perhaps she'd seen him...

Now what sort of a project could he make with her, he wondered? He adjusted the finger screen. Could she be a candidate for their next sting?

It had been a hard week for the Gorillas household, he reflected. As always, Devon would have planned *Forest Frolic* meticulously, rehearsals repeated over and over. Preparation involved days of painstaking research: single out the victim, observe and understand habits and patterns, discuss times, locations, customize the camera equipment. Practice. Repeat.

Choosing a girl might have been his responsibility. But Johnny had muscled in several weeks earlier, said he had the perfect candidate. For once, he was right. She was pretty, much prettier than Alistair had expected. A tight package—or "toit," as Silverman would say.

If Johnny had had his way....An image of Johnny Jackson closing his rough arms around Terri sent a shudder through him. He was glad he hadn't chosen her.

Johnny had discovered that Terri ran early on Sunday mornings with her friend, Katie. She was clean living, rag royalty, in bed before midnight, leaving the boyfriend to down tequila with the rugger buggers. The two girls always followed a route above Rhodes Drive that passed Newlands Forest, before making their way back through Claremont and Rondebosch to Tugwell Residence.

For a three minute video, the operation had started at four in the morning, with Johnny driving to Observatory and sticking a nail in Katie's car tire. No girl changes a wheel at six a.m. on a Sunday, they'd figured. From there, there were three possibilities. Ideally, Terri would run alone after a call from stranded Katie—green light. But what if Katie borrowed a housemate's car or knew how to handle a car jack? Two girls was risky. They'd have to be more confrontational: Johnny would bring along a knife for show, they'd gag and blindfold Katie, disable her with masking tape and deposit her further up the mountain; she wasn't the main attraction. Then there was the chance that Terri might simply abandon the run—the planning would have to start over.

But Terri was a disciplined girl, it turned out.

Alistair flicked through his remaining messages from Maggie: Mrs. Hamilton, the matron, to say they'd located his missing shirt in the laundry; a reminder about the Belsen Sportman's Dance; and his father.

He flipped open his cellphone and speed dialed a number.

"Alistair," said the clear voice.

Alistair could picture his father in a dark, fitted suit, the collar of his white shirt pressed flat against his neck, the knot of his tie immaculate.

"Dad."

"Thanks for coming back to me, Alistair."

"You should've phoned me on my cell."

"Oh. That's Alice. New secretary. A real secretary.com hire. Probably saw both numbers."

"Cool," said Alistair.

"Cool," said John Morgan.

"So what's up, Dad?"

"How's the work going?"

It was a standard opener, not the reason for the call, but neither an unimportant aside. The father gaining a few measurables to satisfy his curiosity.

"Ninety percent for ethics."

"Not bad. Always good to get the right ten percent wrong in that one." He chuckled on the other side of the line.

Alistair didn't mention that he'd only scraped a high second for his most recent corporate law test. Not up to his usual standard. He'd have to put some actual work in for the next one.

"Listen," his father continued, appeased by ethics. "It's your mother's birthday in two weeks. I'm taking her to Arniston. We'll fly in to Cape Town. Are you available?"

"If I'm not, I will be."

"Excellent. Your mother will be thrilled."

Alistair heard voices in the background and John Morgan's voice dropped to a whisper.

"I'm in a conference call," he said. "Dead boring. Got to go. Will text you the details. Big love, my boy."

"Big love, Dad," replied Alistair, but the line was dead.

He shrugged and reached for his suntan cream; spread it over his face, nose, the tips of his ears. The girl in the red and white bikini discarded her book and strutted confidently toward the pool. She sat down at the concrete edge and dangled her feet into the water. Alistair fancied a swim too; the sun baked down, perspiration pooled in the small of his back.

What was the exchange rate? Eight or so? Multiplied by ten thousand. Eighty thousand rand divided by four. Twenty thousand in his back pocket —but he knew it would be less. Devon would deduct expenses. Ten percent channelled into the "company" pool to enhance electronics or spend on other matters of mutual interest. Maybe seventeen or eighteen thousand? Not a huge amount in his books. John Morgan would send him that much if he asked for it. But independence was desirable.

Alistair was the golden boy, only son, youngest child. Provincial schools rower, like father; talented ball player, like father; gifted law student at UCT, better than father—when he put his mind to it. John Morgan idolized him, and his mother, Glenda, adored him.

Alistair licked his lips as the girl positioned her hands on either side of her, raised her ass, and eased into the water without a splash. A ripple floated from her point of entry across the pool. Alistair watched it make its way toward the far edge, bounce back and lose shape, colliding with the next ripple. The girl kicked off the bottom of the pool and burst out into the air, face sparkling in the light, water showering about her.

She was definitely a candidate.

Eighteen thousand, he thought. Not much. But *Forest Frolic* was their first production for Carlos—no need to push him too early. And Devon made a good point: the risks and dangers increased exponentially on the bigger ticket items. Besides, how do you come up with a big seller that's...morally acceptable? Where do you draw the line?

Alistair thought it appropriate, given his area of study, that the law—or his best interpretation of it—be his guiding influence. What was the worst that could happen if they'd been caught with Terri Phillips in Newlands Forest? It would be laughed off as a silly student prank. Maybe they'd be suspended from university, disciplined. Community service once they'd repented. But Johnny, that fool, talking about "prison." Get real! Sure, Alistair wouldn't want his parents to know, but his father was a student once, in Belsen himself—he'd probably secretly approve of his exploits. My boy! Hadn't he told Alistair about the day they spied on the Warden's daughter?

But he knew it wasn't really about the money. It was the thrill. It made life...invigorating. The Gorillas three were so unlike any of his normal varsity friends, the private-school types he was supposed to hang out with. Devon, what was he? Portuguese? Lebanese? Johnny, an Afrikaans speaking Rhodesian, if that's possible. Richard, a computer nerd with moony skin and blotchy complexion, from the other side of the tracks, a small school in Fish Hoek, or was it Muizenberg? They made his skin crawl and yet he was drawn to them.

How could he forget that first meeting with Devon? At a big twenty-first party in Wynberg, Devon the deejay. Alistair had been bored, the girl he'd been stalking all over some other guy. He'd given up, sidled over to Devon to request a song. Next thing they were chatting like old mates. The variety of music on Devon's laptop hard drive had astounded him; Devon was a computer wizard, it turned out, specializing in downloading pirated CDs; earned ten grand a month on the side playing music and selling CDs. Easy cash. Interesting guy. Made videos, too. A little later, Alistair was flirting with a girl called...what was her name again? Alistair told her to meet him in the upstairs bathroom. She did. But so did her meathead ex-boyfriend, a part-time bouncer. Alistair knew he was in trouble as the first blow landed to the left of his nose, knocking him against the shower stall, the bouncer finding his sights. He'd braced himself for the second, knockout blow. But it never came. When he opened an eye, Devon was standing behind his attacker, one hand on his shoulder, the other gripping tightly between his legs, the bouncer's red face contorted in pain.

"This here is my friend," Devon had said, giving a squeeze; the bouncer nodding agreement—under the circumstances there wasn't much alternative—as Alistair eyed the girl in the corner. Her name was Kirsty. No, Kristy.

As he lay at the pool, an abrupt vision of her flashed before him. He remembered her ribcage; he had felt it a lot that following week. Each bone showing; he'd been able to count them from the bottom to the top; a little corrugated journey ending with the freshest, firmest, fakest breasts he'd ever felt. Beautiful.

His new friend had restrained his assailant by the balls, all fight gone, tamed, a neutered cur. Alistair had considered an overhead right, but the thought of fist on bald skull dissuaded him. A head butt? He'd never delivered one before. Devon had sensed his hesitation, swivelled around, hooked his index and middle finger into the bouncer's wide nostrils and thrust him backwards, his head smashing against the mirror above the basin. Amazing, Alistair had thought, that's all it takes; the bouncer prostrate on the ground, the mirror shattered. And his new friend had shoved a business card into his hand, as the girl—Kristy, Crystal, whatever —had tucked up next to him.

That was a little over a year ago, the beginning of an intriguing friendship.

Alistair shifted on his towel. A boy on the grassy slope aimed his cellphone at Red And White Bikini. Alistair chuckled. The whole world was paparazzi now.

Devon's words resounded in his ears: "You think we didn't harm her, Alistair?"

He wondered what Terri Phillips would be doing? Sitting on her bed at Tugwell, tissues on the floor, hugging her knees, rocking back and forth...

Nah, he thought. It wasn't a big deal. She hadn't been hurt. She looked like she could handle it. And she'd never know that her terror was being scrutinized in darkened rooms across the globe. It was Devon who'd said she'd probably blame it on her boyfriend's ex.

But there was something she'd said. What was it again?

"I feel so violated. As if someone has taken my most precious possession."

Come on! She didn't know how lucky she was. It could have been so much worse.

Alistair rolled on his back, the world upside down as he watched the girl swimming lengths of breaststroke.

The ante of their video projects had been raised, that he had to concede. From completely consensual to "what you don't know can't harm you." What would he have thought a year ago if Devon suggested they strip a girl naked by force?

It had always been consensual.

He remembered their first Cavendish assignment. He and Richard had been dispatched to the mall to find two teenagers willing to have sex in the public toilets. It was a trend at the time, in all the papers; horny youngsters with their cellphone cameras; concerned parents outraged. Devon wanted to produce something "with proper production values." Something that might make a name for them on Watchit.

"Just find them," he'd said.

Easier said than done. How do you walk into a mall and proposition a couple of teenagers?

Devon had provided some pointers. "It's not the obvious ones. Not the painted little chicks with lots of hair and earrings and short skirts. Or the guy with the gelled hair. Look for the ordinary ones. They hide behind their normality."

Alistair remembered feeling uneasy even then. As long as it was consensual.... But already it was distorted. Two consensual minors....

Richard had geeked it up with a young guy in black jeans, spotty face. It could have been a young Richard. He'd raced over to Alistair.

"Sounds promising. But he's gay."

A couple of texts and they had the go-ahead from Devon. Alistair and Richard had arranged to meet the kid later that evening near the McDonald's, but when they'd arrived, the boy was waiting with an elderly man.

"I want to know what's going on," he'd demanded. Tall and slim, bespectacled, furrowed brow, anxious, outraged. "I know what you two are up to. You're in big trouble."

Alistair had bolted first, Richard close behind. Dashing across the slippery floors of the mall like two thieves, the voice of the man ringing behind them.

"Stop them! Stop those perverts!"

Alistair wiped a thin line of perspiration from his top lip. Red and White Bikini was getting out of the pool.

Their next projects had been more successful. Night shots of couples having sex in their cars on Rondebosch Common. Usually prostitutes on payday. A hidden camera in Devon's sleeve that recorded some graphic table dances at Gorky Park Revue Bar. Johnny had loved those ones.

And then a camera mounted for a month in the bushes above Hospital Bend, which produced a highlights package of car crashes, including a minibus taxi flipping spectacularly on its head—the stroke of good fortune they'd needed. The two minute clip had received half a million hits on Watchit and YouTube.

That was the one that had caught Carlos's eye. He'd spotted it, viewed all their postings, particularly liked the facial expressions of the couples in the cars. Then he'd contacted Devon through his Watchit profile. Exactly what Devon had been hoping for...

Red and White Bikini dried herself carefully. First her long brown legs, then her stomach. Slow downwards strokes, missing nothing. People paid good money to see this, thought Alistair, as he sat up to get a better view. He longed for a tall glass of iced lemonade.

How long had it been since he hooked up? A few weeks. It was rare. Alistair Morgan had never battled for female attention. Charming, not afraid to use his looks or, if necessary, his family wealth. And happy to chance his arm when necessary. His extremely poor reputation at the girls' residences ensured he remained in demand.

Without taking his eyes off the girl, he flicked open his cellphone and dialed Maggie.

"Maggie, can you get me a cell number for a Terri Phillips at Tugwell?"

The girl bent at the middle, drew her towel slowly up the inside of her thighs. He would have to roll over.

We have a super highway, Alistair mused, from eyes to cock; a big digital channel sucking down images, converting them to something the little man understands. A simple, single-stranded network cable. Different with girls. The path to the panties comes from the heart, with numerous little side alleys from the ears, nose, eyes, senses; a complex network with unpredictable routing tables. But sometimes you could find a short cut.

The girl pulled on a tight pair of denim hot pants and strode in his direction. He turned on his side at the appropriate moment. She paused, lifted her sunglasses to reveal a set of cat-like green eyes.

"Not bad," she said.

"Do I know you?" Alistair asked.

"I know you." She licked her lips, gave his body a slow once over before lowering her glasses.

Hell, what's there to lose?

"Would you like to...I'm sorry, what was I thinking? So presumptuous. I'm sure a girl like you would never..."

"I'd love to. Where?"

He smiled, ran a hand down his chest, and gestured with his head. "Green 212. I've got a bottle of wine in the fridge."

The girl paused for a second, considering her options.

"When?"

He looked at his watch, a silver TAG, gave it a flourish. "Say, six."

She twirled around and left.

He flopped back onto his stomach. There were other people at the pool, he noticed: an elderly man with a bloated stomach, a mother with two small children, two Belsen boys in the pool tossing a water-polo ball.

Where'd they all come from?

He cast an eye over to the empty patch of grass where the girl had lain.

Nah, she'll never come, he thought.

A HOME MOVIE

"Why can't I just snap out of it?"

Katie touched Terri's arm and peered back at the therapist, who sat on a grey plastic chair near the door. First years at Tugwell got small rooms, two beds squashed into an area five by five. But Terri's roommate had dropped out and the room was her own. The therapist, Katie's cousin, had agreed to a house call.

"I've got a feeling I can't describe," Terri continued. "As if my body needs something, but I don't know what it is. Normally it's food." She spoke softly, staring ahead.

Katie smiled at her and patted her arm again. They sat on Terri's bed, among the cushions and teddies, Terri in a pink tracksuit, zipped to the neck, facing the therapist, Katie side on, turned to face her.

"Let's go back a little," said the therapist. "What happened afterwards?"

"After we went to the police station?"

The therapist nodded.

"He—Alistair—dropped me off. I came up to my room and tried to sleep. I didn't want to tell anybody. Not even Katie."

Katie passed her a tissue and she blew her nose.

"But I had to. Katie knew immediately that something was wrong."

"I heard it in her voice when I phoned," said Katie. "We were supposed to run together."

"You had a puncture," the therapist completed the logic.

The girls nodded.

"I got a lift over and she told me everything," Katie continued. "About the attack, the voice, Alistair Morgan, the police station. At first I thought she was handling it well. She was angry. She....What did you say?"

"That I'd pepper spray them next time." Terri forced a gritted smile.

"But then when I left, she phoned me. Said she had these feelings she couldn't control. She'd been staring out the window..."

"You had feelings of suicide?"

"Not suicide. But emptiness. I feel so empty. I can't imagine a time when I'll be happy again. And nothing will ever remove this feeling. I still have it."

"Tell her what happened when Henri wanted to come around?" prompted Katie.

"Henri's your boyfriend?"

"Was. I think." She bowed her head and started to cry. Katie leaned forward and embraced her. Terri's gentle cries became sobs, her body wracked with sadness.

"Terri thinks Henri's ex-girlfriend instigated the attack. But she's too embarrassed to speak to him about it. He can't understand her problem. Why she's changed and gone frigid."

Terri broke free with a mock slap at Katie.

"Not frigid." She laughed as she cried.

"You said..."

"Oh Katie. I know what I said. Let me tell it. It's as if something has changed. I can't help it. I don't know why or for what reason."

"But you blame him? And his ex-girlfriend?"

"Who else could it be?"

"Shouldn't you at least give him a chance to defend himself?"

Terri shook her head vigorously.

"And the other student? The one who..."

"Alistair?"

"He's a student at Belsen," said Katie.

Terri buried her face in her hands. "I hope I never have to see him again. It sounds like a small thing. Being naked in a forest in front of a boy. But it's not that. It's the way it happened. The fear I felt when they pulled me off the path..." Her voice trailed away.

"And it would have to be Alistair Morgan," interjected Katie.

"What does that mean?" asked the therapist.

"He's a very popular boy at Belsen. Third year, Law. He's dated half the girls in Tugwell." She intimated quotation marks as she said the word "dated."

Terri stood up and walked to the window. Below, students like ants were returning from morning lectures.

"He was very kind to me."

"Oh for sure. He's more charming than the groom on his wedding day."

"You were blindfolded?" asked the therapist.

"Yes."

"And the person who grabbed you definitely wasn't this Alistair?"

"No! I will remember the voices anywhere."

"Voices?"

"Well....One voice. Only one spoke."

Katie walked her cousin to the lift after the session.

"I tried to make light of it," Katie said. "Say, what the hell, we all get naked here and there. So what if he saw you starkers? She's skinny dipped with Henri at the Reservoir before."

"It's not the nudity. It's the violation of her person. The power, loss of control. They've mentally raped Terri. Even though they didn't touch her. But something else is a problem. That's why she has the feeling..."

The lift button illuminated. They entered the lift and descended to ground floor.

In Terri's room, her cellphone rang, a new number, not on her contacts list. She pressed the silent key and waited for her voicemail message to beep.

"Terri, it's Alistair Morgan. I wanted to find out how you are. I hope you're doing OK. Please give me a call back on this number."

She deleted the message and voicemail then lay back on her pillow, closed her eyes, and relived the morning in the forest.

⊙

Having been voted onto the Kopano House Committee at the end of the previous year, Alistair was entitled to a choice of one of the fourteen larger rooms in the residence. He chose Green Block, second, room 212, due to its proximity to the canteen, the mess, the A3 and the residence entrance.

His neighbor Silverman called 212 the Va-va-vroom! A fridge, some half decent furniture, and a Persian carpet set Alistair aside from the other students.

Most of Alistair's contemporaries had moved out of res after second year, finding a digs in one of the surrounding suburbs; the poorer guys to Mowbray or Observatory, the flusher friends to Rondebosch and Claremont. But Alistair enjoyed the easy life of residence—washing organized, food prepared, the recognition bestowed by his senior status.

And everyone seemed to enjoy having him there. Even Mrs. Hamilton, the impossible, grey-haired Belsen matron. Alistair's receipt of special attention was legendary: clothes drycleaned; a double plate of steak, egg and chips on Friday nights; room cleaned twice a week.

He'd drop into her office with a smile.

"It's your birthday coming up, Mrs. Hamilton." She wore her customary white tunic. The room smelled of washing powder.

"Oh Alistair. Don't remind me. At my age."

He put his hands on his hips.

"You're a spring chicken, Elana!" He seldom used her first name— once or twice to underline their special relationship, but mostly "Mrs. Hamilton" for respect. "You need a cup of tea and some time off your feet." He patted a chair. Shameless.

"Oh Alistair. I can't. So much to do."

"It can wait. I'll turn the kettle on and you put up your feet. You do so much for us. We need to do something for you once in a while."

"Smoother than the shiny-assed shoes of a rap boss," heckled Silverman from Green 214, after Mrs. Hamilton's staff delivered pressed shirts to his room. Her darkest contempt was reserved for Silverman. In first year, he had vomited behind the door of his room; the cleaner's entrance had shoveled the mess into a toxic puddle.

"Manners maketh man," replied Alistair, inspecting the collars of his shirts and shutting the door in Silverman's face.

He whistled to himself, inserted his prized copy of *Withnail and I* into the DVD player, hopped onto his bed. It remained his favorite movie; he had a copy of the screenplay as well. His lips moved in unison with words of the characters, Withnail, Marwood, Danny and Monty. Last year, after final examination, he, Silverman, and Macintosh in Green 215 had matched Withnail drink for drink, tequila substituted for lighter fuel, Tassenberg for the '53 Margeaux.

"Your hair are your aerials," Danny lisped.

Alistair dozed off, laughing to himself, woke to an insistent knocking at the door. He sat up, ran a hand through his hair, checked the time: six fifteen p.m. He jumped up and ran to the door—the girl from the pool, freshly showered, in a strappy red dress, gold hooped earrings, little black bag clutched in one hand. No bra.

"I believe we had a date."

(▶)

The cold Sauvignon blend formed dew on the side of the wine glasses, crystal Riedel Sommeliers collection, a gift from John. Alistair fingered the fine condensation, then held up his glass.

"Do you know wine tastes better in superior glasses?"

He'd made a quick recovery, pulled on a clean shirt, complimented her on her dress. Not bad, but Alistair wished she'd come in her red and white bikini.

"And these are superior glasses?"

"Bowl, stem and base. Form follows function."

"Ah," she replied with a strange look. She raised her glass to her lips and tasted the cool blend. He watched her intently, the shine of her lip gloss, the way the glass touched her lips, the way she drew the wine into her mouth, swirled it, swallowed it.

An amateur. What type of video could they put her in?

He dimmed the central light.

"Buitenverwachting—a quality wine," he said. "You taste the figs?"

She shook her head. "I didn't know there were figs in wine."

⊙

Two empty bottles cut forlorn figures on the counter beneath Alistair's window. His drapes were drawn; Katie Melua sang soulfully about "blaming the moon."

The girl from the pool sprawled across Alistair's bed, her head on his chest, his hand rubbing gently on her shoulder, shifting the straps of her dress back and forth, teasing.

"You don't want to go out?" he asked.

"What can be better than this?" Her eyes sparkled in the dim light.

He'd finally caught her name: Becks. She was a student nurse at Kingsbury. The nurses there all knew of him, she'd told him—at least by reputation. It was news to him. Good news—although he suspected she was about as good as it got as far as the "Kings" talent went.

She turned onto her stomach, her feet kicking up behind her, lifting her dress tantalizingly higher.

"So."

"So," he echoed. "More wine?"

She shook her head, her hair falling into her face. "I think I'm over the limit." Alistair felt a fresh tinge of desire.

"Oops." The remains of her glass spilt on the carpet.

"Best place to spill it," said Alistair. "It's a Persian."

She made a face and placed her glass on the table.

He really loved women, Alistair thought. Look good, feel good; each a unique package of smells and curves, eager to please, tempting and naughty.

Most of the time, that is. After sex, curves became sharp bends; lithe bodies became heavy; the cute voices, whiny; the anticipatory mood, expectation. Sex spoiled the fairy tale; there was more to savor in the anticipation than the course itself. No matter your charm, the aftermath was a debt owed.

"So," she said again, running a finger along his cheekbone.

"Mmm?"

"Are we going to get naughty?"

He laughed and fell back on his pillow, put his hands behind his head.

The nurse ran her hand under the hem of his cotton shirt, moved it up and down against his hard stomach.

"What's that?" She pointed to a Sony Handycam resting on a shelf against the far wall.

"A camera."

"Are you taping me?"

"No!" Pause. "But I could."

She giggled and got up, danced across to the shelf, and checked the recorder on her tip toes.

"It's on!" she exclaimed.

"It's not!" replied Alistair, indignant.

"Well, get it on then."

She turned toward him and gripped the hem of her skirt with her hands, shimmied back and forth. Alistair jumped to his feet, found a new disc in his drawer, broke open the wrapper and inserted it into the camcorder.

She placed her hands on her hips, watched as he balanced the camcorder on his desk and aimed it toward the bed, brightened the overhead light slightly, then checked that the door was locked.

"You've done this before!"

He grinned, closed the gap between them, slipped his arms around her waist and eased her before the lens.

"I blame this on the moon," she said, as Alistair slipped a strap off her shoulder, freeing a breast.

It occurred to him that he'd been thinking about this moment since that morning at the pool; since he'd first spotted her perky little tits in that perfect little bikini. He wasn't disappointed. No matter how experienced you are, there was always something special about this. About seeing a woman naked for the first time. Slowly revealing her secrets. Every one different. More so when you hardly knew her.

He bent down and took her nipple in his mouth. She groaned. The other strap came down, her dress slipping to the elastic waist. He moved in behind her, facing them toward the camera, cupped her breasts with his hands, created an unlikely cleavage as he kneaded them together. She giggled and threw back her head. Alistair rolled her hard nipples in his fingertips.

"Is it really on?" she asked, gyrating her hips.

"Mmm." He nibbled the rim of her ear, ran his tongue across the fine, velvety hair on the nape of her neck, down her spine. His thumbs tucked into the waist of her dress.

Now, where to from here?

"You on the pill?" he asked. She nodded. In a fluid movement, he slid down her body, rolling her G-string to the floor; back up, hands on her legs, the dress riding up, a crumpled band around her waist. He looked down: her firm ass was a startling white contrast to the brown of her back.

"Come on, baby," he whispered in her ear, edging her around and toward the bed, as his right hand slid down her stomach. Another groan as he discovered her preference for shaving. Beautiful. This film was getting better and better.

A moment later, he had her positioned next to the bed, left knee on the edge, right foot on the floor. Hands grasping her ass, thumbs up, he stood behind her, opening his stance for a clearer view. He looked to his right and smiled for the camera.

$\odot$

"This is mine," said the nurse, slipping the disc into her handbag.

Alistair nodded. What had he been thinking? Quality poor, a scrum of heaving white bums, belly ring flashing. She'd managed a few slinky wiggles for the camera, but she wouldn't be table dancing at Gorky Park any time soon.

Recklessness had turned to regret. Why no protection? Why film it when you just want a fuck? Why let her walk away with it as a keepsake?

What would Devon think?

But at least his little drought was a thing of the past.

He walked her down the stairs to the reception area.

She threw heavy arms around his neck, pulled her body tautly against him, rubbed herself provocatively at his middle, all the time looking into his eyes.

"You blame this on the moon," he said weakly.

She held up the silver disc. "This'll keep me going through the dark hours of night duty." She winked at him and spun around. Visions of a nurse's uniform and a helium machine danced like candy sticks in his mind. He slapped his face, trudged slowly back to the reception. The office was closed; Maggie long since lumbered home.

He checked the messages on the board.

None for him.

He glanced at his cell.

None there either.

THE TRUTH ABOUT JOHNNY

Morning. A knock on the door.

"Who is it?"

Alistair, towel around his waist, stowed his shaving apparatus in a fitted cabinet on the wall, wiped an errant line of shaving gel off his ear. Paco Rabbane splashed into his hand and patted onto his face. One more left-right check in the cabinet mirror.

Another knock. He opened the door, a first year passed him a fresh copy of the Cape Times.

"Thanks, pal."

He tossed the newspaper on the bed, dropped the towel; inspected his body, this time in the full-length wardrobe mirror. Damage: scratch marks on his chest and back, bite mark on bum, a three to five day recovery. The smell of the nurse clung to the room.

He slipped on a pair of striped boxers, checked the headlines. A short article on the front page caught his eye.

MAN SHOT EXECUTION STYLE IN CAMPS BAY

Police are investigating the murder of a 45-year-old Camps Bay man found dead in his home yesterday morning. The man, identified as Dean Campher, had been shot at close range in the back of the head.

Police spokesman Trevor Mabunda said the victim's body was discovered by his domestic worker at approximately 10am, slumped in front of his computer in his Geneva Drive apartment. His hands were bound behind his back.

The motive for the murder is unknown. Mabunda told reporters that there were no signs of forced entry and that robbery did not appear to be the motive. Campher's wallet, laptop and cellphone were found near his body.

Mabunda would neither confirm nor deny allegations

that Campher was a convicted sex offender,
after it was alleged that graphic pornographic
material was discovered on his laptop.

Campher, a systems administrator for ABSA Bank,
was unmarried and lived alone. A neighbor
described him as withdrawn and courteous.
Police are investigating.

"Two bottles?" Silverman, in a scanty pair of once white now grey underpants, pushed the door open and surveyed his neighbor's domain. He sauntered over to the silver popup dirt bin and peered inside.

"Hmm."

Alistair ignored him.

Silverman examined the wine bottles, raising his hand to his mouth in an exaggerated take on Hercules Poirot. "Buitenverwachting—the good stuff! Oh my! Either you're a sadder case than I realized or you've recently had a visitor. Sexual relations quite possibly occurred."

Alistair showed him the newspaper. "Check it out. A pervert got shot execution style."

"I've never tried that style myself," said Silverman. He pumped his pelvis, made slavering noises with his tongue.

Silverman was a fellow law student. Somehow he'd made it into third year. They hung out at campus; Silverman, source of mirth, a court jester—every group needs one.

Now he sniffed the air, expert eye looking for a show. "She's a first year with a learning problem, on the pill, obviously. Who was she?"

Alistair ignored him, flicked the paper over to check the sport.

Silverman scoured the bin a second time.

"You are aware of the hazards of AIDS and various other nefarious venereal diseases that you expose yourself to when you don't stick a helmet on your astronaut?"

"Whatever."

Silverman"s gaze settled on the Handycam on Alistair's desk. It was open. Silverman's eyes lit up. "You filmed her," he gasped conspiratorially.

"Keep on fantacizing, you weirdo."

Silverman ran around and positioned himself dead in front of Alistair. "Look me in the eye. You filmed her, right?"

Alistair pushed him away and laughed. "Whatever. You're delusional."

Silverman hurried to the desk, pushed books and papers aside, and scanned through the drawers. "Where's it?" he demanded.

Alistair pulled a red sweater over his head, a small white Nike swoosh over his heart. Then into a pair of khaki G-Star shorts.

"Well? Where?"

"She took it."

Silverman put his hand in front of his mouth in mock shock. "I love it! Who is she?"

There was a soft knock at the door. Silverman opened it with a flourish.

"I'm sorry. I must have…"

Alistair pulled Silverman back and peered around the door.

"Terri!"

She looked pale and small, her face blotchy, nose and eyes red, cheeks colorless. Alistair adjusted his pants and fastened the button.

Silverman slotted in behind, hand on Alistair's shoulder, his straight donkey brown hair brushed forward, fringe hanging over his eyes, hot breath on Alistair's neck. Alistair turned and looked at him. Silverman's mouth formed a perfect zero.

"I'm sorry. Is this not a good time?"

Alistair turned back to Terri. "He was just leaving."

Silverman wormed his way past and out the door. Behind Terri's back, he unleashed a frenzy of silent questions, waving arms and pogo jumping. Alistair ignored him and shut the door.

"Sit?" he offered, pointing to his small couch, regretting the two empty bottles of wine next to the bin, hoping the excess cologne he'd just applied would mask any traces of last night's romp.

She looked back at the closed door. "No. I can't stay." She folded her arms and remained standing with her back to the door.

Alistair picked his towel off the floor and sat down on the bed. He rubbed his wet hair. The open video camera was on his desk.

"I want to say thank you again for helping me," said Terri. "I know you phoned and I didn't reply. I wanted to deal with this on my own."

Alistair nodded, watching her, taking her in: hair clipped up, a blue denim skirt, tackies without socks, shapeless UCT sweater, a size too large, two silver bangles, no earrings, no makeup.

"Sometimes it helps to have someone to talk to," he said.

"I have someone to talk to."

He wondered who, decided not to ask. Why couldn't he think of something suitable to say? Distraction, distraction.

"You haven't told anyone?" she said. The intensity of the expression on her face jolted him.

"No, of course not."

She relaxed a little. "It's just..." She took a deep breath. "I keep thinking, Henri, that's my boyfriend...rather, was my boyfriend...had something to do with it."

Alistair's mind worked furiously.

"Not Henri, I mean...his old girlfriend. When they look at me..." She stumbled over her words.

"I want to help you. Please." He took a step closer.

"No. It's fine. Really."

"But this chap Henri..."

"Uh. It's probably all my imagination. I've got lectures now. I don't need any help. But thank you. I just wanted to be sure..."

"Can I give you a lift?"

"No. Thank you."

She turned, opened the door and was gone. The door burst back open immediately: Silverman, still in his underpants, eyes darting at the video camera, hands pulling at his hair.

"Fuck, fuck, fuck! That's Henri Brink's girl! Do you know how much trouble..."

"Silverman, you're an asshole. It wasn't her."

"Wasn't her? Now who's the asshole? I saw her with my very eyes. That was Terri Phillips."

"I meant, it wasn't her in the video."

Silverman shook his head and grinned. "So there is a video!"

Alistair groaned.

"Don't worry, bud. Your secret's safe with me." He put his finger on his lip. "But I want to see the video."

"There's no video, you big dick. Now get out of my room!"

$\odot$

"Let me show you something."

Breakfast finished, back in 212, Silverman assumed control of Alistair's laptop, connected to the net and fired up Facebook.

"Terri's one of my friends," he continued, a page appearing: Candy Smith.

"You're Candy Smith, large-breasted Tugwell resident?" Alistair laughed with disbelief. The picture showed a raven-haired beauty in a see-through top. "Interested in women!"

"I was in Tugwell," corrected Silverman. "But I've moved into digs. It was getting hot in the group. I think I'm the only lesbian."

He twirled the trackpoint device on Alistair's Thinkpad. Terri Phillips's page filled the screen, her profile picture taken at a formal dance, probably Matric Ball, face younger; she'd matured into a young woman.

Alistair scanned the screen.

One hundred ninety friends. An even spread of girls and guys. None of the girls he'd poked before, he hoped. Maybe a couple.

Nineteen. Great age. In a relationship with Henri Brink. Later for that...

Alistair scanned her profile. Looking For: Happiness. Interests: Find out for yourself. Favorite Music: Cassie. Favorite Book: *Heat* magazine.

Heat magazine!

"Pictures, pictures..." Thumbnails of a happy young girl. Playing tennis, running a half marathon, modest bikini on Clifton Fourth beach, or maybe it was Llandudno.

"No nudes, I checked," said Silverman.

"What do you mean you've checked?" Alistair slapped Silverman on the shoulder.

"I told you. She's got a big fan club," said Silverman. "Look at her friends! Cindy Jones..." He flicked to Cindy's page, another stunner, looked like a young Cindy Crawford. It was Cindy Crawford, a younger pic from her early modeling days.

"That's Macintosh," said Silverman.

"Macintosh! I can't believe it," said Alistair, shaking his head. "A network of deceit."

"It's fun," said Silverman. "Everyone's doing it."

⊙

The text from Devon arrived midmorning:

Come pick up your $$$.

Gorillas was a five minute drive from Belsen: down the hill into Rondebosch, through the student back yard, up into Grotto Road, left at the T-junction. Third house up on the left.

Alistair turned into the driveway and parked behind a rusty blue Cressida, Johnny's ride. Devon's silver C-Series Mercedes stood under a shade cloth covered bay.

Alistair hopped out and strolled across the unmowed lawn, the grass dry and patchy. A lopsided, scraggly hedge separated the road from the house. Up some stairs to the front door, standing open.

"Hello!" called Alistair. He could hear muffled voices behind a door but received no answer. He didn't feel like conversation, anyway. Devon would ask him if he'd seen Terri.

Why was Terri taking it so badly? Breaking up with her boyfriend was not regrettable, but the way she looked? Sorrowful and empty, sadness without seeking pity. What was her problem? A few pine needles on her ass...

Clearly she wasn't very interested in his offer of companionship either. But she'd come all the way to see him in his room "just to be sure"...

He lifted a fat envelope marked "Alistair" off the telephone table. Underneath it, a book caught his eye: Luke Rhinehart's *The Dice Man*. He opened the front cover, "Devon Deacon" pencilled in as the owner.

He pocketed the envelope, tucked the book under his arm, then performed a quick U-turn and skipped back down the stairs and into the street.

How long had she been in his room this morning? A minute? Two? He wished she'd left some lingering memory.

Imagine if....A sudden chill of paranoia; Alistair straightened his shoulders. What if she comes back to Belsen, to visit again and Silverman asks her about a video? He played out the scene in his mind.

"Hey, pretty girl," says Silverman knowingly.

"Excuse me?" Terri's eyes are puffy.

"Which way did you do it? On the video? Huh, huh?"

Alistair stopped and looked up at the sky. The sun was reaching its zenith; motion was necessary to avoid incineration. Devon was right. Keep away from her. But he'd have a word with Silverman anyway and straighten him out. Best bet: salvage the disc from the nurse and screen it for him.

The bang of the front door distracted his daydream. Johnny marched down the garden path toward the blue Cressida, a reluctant girl in tow. He looked like a Free State farmer: tight khaki shorts exposing massive quads, matching shirt with grey panels on the pockets, angry neck jutting out.

Who actually wears those shirts? thought Alistair.

The girl resisted, but Johnny marched on, pulling her by the arm, uncompromising, intent to drag her to his car.

"Get the fuck in!" he shouted. The girl collapsed on the ground, heaving with tears. Alistair stood dead still, observing from across his car. What was her name? Sasha?

Johnny wrenched open the Cressida's rear door, returned for the sobbing heap, bent, bundled her into his arms, shoved her onto the back seat like a sack of potatoes. He slammed the door and glared at the car parking him in, then noticed Alistair for the first time.

"What the fuck you looking at, Morgan? Get out of my driveway!"

"Jesus, Johnny, what's got down your crack today?"

Johnny wrenched the door of his car open, started the engine and revved loudly. Alistair hopped into his car, put the keys in the ignition and waited. The thick neck swung around, engine screaming, blasting on the hooter.

"Move your fucking car!" he roared.

Alistair turned the key and slipped out the driveway.

He drove leisurely to the bottom of the road, the blue Cressida tailgating, and paused at the traffic lights leading onto Main Road. Johnny swerved to the other side of the road, overtook and jumped the red light.

⊙

Alistair was leaving the parking lot behind Pick'n'Pay when his cellphone rang. Devon.

"Have you stopped in already?"

"Yip."

"Get the cash?"

"Yip."

"You count it?"

Alistair laughed.

"And I took a novel I found on the table. *The Dice Man*. Hope you don't mind."

"Thought you might like the look of that. Can you come back?" Devon could elicit a command in the form of a question.

"Be right there."

Five minutes later, Alistair was back in the Gorillas driveway. No sign of the blue Cressida. He parked in the road to avoid being parked in if Johnny returned.

Devon, immaculately dressed, muscular arms accentuated by a tight-fitting short sleeve shirt, was perched in front of one of the PC work stations in the lounge. He was clean shaven, hair slicked back, smelling of cologne.

"Sorry I missed you," said Alistair. "Where were you?"

"I must have been dressing."

Dressing, thought Alistair. Ten o'clock in the morning?

"I didn't sleep last night." Devon seemed to read Alistair's mind. He gestured for him to take a seat.

He was a package, thought Alistair, serene and relaxed, oozing composure. Not your average tech whiz.

Alistair sat down.

"Alesandro," Devon said, deliberately spinning around on the computer chair. He wheeled across and placed a hand delicately on Alistair's arm. It was a name only Devon called him.

"Alesandro, we might have a problem."

"Oh?"

"Johnny."

"Johnny?" Alistair wondered whether to tell Devon about the earlier incident. "Funny you mention him. I saw him this morning with the thin girl, the stick insect. Was roughing her around a bit. What's her name?"

"Sasha." Devon knew everyone's name. It was his business.

"He was pulling her..."

Devon stopped him. "I know. I saw you."

Devon took a long breath and exhaled slowly. He pointed toward the television with the DVD controls.

"Take a look at this."

The screen filled with images of a room, dimly lit. A second and then Alistair recognized it: Gorillas, this house. A black and white duvet: Johnny's room.

The door opens. In walk two people. Johnny and a girl. Sasha. She looks barely conscious. He props her up, her legs bandy and elastic; lets go and she falls onto the bed. She is laughing, definitely drunk. Drugged? Johnny obscures her face; he stands beside the bed, back to the camera. Who's doing the filming? Johnny roughly unfastens the buttons of his shirt, rips it off and throws it to the floor, turns toward the camera with a big smile, puffs out his chest, starts on his fly. Some muffled words are barely audible above the shuffling sound of Johnny undressing. Sasha saying something. Johnny's trousers slip to the ground, he turns back to the bed, pulls down a tight pair of blue Y-fronts. The camera zooms in on his large white bottom. A snigger from the cameraman. Johnny reaches for Sasha's jeans. She tries to swat him away, but one hand pins hers and he undoes the button, unzips her, pulls them off from the ankles. She kicks her legs, laughing; crying maybe. They are off. No panties under-neath. The camera quickly zooms to her crotch, a thin covering of curly black hair. Johnny pushes apart her thighs, holds her legs open for the camera for a moment. Then he climbs on top, licks his hand, and shoves an open palm between her legs. The camera moves to her face. Her eyes are closed, barely an expression. "Hey!" Johnny's clear voice. Sasha's eyes open, the camera pans to a thick erection, he steers it deliberately home, pushes, slowly first, easing and feeling, then in and out, faster, increasing momentum, his ass rising and falling in slow, even movements. He turns to face the camera again, a huge smile on his face, a hand raised with thumbs up. The camera focuses on her face, her willingness is unclear, her eyes are closed, lips move slowly, a murmur, pleasure?

Her eyes flicker open and the lens retreats to a wide angle. He lifts her, carries her, still inside, one arm under her buttocks, one behind her back, toward the open window. He disengages; a monstrous penis shines in the dim light. He rotates her body and presses her against the window ledge, her body limp, resistance free. He fumbles below, transferring lubrication, insert himself slowly, higher, more resistance, parts her buttocks with his hands for a good view, fucks her rhythmically from behind, her head in her arms resting on the window sill, face obscured.

Johnny looks around to the camera again, big smile, one arm around her waist holding her up, the other beckoning to the camera. The camera moves toward the couple. Shuffling and rustling noises. Johnny shifts across, still holding her with an arm around the waist, the screen locked on her buttocks. The camera jumps around, shaky images of her thin white bottom, two flapping penises. The picture steadies and zooms out, light back on the couple, the angle widening. The man behind the girl is different now. Thin, wiry, he heaves and thrusts vigorously. He turns to the camera with a wide smile, a single image of his face. Who is he? The camera turns on its operator. The face is Johnny's. "Now let's have a little fun," he says, his eyes shining, grinning. The camera moves through the bedroom door, down the passageway, to the front door, sound of the door opening, footsteps crunch across the grass, turn left, shaky images of the night, zooms into an open window, Sasha, her arms resting on the window sill, eyes closed, body nodding back and forth to the sound of grunting from behind her. "Not yet," a voice says through the window. The rocking intensity increases, the girl's head bangs against the window and she opens an eye. The image is dark. A torch suddenly illuminates the girl, arms on the sill, head resting on her arms, short dark hair.

"Sasha, what the fuck are you doing?" Johnny booms.

The girl lifts her head, squints into the bright light.

Behind her a shout: "Argh! I'm coming."

"What are you doing, Sasha?"

She twists around, confusion all over her face. "Johnny?" she says, looking behind her.

"Here I am," says Johnny loudly. "I'm out here. What the fuck are you doing, Sasha?"

Realization sets in. The camera captures every moment. The money shot. Her eyes widen and her elbows spin around. Johnny's laughter is raucous. Behind Sasha, his accomplice pulls up his pants, a glimpse of his laughing face. She is naked, her hands at her face, eyes wild, uncertain.

"You're a very naughty girl, Sasha," says Johnny's voice clearly. "A very naughty girl."

Sasha starts to scream hysterically...

Devon flicked off the picture.

"Phew," said Alistair, his back stiff and rigid, perspiration dripping under his arms.

"Three hundred and forty seconds. What do you think?" Devon turned to face Alistair, rotating the controls in his hands.

"Jesus. What do you want me to say? It's a..." He almost said "turn-on," looked up at the blank screen, felt suddenly appalled. "It's pretty shocking."

Devon opened and closed his fist. "Johnny did this on his own. Last night. My camera."

Alistair knew Devon wasn't partial to anyone borrowing his equipment under normal circumstances. This, though, was something else altogether.

"Did he show it to you?"

"No, I was out last night. When I got back, I noticed some of my equipment had been moved around. Checked my computer and I see there's a new drive mounted on the network. I click play and it's this." Devon pointed to the screen.

"Does he know you've seen it?"

"No."

"Hasn't he asked for it?"

"Not yet."

Devon stood up. He straightened a poster on the wall, a picture of King Kong brandishing a giant tree trunk, people with arms outstretched tottering on the edges, the caption: "Consideration. In everything you do, try not to piss off the giant fucking Gorilla."

"It's unacceptable. In my house, with my camera, he shoots this, this...sordid fucking."

Alistair sat silently. He'd seldom heard Devon swear. He wondered what he would think about his effort with the nurse.

"What are you going to do?" Alistair asked.

Devon shrugged, sunk his hands in his pocket, and paced to the other end of the room.

"It gets worse," he continued. "I removed the disc from the drive and went to bed. Head on the pillow and my cellphone rings. Carlos from Dark Video. Frothing at the mouth. He says someone I know contacted him about becoming an agent. He asks the guy where he's from, how he heard about DV, how he got his Skype address. Says the guy is cagey but tells him he has some great material. An assfucking rape, double team—can you credit that? Carlos is spooked. He wants to know how this guy knows about him. I mean paranoia is Carlos's middle name. "

"How did Carlos know to call you?"

Devon laughed humorlessly and shook his head. "Johnny! The world abounds with stupid people who think they're clever."

Alistair swallowed hard. Was he one of them?

"Johnny configures himself as a Skype user from Canada. Carlos listens to his accent, his style. Is suspicious anyway. How did this guy get his contact details? He asks Johnny where he's from. Johnny says, 'Toronto.' Carlos asks 'Where in Toronto?' Johnny says 'Never mind.' Carlos smells a rat. So he checks through Johnny's profile—you know you can share stuff with Skype?—Johnny's got a shared directory from a previous setup. Carlos looks in it. There're the names of all Johnny's mates' contact details. Including mine."

"Shit."

"Luckily, Carlos trusts me. I explained as best I could. But it's embarrassing. Johnny's an accident waiting to happen."

Devon restarted the video from the point where the swap takes place. He froze the face of Johnny's accomplice on the screen.

"Who doubled for the lucky leftovers?" Alistair asked.

"Jeff."

Alistair frowned.

"A dealer," Devon explained. "Sasha's supplier. Trouble."

"Is the clip worth anything?"

"Not to Carlos, that's for sure," said Devon. "Sasha's high as a kite, doesn't know where she is. After I explained to Carlos, he wasn't interested at all."

Alistair was surprised. He figured there would be a huge audience for this kind of thing. Surely this kind of shit was perfect for all sorts of sickos out there?

"It's disgusting," emphasized Devon.

They were quiet for a moment. Alistair was feeling uncomfortable, keen to get away. He changed the topic.

"Speaking of distasteful. You heard about the murder in Camps Bay?"

"Camps Bay?"

"Shot through the head, in front of his computer. Porn on the laptop apparently."

"Oh right. Heard about it. You walk in shit, you start to stink," said Devon without interest.

Alistair stared at him. "Jeez, man. Bit harsh maybe?"

"Look, who knows what the scene was? I have no sympathy for the freaks who watch this shit." He indicated the screen. "I do it for the money and that's it. People on the other side of the screen are pure scum."

"Could he have been a Dark Video client?"

Devon ignored him, advanced the sequence frame by frame, froze on Sasha's expression.

"Could he have been?" Alistair persisted.

"Could be. Could be," Devon said, trancelike, Sasha's frozen face etched with recognition. He looked away from the screen. "But he could have been a million things. Probably just some pervert. You've read one newspaper article and you're as paranoid as Carlos!"

Alistair looked back at the screen. Sasha stared back. He swallowed. Imagine if she were his sister?

"So what do you think I should do about Johnny?" asked Devon, killing the picture again.

Devon always knew what to do, thought Alistair. Why ask his opinion?

"Simple," said Alistair. "Keep the DVD. Johnny will look for it. It'll be gone. What's he going to do? He can't ask you for it."

Devon smiled. "A bit lenient, don't you think, Alesandro? This guy could prove to be very dangerous to us."

"Hide it. It'll drive him crazy. He'll imagine he misplaced it, he'll go crazy looking for it."

Devon allowed himself to smile. "I like it. But there's a bigger issue. If I—if *we*—can't trust him, then what? What about the girl? Suppose she goes to the authorities?"

"We didn't do anything."

"Do you really think if the shit comes down on Johnny, he'll shoulder the responsibility quietly?"

"But what could he say?"

"Alesandro. You're in denial, my friend. Need I remind you? A young girl in the forest."

Alistair ran his hand through his hair. "There's no proof."

Devon put both his hands on either side of Alistair's cheeks and squeezed. "Such big blue innocent eyes." He slapped the cheeks lightly. "Do you want me to spell it out for you?"

Alistair shook his head. Devon was right.

"I don't want to piss Carlos off," said Devon. "I'm not scared of much. But those guys…"

"Listen Devon," said Alistair. "Johnny has Terri's bra. That wasn't in the plan. What did he do that for?"

"Souvenir."

"We must get rid of it. It's probably marked with her name, that's what the chicks in res do."

"I'll deal with it. You think I should have a talk with Sasha?" Devon asked.

"She was drugged. She won't remember a thing."

"And if she does?"

Devon stared into Alistair's eyes as if he was watching for the words to travel through the ether, into Alistair's brain, see the gears of logic and understanding shift, return an obvious result.

"Should I tell Warnabrother about her?" Devon continued. He seemed to be enjoying Alistair's uneasiness.

BUMP AND GRIND

Alistair looked himself over in the mirror. The Sportsman's Dance at Belsen, dress up in sports gear, boys in white cricket flannels or tight McEnroe tennis pants, girls in sexy little hockey skirts or, if they dared, bikinis.

Keep it simple.

He settled on an angle of attack: red baggies and a pair of slip-slops. He had the ripped stomach and slim body to pull it off.

From his bedroom window, he observed the crowd gathering outside in the hall below, the music volume rising, tempo upped, the sound of excited voices. He opened his door and stepped into the corridor. Now to find a henchman.

He banged on Green 215, diagonally opposite. Colin Macintosh, masquerading as Cindy Jones on Facebook, second year, white hair, round head, freckle face, good sense of humor. There was no answer. Macintosh was a useless wingman, anyway; too childish, insufficient focus; he'd be downing beers and giggling with his friends.

It would have to be Silverman. He knocked on Green 214. No answer; not unusual.

A dull noise emitted from within and he pushed open the door. Silverman lay in a huddle on his bed, a haze of sweet-smelling smoke hovering like a pest, the room in squalor.

"Where's the video? The princess?" Silverman railed.

"I wanted to speak to you about that, Silver. A serious chat." He looked at Silverman's red eyes, his one hand tucked into his underpants.

"The video! Let's watch the video." Silverman straightened up and giggled moronically.

"Silverman, this place reeks." Alistair took a look around: rotten apple cores on the desk, windows closed, ashtrays full, dirty clothes strewn across the carpet. Not an item in its original place. Alistair walked to the window and threw it open.

"You'll asphyxiate in here."

"Wholly," said Silverman. He lay on his bed, naked, but for torn green underpants that had lost their elastic.

"I thought it was 'fully.'"

"Fully," agreed Silverman, drawing deeply on a little stub of burning paper in his right hand.

"Now, Silver, listen to me: there's no video. I promise you."

"The princess! The princess!"

"I swear to god. Do you hear? She…" Alistair could think of no immediate reason to supply for Terri's visit. "She's a friend. I haven't even kissed her yet."

"The video," Silverman dribbled into his pillow.

Alistair gave up trying to convince him. He hooked into Silverman's underpants and ripped. The material stretched and tore; Silverman contorted on his bed in the clutches of a gigantic, green wedgy.

"You've cleaved my buttocks," he yelled. "You bastard!"

Alistair shook his head with resignation. "Say no to crack," he said as he made for the door. He would have to fly solo.

⊙

Entrance is everything.

Alistair's trick was to pretend he wasn't really going to the party. He eased down the steps of Green Block, turned right, down more stairs past the mess hall, the shiny pine floors silent, more stairs to the entrance hall where the crowd was massing. He had a prop, his washing bag, tossed over the shoulder, confident, ready to bump into…

The nurse. She leaned against the wall, a tennis player, tight shirt, exposed belly, sexy skirt.

"Hello, Alistair," she said, all the actions going, eyes fluttering, hair flicking, stomach pulled in, one leg pushed forward.

His eyes darted around the room, a mental snapshot of the opportunities.

"Hello!" said the nurse again for attention, putting both hands on his chest and jutting her chin forward. He gulped and kissed her chin.

"Baby," he said. It didn't really matter what he said. He knew he had her in his tractor beam—whether he wanted it or not.

"Nice outfit," she said, eyes wandering down his front.

"Oh," he laughed. "It's not an outfit. I'm taking out my laundry."

"How are you?" Even bet to be the most overused line for the evening. Alistair sighed.

"I'm fine," he replied, poking a finger in her belly button. "How's the little belly ring?"

"Want to lick it?" she said, giggling. There was something not quite right about her, he thought. Perfect from a distance in the bikini, up close, something…

She flicked her hair back.

Maybe it was her eyes; they were too far apart.

"Now?"

"Right now."

He bent down and wiggled his tongue in her belly.

When he straightened up, he saw Terri Phillips. She was standing against the wall, talking to a friend, wearing a red something or other; he looked away so quickly that he couldn't quite see. Had she spotted him?

"I have to go," he told the nurse indicating the washing bag slung over his shoulder.

"No! Where're you going?" She grabbed his wrist. "You told your friend I go down like an oak tree," she accused.

Alistair wriggled free. "I know my trees. I said a redwood."

He hurried away, in the opposite direction to Terri, hoping she hadn't seen him. The nurse watched him go, fists on her hips.

⊙

"Trouble?" The big black guy who the Gorillas gang called Warnabrother answered his cell, sipping on a margarita.

"Affirmative, Samuel. Where are you?" asked Carlos, naked at his office desk, unable to bear a stitch of clothing. The beautician had murdered him; his skin was red and painful. At least he was hairless again—front, back and crack.

"Tel Aviv. Just enjoying the night life."

"Oh yes. The military fetish. What's it like?"

"Chilled." A table of students stared; he stared back and they turned away. Everywhere he went, he was the odd man out. He checked his reflection in the café window: no surprise, really.

"Everything check out?" Carlos rubbed his hand along his leg.

"One hundred percent."

"Nice to know."

"I was thinking I could do with a li'l holiday cruise now, a horny li'l honey..."

"Later for that, my boy. We're getting some interference." Carlos interpreted the silence as disappointment, but it didn't deter him. "Cape Town. Another one bites the dust."

"Uh-oh. I need that place like a hole in the head."

"That's just it. A second client got one, sitting at his computer. I can't ignore it." Carlos connected the backup hard drive and double clicked a window, the drive whirred; everything he possessed was filed on that drive.

"Can't the polo neck boy sort it out?"

"Deacon? No. Not in his league. I need you there. Tomorrow."

"Right. What are the orders?"

"Nose around. Low profile. Check out Deacon's crew. One in particular might need special attention."

"And who's that?"

"Name's Johnny."

The backup was completed. Carlos unplugged the drive and placed it under the desk. Later he'd hide it beneath his bed. It was the safest place.

"Check your phone. I'll send details."

Alistair leaned against the bar counter of the Verge Inn and sucked on a Peroni. A seething mass of flesh and color bobbed, arms reaching out, the gangsta beat of Dr. Dre ricocheting off the drab grey walls. He'd shot back to his room, changed into a pair of cotton chinos, blue cord shirt and raced back to the ball, found a safe spot in the Belsen bar.

He'd rehearsed his lines.

"Terri. What a surprise!"

If she asked about his earlier entrance in the baggies?

"Oh. I was taking my laundry down."

And if she asked about him licking the nurse's belly?

No, he didn't need an answer for that. She'd never ask.

But there was no sign of her.

Next to him stood Colin Macintosh, Green 215, useless wingman, snorting over a game of "Freckles" he'd played with two fellow Zimbos the night before. A solitary, stocky girl perched on a stool, hanging on their laughter.

She was trying to uncork her woes on Alistair, relating a horror story from the night before when she was urinated on at the annual Zimbabwe Society gathering.

"It was disgusting. I was cross-legged on the grass listening to the speaker..."

"What do they say at those meetings, anyway?" Alistair interrupted, absent mindedly.

"Generally it's about Bob, you know. How bad he is. The economy. How the country has gone to shit."

"Why doesn't someone just knock him off?"

"Have you seen his security? They shoot anyone who drives near his place."

"That never stopped anyone before."

"What's your point exactly?"

She was a tough little thing, Alistair thought. No wonder she'd been pissed on.

"You've seen it, haven't you?" she said.

"Seen what?"

"The video."

Alistair"s heart almost stopped. The nurse! What had she done?

"Of me—being pissed on. On Watchit."

"Oh. That." Alistair relaxed. "They filmed it? Disgraceful. The things that people do for entertainment these days..."

"Hello Alistair."

He turned to find Terri at his side, a lifeguard in a red one piece swimsuit and blue jeans. Her hair was full and loose, her face shone, the patchy skin of her visit to his room gone, replaced by an airbrushed beauty.

"Terri," he turned, blocking the Zimbabwean girl. "What a surprise to see you here."

"I came with Katie. She says I need to get out."

He scrutinized her face, a thin streak of eyeshadow accentuating the blue, pale pink lipstick, no base. The first time he'd seen her wear makeup.

"You're looking...so much better."

She smiled at him. "Thank you."

"Are you *Baywatch*?"

"Trying," she replied.

He kept his gaze at eye level. "Funny, I almost did a similar thing." He scanned about, checking to see if Henri was around.

An awkward silence.

"I'm just trying to get a drink," said Terri eventually.

"Oh!" Alistair swivelled around. "Let me help you." He whistled at the barman.

She touched his arm lightly. "Don't worry. I'm fine."

The Belsen barman arrived. He looked at Alistair and then at Terri. "What'll it be?"

"Two spritzers."

The barman, new on the job, looked at Alistair. "Half wine, half soda," he explained.

Alistair turned back to Terri and smiled.

"And what are you?" she asked.

He examined his clothing. "I don't do dress up."

"Could have fooled me." She smiled and walked away with her drinks.

"What did that mean?" said Alistair aloud, shifting to one side. "Could have fooled me?"

"I couldn't hear. Your ass was in my face," said the Zimbabwean girl.

"Your face is his ass," Macintosh chaffed her and the other Zimbos roared with laughter.

⊙

Devon and Richard worked shoulder to shoulder behind the computer screens in the lounge at Gorillas.

"Can I get you another cup of coffee, Dev?" said Richard, removing his spectacles and placing them above the unused fireplace.

"I'll be awake all night. How about some wine?"

"A good idea. I'll open that nice Rosé."

"Rosé? That's terrible. I put a bottle of Chardonnay in the freezer."

"And what if I want Rosé?"

Devon smiled and waved him away.

They'd spent the evening working with a new video editing package. Given a selection of clips, images and music, the software automatically created a professional video. They experimented, interchanging images of famous people and settings pulled from the internet with photographs of themselves and surroundings. Richard had superimposed Desperate Dan into Johnny's blue Cressida.

"Alistair asked me about the Camps Bay murder," he said to Richard when he returned, Rosé in hand.

"Really? How did he know?"

"Read the article in the newspaper."

"Alistair reading?" said Richard bitchily.

"He's a law student," reminded Devon.

"I rest my case. Why didn't you tell him?"

"For what purpose?"

Devon picked up the bottle of Rosé, sighed, and filled his glass.

"I have to hand it to Carlos. He's in touch. A client doesn't contact him, he checks up. He knew about the murder before we did."

"Are you concerned?" asked Richard, picking at his skin, his forehead oily and red.

Devon shrugged. "I'm curious."

Richard turned and looked at Devon. "Thank you for sharing things with me," he said softly.

Devon pointed at the screen, "Let's work out the code for this application."

Richard isolated the object code and dragged it into a disassembly program.

"When did you speak to Alistair?" asked Richard, fingers rubbing and scratching at his face.

Devon raised his eyebrows. "Stop picking your skin!"

Richard, told off, pulled his hands away from his face and turned his attention back to the screen.

"When did he ask you about Camps Bay?" Richard tried again, as he scribbled down the list of compatible file types that would operate with the software.

"Yesterday afternoon."

"What was the occasion?"

"He'd come to fetch his cash."

"Did you talk for long?" Richard kicked off another background process and a list of subroutine calls flashed across the screen.

"No. I'm getting tired of this." Devon pushed his chair back and stretched his arms in the air.

"Of what?" Richard let go of the cursor and faced him.

"No, I mean of this work. Even if we disassemble the code, what's the point?"

"We can use the subroutines in our own programs."

Devon yawned. "Have you heard anything about Alistair?" he asked, changing the topic.

"What sort of things?"

"Him seeing Terri Phillips."

Richard shook his head.

"I wonder if he has?"

"Don't worry so much about him, Devon. You're always on about him. Alistair this. Alistair that. You'd think..."

"What?" Devon interrupted, his voice sharp.

Richard raised his hands in the air and pushed his chair back.

"What? Richard! Think what?"

Richard got up, hands still in the air as he walked toward the door.

"Richard! Answer me!"

"I can't talk to you when you get like this, Devon."

He walked to his room and locked the door.

A MATTER OF SHARKS

"My ass looks like the Japanese flag," Silverman moaned from within a cubicle in the communal ablution area on Green Second.

Alistair leant against the door of the cubicle. "What ails, Silverman?"

"I have a grass burn in my crevice."

"Ouch."

The remnants of Silverman's green underpants lay on the concrete floor; they looked as if they'd made a journey too many through Mrs. Hamilton's washing machine.

"Look, Silverman. I want you to understand something. I never made a video."

"Liar!"

"Seriously, I didn't."

"Why was your video camera open on your desk?"

"I was cleaning it."

"Why was there a plastic DVD wrapper in your waste paper basket?"

Alistair thought hard. "I downloaded a video online and cut a copy on my laptop."

"Have you retained the evidence for this court?"

"Yes."

"Why was your room reeking of perfume and sex?"

The cross examination had taken a bad turn. Alistair floundered. "It wasn't."

"We have witnesses who'll say it did."

"But are they credible?"

"I want to see the video, Morgan. I won't rest until the truth emerges. I'll call the princess to the witness stand."

Silverman yelped again.

"OK. The truth," announced Alistair.

"Nothing but."

"I did make a video."

"Whoopee. State's evidence. Please present."

"But not of Terri."

"Pray continue."

"I met a girl at the pool. She came up to my room later."

"You didn't know her. Before?"

"No. I think I'd seen her around."

"Seen her around? Filthy girl! Name, please?"

Alistair hit a blank. "She's a nurse."

"OK. I'll cut you some slack. Present the video and we'll examine the evidence."

The toilet flushed and Silverman appeared.

"I have a bit of a problem with that," explained Alistair. "She's got the video."

⊙

Campus, lunch time. Alistair received a text:

Rwanda. 1600. NB

He idled at the Leslie, sipping on coffee, scouting talent on the move, noting the different speeds and intensities. The conscientious girls skipped, bums taut, books clutched, intent obvious. The flirty girls dawdled, wiggled ass, dropped pencil cases, flicked hair.

He examined the message, from Devon, an important meeting at Gorillas at four.

Alistair stood up, still sipping on his coffee. He spotted two girls waving. He smiled a shy, cheeky smile and waved back as if he knew them. Not bad, he thought: definite maybe.

He attended class after lunch, slipped a text to Terri:

U on campus? Keen 4 a coffee at leslie?

He had time to kill before four. No answer, though.

⊙

The gang sprawled across the lounge furniture. Johnny in a pair of shorts, scratching his chest, Richard flicking through muted DSTV channels. Alistair sat in the chair next to Johnny watching Devon, who paced restlessly back and forth. Devon sucked in his breath purposefully and heaved out an artificial laugh. The speakers resonated with obscure electronica, a German band Richard had found, the tune lost in excessive bass.

"This is outrageous," said Devon. "But authentic, a one hundred percent for real request from Dark Video."

Richard continued to flick the remote, Johnny rubbed his hands on his pants and looked up, a hungry wolf anticipating his dinner. He removed a crumpled packet of cigarettes from his top pocket, banged the pack to unseat a unit, saw Devon's disapproving expression, fed the cigarette back and replaced the packet.

"They want a clip of a great white shark attacking..."

He paused as they digested the news. Alistair stared ahead, gaze directed at the poster of King Kong without conscious thought.

"Attacking what?" asked Richard, putting down the remote, eyes huge behind the lens of his glasses.

"A person."

The music thumped in dull monotone.

"No way," said Richard, pressing his face into a cushion. "No way!"

"Way," replied Devon, his head scanning the room in a slow arc. "Big cash offered."

"Can I just turn it down and leave right now?" Alistair sitting forward, addressed the amplifier.

"How much?" Johnny asked.

Alistair sat back again, the volume squeezed out of the room, a light wind flicking at the closed curtains in the lounge.

"Two fifty US."

Johnny whistled. The math was easy: over two million rand.

Devon paused for effect. "An additional two fifty if it breaches."

"What?" said Alistair. "Five hundred thousand dollars?"

"No way," repeated Richard. He laughed nervously.

"Snuff," said Alistair, shaking his head. "I'll be leaving, I think..."

"Just wait a moment," responded Devon. "Let's just think this through slowly. We've got a lot of sharks right on our doorstep and there may well be a chance to take advantage of our location."

Like most Capetonions, all four of them knew about the infamous shark population off the Cape coast to a greater or lesser degree: that the coastline was home to the largest population of great white sharks in the world; that False Bay, ringed with popular Cape Town beaches, was one of only a few known great white breeding grounds and harbor to the infamous Seal Island which, overrun by thousands of Cape fur seals, attracted the fearsome predators by the score. One thing they all knew for sure: it was the only spot in the world where great whites have been regularly filmed breaching as they race up from the murky depths in pursuit of their prey. Devon, Alistair, Johnny and Richard had all seen the *National Geographic* footage and images of gaping jaws clutching at flapping seals; muscular bodies thrashing in midair, filled their minds.

"But I've seen footage of shark attacks on people," said Richard, breaking the silence.

"Coincidence," said Johnny. "Those are right time, right place events. You can't follow a shark around hoping it attacks someone." He removed the pack of cigarettes again.

Alistair unlaced and retied his tackies. The repetitive beat of the music irritated him. "Devon, you're not being serious are you?" he said.

"I'm serious that it's a DV request. I'm serious about the cash offered." A little smile appeared at the side of Devon's mouth. "But I haven't got a serious suggestion for how we go about getting the shot."

"A shark cage outing, someone gets knocked overboard. We film it," suggested Johnny.

Richard shook his head. "How'd they get knocked overboard? What are the odds?"

"Exactly," agreed Alistair. "And we can't exactly arrive on a chartered boat with tons of video equipment and then someone falls over? Come on!"

"Good point," said Devon. "We'll need an underwater camera and at least one on board. We'll definitely need our own boat, which I can organize."

"Easy, we stage it," interrupted Johnny.

"We can't do that," said Devon. "It has to be real."

"So let's get this straight," said Alistair. "Someone has to die."

Devon nodded.

"And we're still having this conversation? Have I gone crazy or something?"

"No way! No way are we going to kill someone for bucks," said Richard.

No one spoke, just the relentless bass. Then Devon: "What if the person wants to die?"

"What the hell does that mean?" said Alistair. He stared again at the picture of King Kong. He imagined being one of the people trapped on the branch. "Please can't someone turn that flipping music off!"

Devon pointed the remote at the sound system. The volume diminished.

"It's simple. Find someone who wants to die."

Richard laughed hysterically. "What moron wants to be eaten alive by a great white? Have you watched freaking *Jaws*? I wet myself when I'm in a swimming pool sometimes."

Johnny raised his hands to allow Devon to continue.

"Dark Video don't care how we do it. Other agents will be prepared to cross the line, whatever the method. But we have a moral line we won't cross."

"Then how?" Johnny tapped the packet of Camels, took out a single cigarette.

"What if a person is dying anyway? Terminally ill, three months to live. No pension or reserves. Leaving behind destitution. We offer a million rand to be paid to the family on his death."

Devon's words turned the questions into imagination, into blue water thrashed by a savage black beast, gaping mouth, rows of serrated teeth, red blood spurting in the air, screams and frantic splashes. Would the victim resist or accept death gracefully? Would a primal instinct to survive engage and a desperate struggle ensue?

"Beers!" Devon broke the silence.

Johnny volunteered, disappeared to the kitchen, returned with four Black Labels and passed them around. Alistair placed his can on the table. Not his drink of choice.

"Now this *is* exciting!" said Johnny. "Cheers."

Technically it was possible, Devon explained. He possessed a skipper's license; his uncle owned a decent sized ski boat. He revealed a plan for an automated camera attached to a pole to focus on the action underwater, and on board cameras recording the breach and the action above—one of the big Canons mounted on a tripod, and a camcorder, just in case. He would acquire the waterproof casing required for the underwater camera, as well as a suitable telescoping pole, then work out an easy fitment and removal mechanism, and cabling to control the angle from above.

"Why not just get in the water and film it?" asked Johnny, gulping from the red and black beer can.

"You crazy?" said Richard.

"I'm not scared of those things," Johnny retorted. "You know how hard it is to get a shark to attack someone? That's the whole problem, not avoiding being attacked."

"Oh yeah, know-it-all!" Richard replied.

"Fuck off, you fag. Just because all you know is computers and rent boys..." Johnny glared at Richard.

"Alistair, what do you think?" Devon stepped in.

The sound of his name shook Alistair from muteness. He lifted his beer then put it down again. "I think it's madness."

"But if the victim was willing..."

Alistair shook his head.

"An old age home," Richard interjected. "Good evening, sir! Sorry to hear about the cancer. Skin or prostate? Oh, lung. Nasty. Can I interest you in a little sea safari?"

Johnny drained his beer, lumbered away for a refill. Alistair's can remained undrunk on the table.

Richard continued his charade. "We design a pamphlet. Are you tired of living? Picture of old timer in pain. Are your loved ones taken care of? No? Picture of homeless family huddled in the rain. Then why don't you—dun dun dun—just get eaten by a shark? Picture of great white with old timer in its mouth…"

"OK, enough," Devon interrupted, annoyed. "That's the challenge. There wouldn't be so much money involved if it wasn't a challenge. Finding a willing participant is the key."

"Are you for real?" said Alistair. He lifted his beer and took a solitary sip. "Imagine the first person you approach declines. Then someone accepts. What happens a few months later if we actually get someone to do it? The first person comes forward and you're busted."

"Now you are thinking, Alesandro….Carry on."

"You're asking for someone who has cancer or something, can swim proficiently, has destitute relations and is prepared to die, in a horrifying manner." Alistair's low voice muffled the enthusiasm of the room like soot over glowing embers. "Then you have to find a shark who's happy to eat the guy on a given date. Like Johnny said, we may be shit scared of them but they don't just attack humans. And breaching is extremely rare, happens at Seal Island when they're attacking seals from deep down, virtually nowhere else in the world, so chances of that happening are less than zero…"

"Now who's the know-it-all," interjected Johnny quietly.

Alistair ignored him. "So," he continued, "we might get two fifty thousand if—if—we can convince some demented old guy to be mauled to death in front of us. Hmm, might pay for the therapy bills for the rest of our lives."

"OK, relax, Alesandro, relax," said Devon. "Let's all take a deep breath and have a think."

"You never know until you try," said Johnny, banging down his second empty beer can on the table. "I reckon there must be a way."

Alistair looked at his watch. Five o'clock. He had better things to do. Richard turned the sound up on the amplifier, threw out an ungainly dance move. Thump, thump, thump.

"I say we make a victim," suggested Johnny. "We lay bait in the path of some early morning swimmers."

"Ridiculous," muttered Alistair under his breath.

Johnny swung around and grabbed his shirt, the button on the sleeve popped off.

"What did you say, huh, rich boy?"

Alistair yanked his arm free. "It's murder, you fuckwit," he said, brushing down his shirt.

Richard jumped up and unleashed a series of mock karate chops in Johnny's direction. "Murder on the dance floor," he laughed.

"What the hell is wrong with you guys?" Alistair was astounded; it was almost surreal.

"Look, it's not easy," said Devon. "Perhaps we laugh it off. Wait for the next one..."

"Fuck that, this is a great opportunity," said Johnny. "We've got the largest great white population in the world, take a boat a kilometer out of Kalk Bay, and they practically swim right up to you."

"Laugh it off," Alistair advised. "It's not legal." He stretched his legs, motioning to move.

"What would we, Mr. Fucking LA Law, be guilty of, if the participant was willing?" asked Johnny.

Alistair threw his hands in the air, fed up; he made to leave.

"Sit, Alesandro. How's your beer? We're just debating. Intellectual banter."

Alistair halted in mid-dismount, remained flexed on the edge of the couch.

"Hypothetically, Alesandro. Think John F. Kennedy. A guy with a motion camera, Zapruder, just happens to be filming. In 1963! Think the Twin Towers. Aeroplane flies over and you get the shot that no one else got. Now, if you're filming on a boat and some guy swims past. Next minute— whoosh!—out the depths, this monster grabs him. You've got a problem with that?"

"That's coincidental."

"And you wouldn't sell that video?"

"I might," Alistair replied reluctantly. "Sure, if this were not under-hand, the video would be public domain. We'd sell it to media. The fact that we'll sell it to Carlos means, by definition, it's illegal."

"Alesandro, please humor me. Mental challenge only. You know I'd never get involved in snuff."

"OK, fine. But even watching people die is sick, man. Do you really want to watch someone die in front of you? Intentionally set out to watch that?"

Richard laughed nervously again. "I tried to watch that US journalist, whatshisname, Daniel Pearl, getting beheaded on the net," he said, pointing at his computer. "Couldn't do it. And those other guys in Iraq. I've downloaded about five of those clips, never actually been able to press play."

"You're so pathetic." Johnny on the attack again. "I've watched them. It's pixels on a screen, the guy dies. How's it different to a movie?"

"These are real people!"

"Real people die every day, thousands of them. It's the way of the world, so what? What does it matter if you watch it?"

"Look," said Alistair, keen to end the discussion, "that's just one point. The ethics of legitimately filming a victim, even by coincidence, is questionable. If you staged it, you'd go to jail."

"You'd go to jail for what you did to Terri Phillips, golden boy," replied Johnny with a relish. He tapped his pack of cigarettes rhythmically against the table.

"What I did?" Alistair blinked twice.

"Forget about this fuck, Devon. Take us through the plan," continued Johnny, pleased to have silenced both Alistair and Richard. He replaced the cigarette pack and squashed his fist into a ball, clenching and unclenching, unconsciously examining his blunt, nicotine-stained fingernails. "We identify a willing candidate. What do we tell him?"

"Well, we have the equipment and ability to film. Our challenge is to find the right candidate; if he declines then we've got a risk. We have to abandon the project until he passes on. The negotiation process is key: select the right prospect, win their trust, create a situation where the target is propositioning us, and not vice versa."

"They need to trust we'll pay the money," said Richard.

"Contractual. We'll get ourselves a tame lawyer. Legal confidentiality and all that."

"Surely he's going to tell his family, though?"

"No. He cannot. No one can know about the transaction except us and him."

"A brainwave, a brainwave," Richard injected, waving his arms around. "We get a dead guy. Two people in the water, one swimming, and one already dead. Dressed identically. We shoot on the live swimmer and when the shark nears we hoist him out."

Alistair tensed his legs. He should have left already. Or missed the meeting entirely.

"Sounds workable," said Johnny.

Devon shook his head. "It's got to be real. If we scam Carlos..." He drew his finger across his throat. "We agreed before. It's a rule. We'll never deceive Dark Video. Rather walk away. The money's not worth it." He paused. "Do you think we should ask for more, Alesandro?"

Alistair shrugged.

"Come on Alistair. Apply your mind. You're not being asked to commit, I promise."

Alistair reluctant, spoke quietly, desperate to get up and leave. "Even if you had a willing candidate, like we've said, sharks don't naturally eat people."

"That's what the experts say," smiled Devon. "Find me someone to test the theory and our problem is solved."

"What the fuck—I'll test it," said Johnny. "I believe it. If the sharks wanted to munch us, there'd be a bloodbath at Muizenberg every day of the year."

"The water's shallow just offshore," said Richard. "I read that it's not their natural feeding ground. If there was a surfing break at Seal Island, you'd see the body count rise."

"That's a thought, though," said Devon pondering Johnny's input. "We give the guy a choice. He goes in. If the shark takes him, we win. If it doesn't, we lose. We could cover the cost of a losing bet by asking Carlos for a deal on filming the gamble. Wouldn't that be better?"

"Freak out," said Richard shaking his head. "I can't get my mind around this."

"I'll volunteer," repeated Johnny. "One million and I'm in."

Alistair shot a sideways glance at Devon. Devon's lip twitched.

"You're insane, Johnny," said Richard, laughing.

"Keep laughing, asshole! You're just a pussy. Swim aggressively at a shark and it swims away. It's all about confidence. Four people killed last year. Worldwide! I'll take those odds"

"But if the odds of attack are so low, Carlos won't go for the bet," Devon replied. Alistair stared at him. He was amazed that Devon was even entertaining the idea.

"Yeah, Johnny," taunted Richard. "We choose the parameters. Early morning, virgins' blood in the water, low visibility, vibrations of dying fish..."

"Bring it on," said Johnny.

"Big freaking talk! You'd bail," countered Richard. "The waters churning and the beasts are going wild. We say, 'In you go, Johnny. No way. No way!'" Richard hugged a pillow to his chest.

"OK, OK," said Devon. "This wasn't what I had in mind. I think I'll just Skype Carlos tonight and tell him we'll pass."

⊙

"What's the problem here?" asked Devon a few minutes later. Alistair had been making his way out but was cornered by Johnny.

"This rich prick has taken a video of mine."

"Really, Johnny. What sort of video?"

"Personal." Johnny hid his cigarette hand behind his back and stepped away from Alistair.

"Personal?"

"My girlfriend and me."

"A bestiality sequence obviously," taunted Alistair. With Devon present, Johnny would never swing.

"You're a fucking stupid cunt," said Johnny, his face flushed scarlet, eyes wide.

"Johnny, why are you smoking in the house?" Richard said, making his way past.

"Fuck off!" Johnny lifted the cigarette to his mouth and sucked in.

"Hey! Cool it!" said Devon calmly, then to Johnny: "You made a video of you and your girlfriend. Who's the girlfriend?"

"Come on, Dev. One of the chicks I'm seeing," Johnny blew the smoke out the corner of his mouth, toward the open door, waved a hand after to make sure.

"The skinny one?"

"They're all skinny." A smile returned to his face.

"Why'd you make it?"

"For a turn on. You know what it's like."

"And what sort of camera?"

"Uh. Hers. A real cranky home-movie job. Nothing special. But Morgan swiped the disc. He was here the day it went missing."

Silence, as they weighed each other up. In the background, Richard retreated into the living room.

"I took it," said Devon eventually.

Johnny's face flushed. "Uh. OK. Can I have it back?"

"No."

Johnny scratched his head.

"I destroyed it."

"What!" Johnny expelled a deep breath and sat down, suddenly unsure of himself.

"You want to know why?" Devon continued. Johnny buried his head in his hand, the cigarette hanging limply from the other. He looked up, hangdog expression; stared miserably at the wall, through murky eyes that looked resigned to disappointment. Devon lowered his tone, menacing, cold. "Because I watched it and it's a piece of perverted crap."

Johnny mumbled inaudibly.

"Look at me!"

Johnny shifted his gaze.

"What you did is...twisted. What about the girl?"

Ash from Johnny's cigarette fell to the floor. Johnny covered it with his bare foot.

"She doesn't know a thing. I swear, Devon. She was out of it." Johnny's eyes darted about shiftily. "Jeff drugged her."

"And Jeff?"

"I told him nothing. He was completely spaced out, too. Look, Dev. I swear. It was just for fun."

"You did it for fun?"

"I promise, Devon." The pitch of Johnny's voice lifted.

"Fun?" said Devon softly, as if to convince himself that this was the word used.

Alistair sensed an imminent explosion. He wanted to intervene, to somehow distract them. If only he'd left earlier.

"Look me in the eye, Johnny." Devon pointed to his own eyes. "If you do it again, I'll kill you. Got that?"

Kill, thought Alistair. As in...kill, dead, bang, slash! A vision of a smoking gun appeared in his mind—then a shark's gaping mouth. He looked at Devon, waiting for a smile. None came. The black eyes bored into Johnny.

Johnny swallowed. "I understand," he said meekly. "It won't happen again."

Devon spun around and walked out, leaving Alistair alone with Johnny. He hastened for the door.

"Oh. Happy Birthday, Johnny," he said over his shoulder.

"What? It's not my birthday, you asshole."

"Well, it should be. It's animal rights day."

He sprinted for the Audi.

$\odot$

Alistair lay on his bed and stared at the ceiling. Devon had just phoned.

"Alesandro. I could see you were uncomfortable with today's discussion. Don't worry. I am too. I would never commit to anything that could get us into trouble."

There was so much Alistair had wanted to say. Johnny's threat—"You'd go to jail for what you did to Terri Phillips"—had unnerved him, even if he didn't really believe it. He felt trapped.

"I'm sorry you had to witness my outburst at Johnny. But I needed to warn him," Devon had told him.

Outburst? Devon had been as cool as liquid nitrogen.

"Alesandro. I hate to ask this but I have to. Have you seen Terri?"

"No, of course not! We agreed."

"She hasn't tried to see you."

Alistair had hesitated for a second.

"No."

"Good. I'm worried about Johnny's girlfriend, Sasha. She's a risk. Don't make Terri one too."

He'd been about to send Terri a text.

He deleted the message.

⊙

Silverman's hovel provided a break from reality. Alistair found him on his hands and knees, jabbing messages onto his cellphone. Clothes were strewn across the floor, noxious smells of old socks and cigarettes repulsed him.

"Have you got the video?" Silverman said, without looking up to see who had entered.

"I'm working on it. What're you doing?" Alistair looked toward the windows for fresh air; they were shut.

"I'm in a Mxit chat room. I'm Candy, a sixteen-year-old cocktease. I'm trying to recruit some kindred spirits to a tickle party."

"Anyone keen?" He squeezed his nose between thumb and index fingers, took a deep breath.

"Three little vixens!" He held up three fingers. "Catholic girls. I've organized to meet them at Cavendish."

"Won't they get a fright when they see who you really are?"

Alistair exhaled loudly and Silverman looked up. He straightened his back and made a face.

"What's so wrong with me?" asked Silverman.

"I won't start. How about some coffee?" Alistair threw open the windows and took a deep breath. Under a tree in the courtyard a couple reposed on a grey blanket, legs intertwined, locked into one another.

"Give me a second."

Silverman tapped away on his phone, Cheshire cat grin on his face.

"You should be careful, Silver. You can get into trouble for that sort of thing."

"Trouble?" retorted Silverman. "This is fun. Sin is trouble." He looked up with a worried expression. "Problem being, sometimes sin and fun look the same. At the outset anyway." He threw his phone on the bed.

"Coffee?"

Incredibly, Silverman managed to produce two mugs of drinkable coffee. "So! You're asking me to believe it wasn't the princess on the video. I can make some enquiries. She's an icon amongst the loose wrists on Green Second, you know."

Alistair's expression changed. "I'm being deadly serious. It wasn't her."

Silverman leaned forward, spilling coffee on the floor in the process. He unlaced his shoes and stepped into the spillage with his socks. "Socks are good for soaking up stuff," he said.

Alistair shook his head. He noticed Silverman's bellbottoms, too short, half-mast between knee and ankle.

"Pity about the princess then. I thought we'd use your cinema as the theme for the Belsen Brand video."

"Dare I ask what the Belsen Brand video is?"

"The Belsen Brand is our approach to varsity. Chicks, dope, partying. All the cool stuff. You eliminate the hassle factor, the work, and the exams."

"Great idea, Silverman. You expecting a large increase in applications?"

"Ten fold."

"Commission a study."

"Are you serious? Perhaps when I meet the three chicks at Cavendish. I'll rope them in."

Alistair stood up. Ten minutes connected to Silverman's cerebellum could frazzle anyone. He hoped he'd got the message across about the video.

"Fifty bucks the chicks don't pitch," he wagered.

They shook on it. Alistair looked at the couple on the blanket below Silverman's window. They hadn't moved; they appeared so peaceful in union, content, as if time were irrelevant.

"What's that shit?" He pointed to a mushroom growing through the windowsill. Since the vomit heap discovery and subsequent cleaner's ban on Silverman's room, it had devolved into an organic mess; it could now pass as a science laboratory experiment.

"Now that you ask?" Silverman pushed up his spectacles and stared.

"Fungus," he confirmed triumphantly.

Alistair pointed to another.

"Fungi?"

BREAK

Alistair's shoulders relaxed and he slipped lower in the seat. The Audi pushed one sixty. Five minutes to the Caledon turn off and another forty five through the Overberg on the R316 to Arniston. Every kilometer was a kilometer further away from his worries.

"It's all about your conscience," his father had told him once. "If your conscience tells you it is wrong, you will suffer until you put it right. If you have a clear conscience, if you can sleep at night, you will be fine."

He hadn't been sleeping well. How could he cleanse his conscience? Why could he not stop thinking about Terri?

He sent her another text:

```
What u up 2 4 long wkend? Am in Arniston
```

It was feeble. And elicited no reply.

Alistair imagined her back with her boyfriend, the granite-like rugby star. "Who the fuck is sending you these messages, Terri? I'm going to kill him!"

He guided the car off the N2 and into Caledon. A timely text reminder arrived from his sister Lindy:

```
Dont 4get bday prez 4 Mom!!
```

He cruised down the Caledon strip, not exactly shopper's paradise, stopped at a leather shop, bought his mother a belt.

Not great, but not bad.

Back on the road, he found his mind wandering back to Gorillas, a thought he was hoping to steer clear of for the weekend.

A shark attack video! What next? Perhaps it was time to say goodbye to the crew.

He drove on, the road quiet, only the occasional car passing in the opposite direction.

How much had Devon said? Two hundred and fifty thousand dollars, double for a breach.

Alistair gunned along the narrow stretch of road leading from Bredasdorp to the coast, each passing tree deflecting the sunlight, like flicking pages of a book. He imagined bringing Terri to Arniston; he imagined bringing the nurse.

He opened a window to smell the sea, his progress watched by a jackal buzzard, perched on a telephone pole, hunched over like a streetcorner gangster. A party of muisvoëls played dare before the wheels of his car.

His thoughts shifted to his family. The whole crowd would be down from Johannesburg; he hadn't seen his sisters since Christmas. Lindy, married to Mark; Jenny to Steve; Shelley, unmarried, three rug rats apiece to Linds and Jen.

Thoughts of an Arniston weekend. A relief to be distracted. The girls gossiping in the kitchen while coming up with new and interesting salads for the men sitting outside by the fire, burning meat and talking fishing, cricket, stock markets, politics. Long soothing swims in warm waters, the camaraderie of family, maternal affection, the reassuring grip of his father's handshake.

A Morgan holiday.

The silver Audi whipped past the Arniston signage. The sea loomed ahead like a big blue lake, not a wave in sight. The location of the Morgan abode never failed to impress him: set against a rocky promenade, like an island on a hill, surrounded by water on all sides but one.

"No wind!" Alistair whooped. "Beach time."

He passed the quaint little Anglican Church on the left, followed through the stop street and spun down Church Street to a large grass parking area. The cars signified Morgans in residence: one large new Land Rover Discovery, two hired BMW X3s.

Beyond the cars and green lawn stood the whitewashed walls of Morganhouse, framed by a floating blue sky; a classic beach house, not palatial and dripping with wealth, but tasteful, understated, location is everything, rambling architecture shaped through years of additions and alterations. The kind of place new money would buy and bulldoze. Except that no money could buy this house. John Morgan knew that, god knows how many offers he'd laughed at.

Children rushed to greet him before the car came to a standstill. "Allie, Allie, Allie!" An avalanche of hugs and kisses smothered him. He was the favorite. He rolled on the grass and let the rats jump all over him.

The adults were close behind, elder sisters circling him in a clinch; only Shelley, the youngest, more reserved, standing back, a light kiss on the cheek.

"My boy!" He felt a surge of emotion and fell into the warm embrace of his father.

"Dad," he smiled, a genuine, happy smile. John Morgan pulled back slightly to examine his son. The blue eyes were cloudy.

"My boy!"

Glenda Morgan joined them.

"Happy birthday, Mom." The composure was restored.

Pumping handshakes with the brothers-in-law and macho threats to out surf, out fish, out drink.

"This isn't going to become another wild drinking weekend," Lindy chastised her husband.

Alistair opened the hatchback, extracted a bag.

John Morgan took his case and led the way. "You're in the Anchor Room. Come on. Let's get you changed and head to Main Beach. Bodysurfing. You and me against these jokers your sisters married."

They moved as a group, chatting, laughing, back into the house. Alistair felt a surge of emotion as he walked; this had been missing from his life lately: love, guidance, normality.

$\odot$

An hour in salt water cleared his senses. Father and son versus brothers-in-law for the bodysurfing competition; John Morgan manipulating the results with a changeable set of rules.

In the Anchor Room afterwards, Alistair washed his face at the basin and applied moisturizer with his fingertips. His youngest sister Shelley flopped on the bed, the mattress protesting with a tired creak, her cerise bikini top making damp marks on the cotton sheets, towel draped around her waist.

"You're very disciplined," she said, watching him apply the cream. He turned and smiled at her, dropped the towel dramatically on the sisal mat. He was naked underneath.

Shelley yelped and buried her head in the pillow. "Alistair! Put some clothes on!"

He reached into a drawer and pulled out a pair of thin cotton drawstring pants. "What's your problem?" he laughed.

Shelley looked up. "You never know when to draw the line."

He dismissed the complaint with a wave of his hand.

"Did you unpack those?" Shelley pointed to the pants.

"Nope, I think it was the fairies, while we were swimming."

"You've got it made, don't you?" She shook her head.

He grinned at her. "My mamma, she loves me, she loves me."

Shelley rose and walked to the cupboard. A couple of shirts on hangers; pants, socks, underpants filled the shelves. She shook her head again.

$\odot$

Friday afternoon, lunch outside: cold chicken on fresh Portuguese rolls, various salads on the side. John debated the finer points of the melting ice caps with the in-laws, while Alistair helped his sisters clear the table.

"Not so fast, little brother," said Lindy, the sisters cornering him in the living area as he made his way back to the patio. "So, what's new?"

He shrugged, squatted on his haunches and fingered the Persian; wondered if it was more valuable than his one at Belsen. Probably. His dad didn't love him *that* much.

The girls sat down next to him. A handless clock gaped down from above the fireplace. Morgan ancestors and family memories abided over from their locations on the wall: John Morgan as a young teenager, brown as a berry; a ten pound kabeljou held proudly aloft; John and Glenda in their twenties; collages of the family; a young Alistair on the beach, three or four, bare as usual, an infectious smile, magnetic.

"Ah, little Allie, you look so sweet there," said Lindy, following his gaze. "Shame, what happened?"

The sisters laughed; he joined in. The smile, not so innocent any more, but they still couldn't help being drawn to it.

"He never tells us anything any more," Jen complained.

"He's got a love bite on his bum," Shelley interjected.

"Shelley!" exclaimed the other two. Then softly: "How'd you know?"

"It was a squash ball!" said Alistair, indignant.

Glenda Morgan hovered in the kitchen, a trained ear listening, cautious of her presence.

"No girlfriends?"

"Not even one?"

Alistair rubbed his face. "Lots of girlfriends, no one special."

John Morgan walked in. "That's my boy. Why have one when you can play the field?"

"Says Father who's been married for thirty years," crowed Lindy.

Glenda allowed herself into the room and conversation. "I just want to say it's wonderful having you all together for my birthday. If I cast my mind back I can see you all lying on the carpet just like that, talking and laughing."

⊙

Alistair woke early on Saturday morning. He walked through to the living area; John Morgan, in a comfy chair, browsed the *Saturday Argus*. Seven a.m. on a Saturday in Arniston; how did he get that right?

He stood up and put a hand on Alistair's shoulder. "So glad you could make it, my boy. It's made your mother's weekend."

Alistair rubbed his eyes.

"Tell me about the semester." The father looking for some numbers.

"Not much to tell. I told you about ethics."

"Yes," he chuckled again. Then serious. "Don't let up, Allie. This is the time when it counts. You want to cream this year then go overseas and have a great holiday. Don't get sucked into the Varsity chaos."

"Like you did?"

John play punched him on the arm. "Never. We didn't have any cash anyway. Even if we wanted to party, we couldn't."

"I don't believe that for a second!"

"How are you for money, by the way?"

"Fine, all good."

"You know if you ever need..."

John Morgan made a pot of tea and took it outside. They sat on the cobbled wall overlooking the fisherman's harbor, the morning crisp, gulls circling below, fishermen searching for bait on the low tide.

"I'm worried about the house," said John, looking out to sea.

"What do the engineers say?"

"Oh, the usual crap. Too much sand and clay, not enough limestone. It'll cost millions to stabilize the cliff face. No guarantees."

"What're you going to do?"

"The question is what are *you* going to do? It won't happen in my lifetime. But perhaps in yours."

"Fall into the sea?"

John Morgan shrugged and stared off into the distance.

"Shifting the intolerable burden to the stronger brains of the future," suggested Alistair.

John Morgan frowned before recognizing an ex-Prime Minister's famous quote. "Touché."

"Let's go take a look," said Alistair.

John Morgan's frown returned. "Are you sure you want to?"

"As long as you've got no new tricks up your sleeve," joked Alistair.

"You never let me forget. One little prank..."

"I was eight years old!"

They walked with their tea mugs through the house to the kitchen, the old vinyl floor tiles worn, in need of an update.

"Don't tell your mother," said John.

A *No Entry* sign was pasted on the inside of the kitchen, red and final. John rummaged in a drawer and emerged with a key.

"Your mother tries to hide it in a different place every time."

The door opened and Alistair felt a surge of adrenaline. He filled his lungs with the sea air. A low stone wall around the back yard crumbled down a steep ascent into the sea; deep fissures visible in the footpath.

"It's not a pretty sight," said John with a grimace, his hand testing the tap of a rusty gas bottle.

"Whoa," said Alistair, feeling the familiar anxiety of heights, the notion that something was luring him to the edge, enticing him to jump. It would only take a moment. His stomach lurched.

They inched toward the wall, leaned forward to peer over, down the cliff face, into the contrasting pea green sea below, a stirred soup with traces of cream on the surface, lines of foam and white water. The waves marched on the outcrop in a pattern, refractory forces gorging at the rock face, eroding sandstone; everywhere jagged rocks and caves like pieces of a broken jigsaw.

"It seems hard to believe."

Alistair tried to imagine the house slipping down the ledge, the implosion of mortar into the sea raging below.

"Let's go down the path," said Alistair.

"Oh. I don't think you want to do that."

"When last did you try it?"

"Yesterday."

"Ha!"

John Morgan placed a hand on Alistair's shoulder.

"I can do this," said Alistair.

Alistair started slowly along the path, one foot in front of the other, to his left the cliff, to his right overgrown shrubbery and clumps of grass leading back to the wall of Morganhouse.

Beyond the house, the narrow path opened out onto a small rocky promontory, a triangular heath of waving grass on a limestone surface. On either side, the sea. A weathered red and white beacon marked a position near the edge; a cairn of white stones the midway point between the pinnacle, the edges and the junction where the narrow path returned to Morganhouse.

Alistair stopped and looked around. The only way back was along the footpath. To, his right, the west, he could see the lighthouse; in front, the horizon of the Indian Ocean; east, across the gap, the other houses of the town. He raised his arms above his head and his stomach lurched.

"I'm going to do this," he said to himself. How long had it been? Fourteen years?

John Morgan stayed behind. He shook his head, looked down at his shoes.

Alistair edged toward the cliff on the western side. A lizard with a bright blue head darted for the safety of a rock. Alistair peered over, moved further along until he saw the narrow sandy ledge. He sank down to his haunches then looked back at his father.

"Careful!" called John Morgan. "What happened to your fear of heights?"

"It's still here."

On either side, a sheer fall into the sea. Alistair lowered himself over the edge onto the sandy ledge.

"Be careful, Alistair, for god's sake."

Alistair dropped onto the ledge, a protrusion three by three, completely hidden from the edge. The boom of the sea intensified, its seismic action launching waves against the jagged rocks. He dared not look down. He turned toward the cliff, placed his hands against the rock.

"Alistair!" He heard his father shout.

Alistair took a deep breath. He raised a shoe into a foot hole, a crevice in the limestone, and hoisted himself back onto the precipice. "I'm OK."

They retraced the path back to the house. John put his hand on his son's shoulder.

"Do you still feel it?"

Alistair smiled. "You had balls, Dad. I don't know what made you do it. But you had balls all right."

John Morgan chuckled.

"I wanted to see the look on your face."

"I was only eight, for heaven's sake. I pissed in my pants. Literally!"

"I regretted the day ever since. It really backfired on me. Your mother nearly divorced me. You had to sleep in our bed after that."

Alistair gripped his father's hand. "I'm fine now, Dad. It's nothing. Don't worry."

A gust of wind swept over the promontory. Alistair shivered, doubted his own words.

⊙

Sunday, mid-morning. A girl in a leopard print bikini sashayed expansively down the stairs leading from the car park to beach; soft serve nuzzled against her mouth, dark hair flicking with the rhythm of her steps. Alistair made a screen with his fingers.

"What are you watching?" Shelley asked. She traced the direction of his stare. "Oh," she answered herself.

Alistair slipped his Varnettes down from their perch on his head;

Varnettes in Arniston with their all round protection; rimless Police in Cape Town for the image.

Shelley flicked some sand onto his towel. "Stop perving!"

"Please! I'm enjoying a moment."

Leopard Print strutted past. Alistair rolled onto his back to maintain the train of his attention.

"Let's go to the cave, Allie."

"Nah."

"Please."

Alistair relented; they got up and headed along the beach.

Shelley. Age difference two years. Only unmarried sister. Only sister from whom he sensed a tinge of jealousy. He was the golden child, everyone knew and accepted that, even him. Especially him. It must have been hardest for her.

"What are you doing with the boys?" he said, making small talk.

"Avoiding."

"Probably a wise choice."

The path sloped down toward the sea. Fishermen were crowded onto an exposed reef, remorselessly hurling their rigs of lead and bait into the sea. He stepped aside to allow Shelley the lead onto the rocks. She was an attractive girl: pretty face, short black hair, slim hips but curvy body. His type of girl. He checked out her bum as she stooped to enter the cave. Not bad...

"What are you looking at?"

"For somewhere to park my bicycle."

"Funny, ha ha." She plucked at her bikini pants where the fabric crept into her bottom.

The cave was dark and damp, the narrow entrance allowing in no light, all illumination coming from the wide opening directly into the sea. They sat down on the rocks together. Brother and sister. Alistair thought back to previous excursions there. How many times had they been in here together? Twenty? Between the first time and now, they had grown separate lives.

"Have you ever done anything bad?" she asked him suddenly.

"Bad. Like what? Something illegal?"

"Or unacceptable."

"Shell, stop talking in riddles. What are you trying to say?"

"Do drugs?"

"No," Alistair answered emphatically. "Not my thing. And I hope you don't." He dipped his toe into a rock pool and teased a red crab.

"I knew I shouldn't bring this up with you."

The crab raised its claws, backed out, and scampered into a crevice. Alistair softened his position.

"What's your conscience say?" he asked.

"Recreational fun."

"Well, there you have it. If you can rationalize it in your mind, then you're all right."

They sat in silence for a while. A swell pushed into the cave, water trickled into the rock pools, the tide coming in.

"You ever liked someone?" she asked.

"Is this twenty questions? Like like? Or love?"

"Yeah. Love."

"No."

"Do you know why?"

"Ooh, Shell, you gonna get deep on me here? Tell me why." Suddenly sarcastic, he'd heard it before—from Shelley, from spurned girls he'd handled badly, even Silverman in a moment of weed induced insight: he was spoiled and vain and everyone gave everything to him, and it all just landed in his lap, and he thought he was above everyone, and and and...

"You can't love because you're loved too much."

"Oh that's bullshit, Shelley." He leaned back, scraped off a mussel.

"It's true. You don't love because you're too busy receiving everyone else's love. It doesn't just go for girlfriends. It's family, too."

"Jesus, Shell, a bit harsh, don't you think?" For some reason, he wasn't as annoyed as he thought he'd be. "Well, for your information, there's someone I think I can love." He examined the mussel and passed it on to Shelley. She tossed it into the pool.

"Can love?"

"I don't know her very well yet."

"Have you slept with her?"

"No."

Shelley laughed and whistled. "Let me guess. First year, blonde hair, narrow waist, peachy complexion, big tits."

"Wrong!"

"Close?"

"Exceptionally so."

"You're a joke, Alistair. You're empty inside."

The light from the mouth of the cave dimmed as a cloud obstructed the sun. Alistair thought he heard a sound, looked around to confirm they were alone.

"It's true," Shelley continued.

"So basically I'm a joke and I can't tell the difference between lust or love?"

"Or honesty and treachery."

"Harsh words."

"Someone's got to tell you. Dad certainly won't. He thinks the sun shines out..."

"Lust is a scourge, Shell, I admit it. It ruins genuine feeling. It makes you desire things you don't want. I can't help it."

"Do you lust after me?"

"Don't be ridiculous."

"You have no feelings for me?"

"Of course I do. You're my sister."

"But you know nothing about me. You know nothing about my life."

Alistair opened his mouth to reply, then stopped. The sun came out from behind the cloud. He was used to Shelley's tirades, but this one was more intense than usual.

"All your life you've been given. It's not even your fault. It prevents you from giving."

Alistair rubbed his hands across his face.

"Who am I?" she continued, hands waving about, tears welling in her eyes. "What do I do? Who are my friends? You don't know."

He made to respond, stopped himself, shook his head slowly. "You're right. Jesus, you're right." He took a deep breath.

"That's the most honest thing I've heard you say," said Shelley softly. She touched his leg, looked across at him.

He stared straight ahead into the pool. "I don't know how it got like this....I want to change."

Shelley stood. "Do you have my number on your cellphone?"

He looked down, shook his head.

"I love you too," she said.

They heard voices behind.

John Morgan entered the cave, made his way over with a couple of the youngsters in his wake. "My boy! I knew I'd find you here," he said, squatting beside Alistair and placing an arm around his shoulder. Shelley wrapped her arms around her body.

"Waenhuiskranz: you can turn an ox wagon around in here. Unchanged for centuries, shaped by infinite days of sea and weather. Long before us, long after us. If you sprinkle thoughts here, they are preserved forever." The siblings had heard this speech a million times.

"It's getting cold. I want to go back," said Shelley. She walked alone to the mouth of the cave.

A fisherman tugged frantically on his line, a writhing silver fish whipping over the edge of the reef, flapping breathlessly on the rocks. Sounds of whoops and excitement. Alistair, John Morgan, and the kids went over to check.

"An elf," said John. "A whopper."

Alistair felt a pang of sympathy for the beautiful creature, gleaming sliver and blue as if a light shone from within. He suppressed a desire to run over and toss it back into the ocean.

"Why don't you fish any more, son?"

"I don't like killing things."

Later that day, over lunch, John Morgan shed some light to the brothers-in-law. "He was a little master. I never managed a moment's rest. If I took an afternoon kip, he'd be peeking through the crack in the door every five minutes. Rods out, raring to go. Then one day, all of a sudden, we're driving home, cold and wet, smelling of red bait, empty-handed, tired and sunburned. And we drove past this young girl in a costume and Alistair says—what was it again, Allie?"

"Next time let's go fishing for one of those," Shelley piped in.

Everyone laughed. John Morgan blew through his hand. "Poof. He was gone. Never again to rise."

Alistair looked across at Shelley and turned his fork in the salad.

The Morgans watched the sun set on the horizon, the golden orb sliding lower, an artist's palette of yellows and reds.

"Where's Alistair?" asked John. He examined the milkwood, regretted not telling the garden services to trim underneath.

"Reading on his bed," said Shelley.

"Oh? What's he reading? What's keeping him away from this?" He gestured to the horizon.

Shelley shrugged. She knew it was *The Dice Man*, had read the blurb while Alistair was showering.

Glenda Morgan put her arms around her husband. She wore a white frock, bare feet, no make up, no jewelry. She'd plucked a crimson bougainvillea flower and planted it behind her ear. In the distance, a fishing boat puttered into harbor, birds in tow, laden with wares. The gleam of the sea darkened as the sun disappeared.

"Thank you for a wonderful weekend."

John Morgan stared into the distance. "Of course, my dear. It's a pleasure."

He kissed her lightly on the head and continued his reflection. Wind slithered across the bay; the sea transformed into a grey expanse as the light faded away.

⊙

Monday morning. Alistair shook Shelley lightly. He was tired after a rough night's sleep; dreams of Warnabrother and sharks. He'd woken in a panic, pillow wet with perspiration. Images of Johnny Jackson with Terri that he couldn't erase.

"You've got a bit of sun," Alistair said, running his hand along her shoulder.

Shelley sat up, pulled the sheets up to her neck.

"I'm on my way," he said. "It's late. You've slept for ages."

"I couldn't sleep," she said.

"Neither could I."

She rubbed her eyes.

"Shelley, I....yesterday..." He couldn't find the words. He wanted to tell her that he knew about her drug problem, and that he had problems too, and that if they spoke about them, they might ease each others' burdens.

"What is it?" she said.

He flicked open his cellphone.

"Your number. Can I have your number?"

⊙

The trapped heat in Green 212 greeted Alistair's return. He sorted his laundry and placed the bag in the corner of his room. A tangle of music filtered down the corridor.

Alistair picked up a dice off his desk and spun it in the air. Luke Rhinehart, here we come...

One. I pursue Terri.

Two. I tell Devon I want out.

Three. I aim to pass Cum Laude.

Four. I do the nurse in the ass.

Five. I go with the shark project.

Six. I become a monk.

Alistair rolled the dice. Six.

I can't become a monk.

He changed Six.
Six. I go to the warden and tell him what we did to Terri.
He rolled again. Six.
No ways.
Again.
Five. Not good.
Again.
One. I like One.

GATE-CRASHER

"Sasha!"

The thin girl spun around, jeans hanging loosely on her hips, a white vest washed to a grey, bra straps protruding. Johnny stared at her out of the car window. Pointy face, small brown eyes sunken in their sockets, prominent cheekbones.

He'd parked the blue Cressida on the pavement outside Fuller Hall, expecting Sasha to come this way after her computer science lecture, making her way down to Middle Campus. Johnny's short sleeve shirt was drenched in sweat—the Cressida's air conditioner hadn't worked in years and he'd expected her a good half hour earlier.

"Get in."

She stood rooted to the spot. The fright washed across her blank, dull expression like an icy stream.

He laughed, caught himself, tried a friendlier approach. "Where have you been, Sasha? I've been calling but you won't answer."

"I haven't been well."

Impossible to dispute; her freckled face pallid, hair dank and un-washed, skin blotchy, an unkempt stick insect. She took a step toward the car.

Johnny patted the passenger seat. "Come on, babe. Get in."

She advanced another step then halted, her bony hands repetitively wringing plastic bangles on her arms, an unconscious obsession, sustain-ing her composure.

"What do you want?"

Johnny laughed and slapped his hand on the steering wheel. "What do I want? Come on, Sasha, we had a relationship."

"What happened to me?"

"When?"

"Don't play dumb, you bastard! You know when I mean!"

A pair of passing students turned to stare, moved along, embarrassed.

"Come on, Sasha. Don't make a scene. Get in."

She jiggled the satchel on her shoulders as if to test it was still there, hands trembled, a full scale nicotine crisis.

"Don't be a naughty girl, Sasha. Come along."

She composed herself with a vigorous twirl of the bangles. "You fucked me over, Johnny. I don't know what happened. But you drugged me. You fucking date raped me."

"Nothing happened, it was just a big night out, we were out of it, fooled around, nothing special."

"Fucking liar!"

Johnny's eyes widened and he looked around.

"Sasha. You're making a scene. Nothing happened, I promise."

She spun around and hurried down the stairs.

⊙

Johnny steered the Cressida down Woolsack Drive, phone ringing. He flicked his cigarette butt out of the window. A lady hooted. He gave her the finger, answered the call.

Jeff. Drug dealer. Accomplice.

"What do you want?"

"She phoned me."

"When?"

"Now."

"And?"

"She's looking for a hit."

"OK. Cool. Phone her back. Tell her to meet you outside the Rondebosch library. Give her one more."

"What about my money, Johnny?"

"You'll get it, man. For fuck's sake, you'll get it. It's taking longer than I thought."

"What's the holdup? You said I'd have the money in a week."

"The disc is gone."

"What?"

"Don't panic. I've got another plan."

"Panic is my middle name, Johnny. You don't understand. There's a chain here. If I don't get the money from you, then the Nigerians are gonna start..."

"You think I fucking don't know that? I said you'd get your money and you will. You shouldn't have given that little bitch so much rope. What were you thinking? "

"You always approved it."

"Yeah, yeah. Those days are over."

"You sure you'll get the money?"

"I'll get it."

Johnny accelerated to catch the orange light into Main Road, swung the Cressida into a hard right, across the front of a BMW cabriolet; the driver, in a dark suit, executive haircut, hooted and gesticulated. Johnny put his hand on the iron crowbar next to his seat.

If I wasn't in such a hurry, he thought.

⊙

She sat on the pavement, didn't try to run this time. Her eyes rolled back and she laughed, mouth open, skinny body loose and flexible like a rag doll. Half an hour and Jeff had done his job.

"Johnny. Ooh, Johnny!"

"Get in!"

She climbed into the Cressida.

"Don't flake out on me. I need some help."

Losing the disc was a disaster. Collectively he owed close to a hundred thousand rand. Drug debts, mainly Sasha. Followed up by a dodgy loan, then some last chance sports betting. But he blamed himself; they—him and Jeff—had been so tanked up after the video, on fire with adrenaline and E. They had watched the video of Sasha over and over, laughing and hooting and drinking neat vodka. Then forgot about the disc, left it in the machine.

The next morning it was gone.

And now this guy Warnabrother was in his face. Big fucking sweet-smelling darkie whistling and telling him little stories. "Where's the video? Carlos wants it, man."

But no disc.

He'd assumed it was Morgan, the prick, fucking golden boy, playing a trick on him.

Then worst fears: Devon had it. Of course it would be him. He wondered if Devon knew about Dark Video.

And just when all seemed lost, an email from Mangle. Where had he heard of them?

        Johnny. We want the video. R30 000. Mangle

Followed by a set of instructions for sending it.

He'd responded:

        how did you get my name?? dont know you.
        the disc has been destroyed

And immediately the response:

> We are Dark Video's competition. We are intercepting
> their comms. Did you ever play the video?
> If so, there's a copy on a cache drive.

Cache? He'd never heard of that. That's why he needed Sasha. Fucking little crack whore, but a wizard on Windows. She'd know what to do.

⊙

"You're a genius!"

Sasha had just located a copy of the video in the temporary internet directory under the user "Guest." Johnny leaned in behind her and kissed her roughly on the neck. He steadied her as she swayed back in her chair.

"I want to watch it," she said, eyelids hanging over her eyes, like a boxer after a fight. Gorillas was deserted; he'd locked his door for certainty but checked it now, just to be sure.

"OK. But I want to explain. I did this for the money. To pay off your debts with Jeff. To get us out of shit. It's a video of us making love. Some rich fuckers in America get their rocks off watching this shit."

She double clicked on the file. Windows Media Player sprang to life on the screen. Play.

"That's me. Fuck, I'm so wasted."

Johnny laughed and put his arm around her shoulder, hugged her, started kissing her. He wasn't going to let her watch too closely—ran a hand down her top, stuck his tongue into her mouth, tasted like an old ashtray. But she pulled back, kept an eye on the monitor.

"What happened there?" She sat forward. Johnny was outside the window, Sasha inside, bent over, her body thumping back and forth.

"Who's that behind me?" she screamed. "Who the fuck's that?"

"It's Alistair Morgan," said Johnny, snatching for the mouse and exiting the window. "The fucker tried to crash our party."

IN THE ROSE GARDEN

"How'd you make out at Cavendish, Silverman? Catch a few rounds of the rainbow game?"

Alistair peered around the door of Green 214. Silverman lay prostate on his bed, taking a deep hit from his homemade bong.

"Cavendish?" He stared blankly, his eyes rotating as he ingested the fumes.

"Remember. MXit chatroom? Candy, the provocative teenager? Three little Catholic vixens eager for a tickle party?"

"Oh that," said Silverman. He exhaled a purple fog from his nostrils. Alistair coughed and waved his hands in front of his face.

"I went to the mall, to our rendezvous point. Dirty minxes didn't pitch. But it was weird, man. Freaky." Silverman pulled the pipe to his lips and inhaled.

"Why's that?"

"Well, the chicks weren't there. But there were three other weird-looking guys hanging about. Bizarre!"

"What a coincidence," Alistair sniggered.

"One reaps what one sows, I guess," said Silverman stoically.

"Poor, poor Candy."

"Indeed. No fun for her."

"If it wasn't fun, it must've been sin."

Silverman's eyes went glassy. In the smoky room, he looked like an old man. "The problem with sin is, at its genesis, you don't recognize it as sin. It's disguised as fun. Sin and fun. You can't tell them apart. But something grows. In your room. It's always there; you just don't see it because you're having so much fun. Getting bigger and bigger. Like a mushroom. Ah, my beautiful mushrooms. Until one day you can't open the door because the mushroom is so big. It's consumed everything. Now you can't ignore it. You want to know what it is. 'I'm sin,' it tells you. You say, 'Where's the fun gone?' And this big thing blows the door off your room. And it spills down the corridor, down the steps, sticking to everything."

"That's insane," laughed Alistair. "You're stoned."

"In sin. As I said."

⊙

A busy motorway separates the university Rose Garden from Upper Campus. Students, when they can find a spot, park their cars at its edges

---

and scuttle through the subway to lectures.

Alistair strode up the cobbled path in the direction of the garden, stepping lightly. Face tanned, hair wavy, he veered left and onto the grass.

Terri sat on a bench in the garden, wearing white linen pants, a blue checked cheesecloth shirt, short sleeves, two buttons open, no cleavage. At first he thought she hadn't seen him, but as he came closer, her face changed slowly and a gentle smile, without breaking her lips, transformed her look of serenity into curiosity.

Driving back from Arniston, his sister's words echoing in his ears, he'd phoned her again: "Terri. I need to see you. It's important."

"So what's so important?" she asked.

He handed her a single rose flower and she accepted it without thanks, held it up to draw the scent.

"I want you to know that I can't stop thinking about what happened to you."

"Oh." she turned slightly on her bench to face him. "I feel so silly."

"Don't." He reached out, lightly touched her hand.

"You aren't making fun of me, are you?" She twirled the rose in her hand.

A couple walked past on the cobbled path, down toward Rondebosch. The guy had his arm around her waist; the girl had her hand in the back pocket of his jeans. Alistair watched them go.

"Alistair?"

"No, Terri. Honestly. I'm not making fun."

"More charm than a groom on his wedding day."

"What?"

"Something someone said," she laughed.

"About me?" He felt his cheeks redden.

"Actually, I'm glad for a chance to chat. I finally feel like I have the strength to talk about what happened. You probably think I'm silly, I'm overreacting, nothing really happened. Katie's been on at me to get out and get over it. But it's been difficult."

"I don't think you're silly."

"It's just that, besides Katie and my therapist, I haven't discussed it with anyone. You're the only other person that knows."

"You never told Henri?"

She shook her head and looked around the Rose Garden, flowing green lawns, beds of red and white roses.

"It's beautiful here. Do you suggest this location often?" She smiled mischievously at him and sniffed at his rose.

"No, first time." He acted hurt, fiddled with his sleeves, pushed them up over his biceps, then down again. "I didn't think you'd want to meet at res. And I wasn't sure that you'd want to be outdoors actually. Just took a chance."

"I came here once before. With Henri."

"Romantic?"

"Is that why you asked me here? Romantic setting."

"No, no," Alistair protested. "I just like it here. I thought you would too."

"I do."

She watched his face, looking for signs. He broke into a grin.

"Alistair, you know Henri and I are over. You seem to be a nice guy, but I don't want to jump into another relationship."

Alistair pointed to his chest. "With me? What gives you the idea I'm after you?"

Terri ignored the question, rubbed her hands together.

"This is my coming out day," she said.

He frowned.

Her gaze remained fixed. "You look like Jude Law, you know?"

"That a compliment?"

"Perhaps. Has anyone else ever told you that?"

"No," he lied. "He cheated on his girlfriend with the nanny."

"Do you have a girlfriend?"

"No. Don't have a nanny either."

She giggled.

"What do you think of Jude Law?" Alistair asked.

"He's not my type." She smiled at him, her button nose scrunched up and her teeth flashing.

Chemistry, Alistair thought, missiles of attraction firing in his brain.

"You went to Arniston?"

"Yes. And you?"

"I stayed in my room."

"Curtains drawn?"

She laughed, didn't respond.

"PJs and tissues, romance novel, slippers?"

She nodded.

"And now you're coming out."

She nodded more urgently. "You know, Alistair, you're the only person —of the three who know—who hasn't told me to get a grip."

"I saw you there. I know what it was like."

"You ever been butt naked on a bed of pine needles?"

"Not since last time I..." He cut off an attempt at humor, put his hand on her hands. "Seriously, Terri. You're dealing so well. I didn't appreciate what it must've been like. But if I look at you and I imagine..."

She pulled her hands away.

"Stop imagining!"

"It's good you can laugh about it."

"It's either that or back to the tissues," she said, standing up. "But I'm coming out. I'm a new person. And now I must get back to Tugwell."

Alistair walked her down the hill, along Woolsack Drive, the route they'd walked on the day of the incident. They cut past the swimming pool into the Belsen parking lot.

"Can I see you again?" he asked.

"What for?"

Alistair was out of his depth. Should he just tell her he wanted to see what she was like in bed? No—he knew that much.

"What sort of a question is that? What for? Must I have a reason?"

"Yes," she replied, poking him with the rose. "I told you, I'm not looking for..."

"Look, you make me happy, OK?"

She threw back her head and laughed.

"Isn't that a good enough reason?"

She continued to laugh, then stopped suddenly, put an arm on her hip and looked at him. "For you maybe."

He nodded. "I understand," he said, with an exaggerated air of sadness.

She picked up his hand. "Look, Alistair. You've been very kind to me. And I appreciate it. But you're not my type. Honestly. I..."

Alistair pulled away his hand. "How do you know what type I am?"

"You're Jude Law!"

He shook his head; she spun around and skipped away.

"You can text me," she called over her shoulder. "If you make me happy, I might answer."

Alistair watched her go, then retraced his footsteps back to the Rose Garden. He lay flat across the bench, his head resting on the slat where she'd sat. He covered his eyes with one hand.

Above him, the sun was high in the sky. The weather didn't match his mood.

⊙

When Alistair got back to Green 212, his door was open.

Devon reclined on the couch. He didn't stand up.

"You don't call, you don't write. You don't love me any more."

Alistair flashed him the Morgan ivories. "I've been away."

"Haven't we all?"

"Tea?"

Alistair wondered how he got in, felt rude to ask, imagined he forgot to lock his door. Again.

"That'd hit the spot, Alesandro."

Silverman moondanced past the open door, reversed and looked in. He motioned a movie camera as if playing a game of charades. Alistair closed the door and turned on the kettle.

"What brings you to Belsen?"

"Can't I come visit you, Alesandro?"

He'd never been before.

"Of course you can."

"Where've you been?"

"You know. I went to Arniston for my mother's birthday."

"No, today."

"Oh, today." Alistair pretended to think. He wondered how long Devon had been waiting. He glanced at his phone on the desk; there were missed calls.

"I popped up to campus to drop off a tutorial, chatted with mates on the steps for a while."

Devon nodded. "Left your phone behind?"

Alistair nodded, pointed to the phone on the desk, set about getting the tea ready. Devon remained on the couch, asking arbitrary questions: studies, cars, weather. Alistair realized how little they had to say to one another.

"I think we need to get away, the four of us, quality time with one another. This shark deal is massive. I need to know everyone's on board."

"I'm not, that's for sure."

"I know that, I know that. So we need to listen to one another. Have a chat, get away."

Alistair remained quiet. He doubted Devon's idea of a good time weekend away corresponded with his. And the shark project scared him.

"Where?"

"My uncle owns a farm near Prince Albert. A Karoo sheep farm."

"Are you seriously still contemplating the shark video?"

"Carlos is desperate. I think he'll up the bounty, might be open to suggestions." He lowered his voice. "Look, *Forest Frolic* didn't really cut it. Carlos says the response hasn't been great, he was expecting more from us. I think he's a bit pissed off. Says we were too..."

"Too what?"

"Lenient."

"Jeez, Devon," said Alistair. "We agreed!" He felt the blood reach his cheeks.

"Don't worry, Alesandro. You know I'm with you. No way I want to see anyone unnecessarily hurt. We won't tell Johnny, that's all."

"Do you really think the shark video's viable?"

Devon stroked the side of his face. "Let's put it this way. We've got a boat. We've got the equipment. I wouldn't mind shooting a few sequences. If we could—miraculously—film an attack, then I'd do it. But I wouldn't break the law."

Alistair nodded, didn't respond.

"So let's chat about it in the Karoo. Leave Friday afternoon. Sunday, we're back."

Saturday night, thought Alistair. Good day for a date with Terri.

"I've got a lot of work to catch up with."

"I need you there, Alesandro. Christ, you're my sanity. What with the kid's squeaky voice and Johnny's testosterone, you're my go-to man."

Devon punched Alistair on the shoulder.

"OK," Alistair said without enthusiasm. "Just make sure Johnny behaves himself."

"Absolutely! Glad you've come around." Devon knelt down and ran his hand along the Persian. "What type?" he asked.

"An Ashfar."

"Knot count?"

"A thousand per square inch. You know your Persians?"

Devon shrugged, continued smoothing the rug. As he did so, his shirt ran up his back, exposing a section of skin above his belt.

"What's that?" Alistair asked, pointing to thick welts of skin; they looked like scars from an operation gone wrong.

Devon straightened up and pulled down his shirt. "What's what?"

"On your back," Alistair realized he'd never seen Devon without his top on, never seen him in a swimming costume.

Devon ran his hand inside the back of the shirt. "Oh these. Some old battle scars."

"What happened?"

"It was long ago."

Alistair waited for him to elaborate but Devon changed the subject.

"Alesandro, you've not been yourself of late. What's up? What's happened to my cheery friend? Something's eating you."

"I don't know. I can't explain it. I feel...nervous."

"All the time?"

"A lot of the time."

"Sounds like a similar ailment to what I've got."

Devon reached into his pocket and extracted a brown plastic phial. Alistair raised his palm, shook his hand.

"I know what you're thinking," said Devon. "Pills. But these are different. They're anxiety pills but entirely natural." He took out two and popped them in his mouth.

"Yeah, yeah. No thanks. Not my style."

"Try one. Look, I'll take two more. They're mild. But they make you relax. Sleep well."

"I should be relaxed."

"We all should be. Alesandro, stop worrying. You have choices. You were hardly involved in the Forest deal. Except as a moderator." Devon winked. "Chill. No big deal. The video will go to File B."

Devon held a small blue tablet between his thumb and forefinger. Alistair took it and swallowed. Devon punched him softly again.

"Don't let me down. I need you."

COOL DOWN

"Devon!"

Carlos was happy, freshly shagged, but he could so easily have been pissed. The baby had started crying just as he was rubbing up against his pretty little wife, the wife he hardly got to touch any more since the kid came along. But he'd done the lullaby rocking, then got hold of her in her dressing room. She hadn't had much choice, moaned about his prickly chest, though.

"How are you, Carlos?" Even straight out of sleep, Devon's voice was clear and even.

"You're the man on the spot, Devon. I hear False Bay is teeming with sharks. Only place in the world where the big fellows leap out the water for their grub. How's the planning going?"

Carlos raised an arm to the light, thick black spikes were sprouting through the pale skin, no area spared, even the top of his hand. He could cover it up, wear long sleeve shirts, but he knew the bitch would keep complaining until....He winced as he imagined the waxy strips ripping off his skin.

"On track. We'll spend the weekend together discussing it. Then go into the dry runs. What did you think of the proposal?"

"I like it. Can you make it happen?"

"I think so."

"I like you, Devon. You and I—we could do a lot of business together. This could be your...big break."

"That's great to hear, Carlos. Really, we appreciate it."

"Now, have you sorted out the renegade yet?"

"Johnny? Oh, he won't be a problem."

"Good. He'd better not be. I didn't appreciate his unorthodox approach."

A buzzer sounded. Carlos stepped quickly over to a control board on the wall and pressed a button—caught it quickly before the alarm was triggered. The outdoor floodlights kicked in and the monitor on the wall displayed a shot of the outside garden.

"Hang on a moment," said Carlos. He grabbed the joystick and rotated it through 360 degrees, watching the monitor as he panned the perimeter. No action. Bloody lasers, he thought, never work properly.

"What's happening?" asked Devon.

"Nothing. The intrusion lasers detected a movement. Where were we? Oh yes. I wouldn't mind taking a look at Johnny's video."

"It's no good, Carlos. But what's the feedback on *Forest Frolic*?"

"A very pretty star attraction. But I don't know why you stopped when you did."

"There are sensitivities."

"I haven't got time for that, Devon. But that's your prerogative. I suggest you take less notice of your ethics in the future if you want to get that break. Now, let me take a look at Johnny's video."

"I deleted it. It was rubbish. Really."

"Now why would you do something like that without asking me?"

"Sorry, Carlos. But you've got to believe me; it was really poor quality, a waste of your time."

"Well, I'll have to take your word now, won't I?" A pause, as Carlos allowed his words time to sink in. "As for Johnny, you want to be keeping an eye on him, understand? My man said he had a word but I don't want any more fuckups."

"It's all under control, I promise. Look, we don't need Warnabrother throwing his weight around here. It just spooks us all."

"Warnabrother?"

"That's what we call him."

Carlos laughed, lightening up. "I like it. Warnabrother. Wait until I tell him. He didn't do anything untoward, did he? He can be...difficult to predict."

"I heard him whistling outside my window at five a.m. What's with him?"

"The sailor," Carlos sniggered. "I think, uh, Warnabrother...he was a slave or a pirate in his last life. Spends his money on themed cruises. Takes a cutlass. Uses it occasionally—on people he doesn't take kindly to. But that's not for you to worry about. Try to forget about him. He's in Cape Town for a purpose."

"The murder?"

"It's a worry. We have to protect our clients. Someone's getting their names."

"Well, keep him away from us. Johnny is under control. And Warnabrother stands out like a sore thumb."

"Really? I thought Africa was black."

"It is!"

"Of course it is, Devon. I'm not a complete fool. Now let me deal with the peripherals and you get the men in *Grey Suit* on the bite."

Carlos replaced the phone and smoothed his hair. His wife called down to him. What was it now? The demands of respectability were never-ending.

Here he was trying his hardest to play the model husband and she tested him at every turn. Hardly moved in bed; gave attitude out of it. Christ, if his ex-wife could see him now. He could feel his old habits on the verge of returning: the backhand, the uppercut.

He stroked his hair again. It was cut short and neat. He used an iron to get the look he wanted; otherwise it went bushy and curly, a wild nest. He ran his hand down his prickly chest. How long could he delay the inevitable? Perhaps he should let it grow. Go back to being hairy. The way he used to be.

Alistair was out of place in the world of geeks. His bags were packed for Devon's team building getaway, but he sat watching Richard and Devon at their computers, waiting for Johnny to get home. Hunched over their screens, cables linking cams to computers, downloading, uploading, transmitting images. Whenever Alistair opened his mouth, it generated mirth.

"Did you get that on tape?"

Richard turned to Devon and giggled.

"We don't use tapes any more," said Devon.

"It's all digital now," explained Richard rolling his eyes. He was the super geek. "The quality remains forever. The data is fixed. If you copy fixed data, you get no degradation. It remains fixed. Even if great-great-great-grandchild Alistair junior watches your video, it'll be exactly the same."

Alistair was nonplussed. "But why do you need such expensive gear? My Sony cost four grand."

"Yes, but there are all sorts of Sonys. It's about quality."

"But you said it was fixed."

"Once you shoot it, it's fixed. But you still have to shoot it."

Alistair shook his head.

"OK," said Richard, used to dealing with Philistines. "If you shake your hand while filming, you agree the result will be shaky?"

"Sure."

"Well, if you use a tripod then it won't shake. The more expensive the equipment, the more features and functions available. Better zoom, better focus, white balance, better audio."

"And CCD," interrupted Devon.

"CC what?"

"Charge-coupled device. That's what translates the light from the world into digital ones and zeros. The more the merrier."

"You can shoot the same scene with two DV cameras. That stands for Digital Video cameras. One creates a file of say ten megabytes and the other one hundred megabytes. Same scene. But the big one contains much more detail."

Alistair followed. Sort of.

"But how do you send the hundred megs across the net? It'll block everything up, surely?"

Devon and Richard exchanged glances.

"You want to send little videos around the net then buy cheap," said Devon. "Not much fuss, not much quality, but small files that are internet friendly. That's not our business. We're into movie quality videos. Carlos's clients have their own indoor cinemas; these guys are hard-core enthusiasts. Grainy schoolboy efforts won't impress. We shoot in very high res, compress to a low-quality format and submit to Carlos. He reviews. If he likes it, then we transfer the real McCoy online. It just takes a while."

"Sounds simple," said Alistair, perusing the array of equipment spread across the lounge floor.

"This is the heavy artillery," said Richard proudly, lifting a Canon XL2 camcorder. A huge two by twenty lens added weight to the firepower.

"How much?"

"Five grand."

"Rand?"

"Dollars."

Alistair whistled.

"Devon has two of them. Twenty four frames per second. Film compatible. You can shoot a freaking movie with this baby." Richard was enjoying himself.

Alistair peered at the computer screen over Devon's shoulder. Devon was logging onto a site.

"Video sharing is booming," he said. "This is a new site. Called Ultra. Check it out. Everyone and his dog is a movie director. Cellphones, video cams..."

The screen showed thumbnails of twenty videos under the heading "Recent Submissions." Alistair scanned the narratives underneath. Devon clicked on a video entitled "Sharking in Japan."

"Look at the counter. This was submitted five minutes ago. The counter is 4,218. That's the number of people who've viewed it." He refreshed the page. The counter said 4,620.

"This must be a hot one," he said, clicking on it.

On the flickering screen, a man in a balaclava approached a young woman carrying groceries. He rushed up to her and pulled down her pants. Richard guffawed.

"Is this legal in Japan?" asked Alistair.

Richard giggled and Devon shook his head.

"But won't this put an end to Dark Video? I mean, if they show anything online. For public consumption."

Devon shook his head again.

"This recent submission page will soon be blocked. The owners of these sites cannot afford to allow just anyone to insert an unedited video. They have legal obligations to filter out unacceptable material. Otherwise they'd be sued."

The man in the balaclava struck again.

"We should totally do this," said Richard.

"These sites get away with this for a while, before the complaints come in, then are forced to accept submissions offline, review them and then only publish the legal ones. You could never put a clip like this on YouTube. And Watchit is legal too. They've had some big problems. You'd only find this in the age restricted section there."

Another Japanese woman was frantically pulling up her pants, parcels scattered on the pavement. Alistair blew a whistle through his teeth.

"5,115! This is big business."

"The future," said Devon.

Alistair was getting tired of the tech talk; he changed the topic. "I'm going to grab a beer."

He marched to the kitchen and picked his way through the fridge. Well stocked. Cheeses, vegetables, mayonnaise; Johnny must go mad for a burger. He pushed aside the Black Labels and located a six-pack at the back of the shelf: Amstel. Much better. He returned to the lounge with the beer.

Devon accepted a dumpy. "Did you learn anything?" he asked.

"That I can't shoot *Jaws* with my little Sony?"

"You gotcha." Devon laughed and took a swig.

Alistair tossed a beer to Richard who caught it awkwardly.

"Just one for you, kid," he said. Richard stuck out his tongue.

"When's the beast getting here?" asked Alistair. Their departure depended on Johnny's return from rugby practice.

"Who knows?" replied Richard. "That Neanderthal probably can't even tell the...."

"Hey!" Devon cut him off. "Johnny'll be back soon. I want a nice, quiet, relaxing weekend. No stirring. No shit. From you or Johnny."

"No shit."

Johnny's blue Cressida pulled into the drive, engine revving.

(▶)

Richard, in the back seat with Johnny, sat reading the newspaper. Alistair in the passenger seat, Devon driving.

"Hey, check this. There's been another porn murder. Same lines as the Camps Bay guy."

"Read it," said Alistair.

"'Police are investigating the death of Ray Naidoo, 55, found dead in his Bishopscourt home yesterday morning. He had been shot at close range in the back of the head. Police spokesman Gerrit..."Blah blah." Richard scanned ahead. "Check this: 'Naidoo is currently under investigation by the Special Branch. He is alleged to have been involved in a pedophilia ring passing child pornography over the internet.'"

"I wonder if this is linked to the Camps Bay murder?" asked Alistair.

"Who knows?" replied Richard. "Cape Town's the murder capital of the world."

"Both wealthy, both executed in their homes, shot in the back of the head—that doesn't happen every day," said Alistair. "Plus the internet porn connections."

"Who cares anyway?"

"Who cares? Dodgy internet trading—that's similar territory to what we do. I reckon it's worth caring."

"Maybe they're Dark Video clients," said Johnny, drumming with his fingers. He was desperate for a cigarette.

The car rollicked on along the dusty Karoo road; dust spewed from the back wheels, blowing a film of red smoke over the green fig trees. Alistair wondered when last it had rained.

"You ever consider nicotine patches?" asked Richard.

Johnny pulled up his right sleeve and showed off the attachments. He opened the back window, the heat outside permeating into the car, dangled a plastic Coke bottle from the window, the rushing wind creating a tuneless harmonic within the aperture of his instrument.

Devon checked the interior temperature on the front dial. "You're messing up the temperature," he said.

Johnny's eyes were closed, lost in his world of winds and sounds. It was a long journey. Three hours along the N1, past places with names like De Doorns, Touws River, Laingsberg, until a turn off the national road onto a dirt road that wound and extended forever.

Devon braked heavily, momentum pushing his passengers forward, Johnny's face thrust into the gap between his headrest and the window arch. Devon fired his elbow, up and to his right, landing a solid blow on Johnny's jaw. Alistair had predicted the outburst, but the sudden viciousness took him by surprise.

"What the fuck!" Johnny sat back in a daze.

"Shut the window!"

Johnny wiped his hand across his mouth and reached for the window button. "Jeez. Keep it cool."

"It's nearly 40 degrees outside. I've been driving for three hours. I'm not cool."

Richard sniggered in the back seat alongside as Johnny gingerly shifted his jaw from side to side.

Alistair turned up the volume on his iPod. This was team building...

⊙

They arrived in darkness to an old farmhouse: thick whitewashed walls, tin roof, wooden floors. Beds allocated, they turned in, happy to sleep off the long journey.

Alistair woke early and strolled down to the orchard, small and unkempt. How do the trees survive here? he wondered. He didn't really get this place. Pretty, in a harsh kind of way: red dust and shimmering heat before breakfast already, stark vegetation able to survive on the sniff of a raindrop. He stepped carefully along a narrow footpath that hugged the inside of an old stone wall. The grass grew long against the edges; Devon had warned of snakes.

He imagined Terri on the farm, blue eyes casting color on the drab environment, like flowers of a jacaranda. Mentally, he selected her wardrobe: blue and white checkered shirt, one size too big, unbuttoned, tied at the waist; faded blue jeans, not tight, the type that hung low, like a gunslinger; short brown boots; hair loose, lace, an Alice band.

A tickle of a breeze released the scent of the orchard: naartjies, figs and lemons. He followed the concrete sluice, water trickling slowly from the reservoir, dripping through a hose against the base of the trees.

He texted Terri:

In karoo. No fun without u. Help

She replied:

sleeping. Call yr nanny

A truck of farm workers shattered the serenity, descending quickly into the valley, dry brakes screeching.

Wait, thought Alistair, wasn't this dream his nightmare? White picket fences and snaking dirt roads leading to a place where he could take a wife and plant his roots. He chuckled to himself. What had he taken last night?

"Just take it," Devon had said. He'd popped the little white tablets in his mouth and slept like a baby.

Whatever it was, his imagination ran wild, a giant wide open Karoo canvas splashed with images of Terri in hipster jeans. He placed her in the kitchen, hands on hips; in the bedroom in a thin negligee, dark nipples visible.

Voices of the farm workers disrupted his thoughts. He tried to recapture the images, but the nurse was there....She reposed naked in the orchard, belly ring glinting, a bed of fallen leaves and decaying fruit, defined leg muscles, her olive skin wet with perspiration, a contrast to Terri's soft pale complexion.

"Breakfast!" Richard yelled from the porch.

Alistair dug his hands in his pockets and turned back toward the farmhouse, the tin roof, silver tinted with orange dust, reflecting the climbing Karoo sun.

⊙

Johnny drove like an animal, foot on the pedal, elbow out the window, cigarette in hand.

They'd spent most of the day discussing *Project Grey Suit*, as Devon had called it, running through different scenarios, reading articles on shark attacks downloaded from the net. Richard had displayed the research on the laptop: pixellated images of a goofy surfer getting nailed in the middle of a cutback at Nahoon Reef; shaky footage of an oceanic research student losing a leg in the South Pacific. Shark attacks had been filmed, but it was low-grade opportunism only. Devon made them sit through a couple of *National Geographic* documentaries: one showing shark experts free diving with great whites in Gansbaai; the other shot off Seal Island, footage they'd all seen somewhere along the line, of seals swimming on the surface and being hit from below, sharks breaching, cartwheeling through the air.

Afterwards, Devon and Richard had slipped off for a walk to the river.

Alistair, feigning stomach cramps, had headed to his bed—but Johnny had come calling.

"We're going to Prince Albert for a drink."

"We are?"

"You and me," crooned Johnny.

Alistair closed his eyes.

"Come on. Don't be a pussy, Morgan. A few drinks will do you good. Besides, I'm not sure how much of this place I can handle without a beer or five."

"Er…"

"Pussy, pussy, pussy," Johnny goaded in a girly voice.

"Fine. I'll drink anything you put in front of me, big shot."

Johnny lifted him roughly off the bed, face against his face. "Fighting talk. I love it."

Three beers each were emptied in less than twenty minutes at Kromby's Bush Bar—quarts, at Johnny's insistence.

Johnny swaggered for the toilet, to break the seal, a big slap on Alistair's back, shaking the legs of his stool. Alistair reeled already, a fighter on the ropes. He stared out the window: a forlorn assortment of old buildings, an empty parking lot, a spread of abandoned, rusty farming equipment. Paraffin lamps blazed on the walls, the smell of kerosene ingrained into the room.

"What's your name?" asked Alistair.

"Who me?" replied the barman.

"No, behind you."

They were the only people in the bar.

Alistair slipped him a fifty rand note. "Here's the deal. If I order tequila, you pour me water. I'll pay for it and you can have the money. But mine are water, his are tequila. If I order a quadruple, you give him four tots and me one topped with water. Got it?"

The barman looked mortified. Alistair peeled off another fifty.

"I'm counting on you."

Johnny reappeared, tucking his shirt down the front of his pants and buttoning himself up.

"How's this fucking shirt?" Johnny wore a loud floral Hawaiian shirt, all but one button undone.

"Two tequilas each," said Alistair as Johnny whacked him on the back again. He was on the offensive.

"You're in good spirits," said Alistair.

Johnny raised his glass. "It's a Saturday night and I just got paid," he shouted tunelessly. Alistair vaguely recognized the song, it had "belly full of beers," and "switch blades" in the lyrics.

"We should've done that chick, Morgan, that little princess. The money would've been tripled!"

Johnny spun around and checked around the bar.

"Watch what you say, Johnny. People might..."

"Chin chin." Johnny raised his shot glass. Down it went. Alistair sighed and followed suit. Then the next one. He looked at Johnny. Not a blink of the eye.

Double the stakes; he ordered another two each and a quadruple Bell's.

"I like this man," said Johnny, throwing an arm roughly over Alistair's shoulder. "Maybe you're not such a prick after all, huh?"

Forty-five minutes later, Alistair had turned the tide. Various quantities of tequilas, whiskey, and beers had gone down; Johnny weaved and slurred.

"Why'd you guys destroy my video? You can't believe the quality—pure show business."

"Devon's a prude." Alistair didn't want to say he'd seen it.

"A rude?" he started to laugh. "I've seen some rude things, I tell no lie."

"Tell me more."

Johnny put a finger to his lip.

"Another quadruple," called Alistair, alcohol to lubricate the flow of truth.

"But fuck him. Fuck him!" Johnny's decibels were on the rise. He cupped a hand to the side of his mouth, pulled Alistair forward off his chair with the other.

"I fucked him. I made another copy."

He performed a victory shimmy, his eyes never leaving Alistair's, whipped out his wallet, pulled out a wad of notes. "Where do you think this comes from?"

Alistair looked away. Johnny grabbed him around the neck again. "You're not going to run and tell Devon, are you?" He was slurring, spittle spraying into Alistair's face. "Because if you do...if you do..."

Alistair raised his hands in submission, brushed off his shirt.

Johnny was distracted by the entry of two men and a woman, the volume of patronage drastically increased. He looked them up and down as they sidled up to the bar. Not locals, but relaxed, part of the place. Green shirt, yellow T-shirt—the men. Purple shirt—the girl. Big tits.

Johnny beckoned them over. "Drinks all round for my friends." A round of beers for the men and a Southern Comfort for the lady. Alistair made small talk while Johnny disappeared to the bathroom. They were from Worcester, working for a building contractor in town.

Johnny returned, shirt hanging out.

"I've got a dare for you fellows. Sorry, and dame." They leaned forward to listen. "Barman, give me two tot glasses, one with water and one with whiskey."

Alistair scrutinized the girl. She looked cheap. Would he give her one?

"Now," slurred Johnny. "I bet you five hundred rand I can make the whiskey and water swap glasses. Whiskey from here to there, water from there to here."

"What, without first pouring them into other glasses?" checked Yellow T-Shirt.

Johnny nodded.

"And your mouth?"

"No interim container, sonny. No mouth, no glass, nothing. It's magic."

"Without spilling?"

"No spilling."

"We don't have five hundred rand," laughed Green Shirt.

"Otherwise you'd be on," said his friend. They clanged their beers together and laughed.

Johnny rubbed his forehead. He hadn't given up on the deal. "Wait. We renegotiate."

Alistair prodded Johnny in the ribs. "Let's get out of here."

Johnny slapped the hand away.

"Your girlfriend does a strip for us."

The two men laughed again. They glanced at their companion. She sipped on her Southern Comfort and ignored them.

"Five hundred for a strip tease, babe," one said. "That's more than you charge for a blow job."

The two men laughed. She cast them a glare.

"Come on," coaxed the other. He slipped his arm around her waist. A thin smile lit up her face. "Just a little dance?"

"Deal," said Yellow Shirt to Johnny, before the smile disappeared.

"Deal!" bellowed Johnny and banged his fist on the bar counter.

Johnny removed a credit card from his wallet. He placed it on top of the tot of whiskey and slipped it across so that a narrow arc of the golden liquid was visible. Then he quickly inverted the tot of water on top of the credit card. The two men stared, dumbfounded, as the water and whiskey began immediately to transfer from one glass to the other.

"Check it out changing glasses!" They clapped and exchanged grins.

The girl looked down, hair falling over her face, flicked her fringe defiantly.

"Look, she doesn't have to do it," said Alistair.

Johnny smacked him hard on the chest. "Like hell she doesn't. Let's see it, baby."

The girl stared at him, the same glare from before, sipped gently on her Southern Comfort. "Screw you," she spat. "I had nothing to do with this bet." Johnny turned to her companions with menace. They nodded.

"A bet's a bet, babe," said Yellow Shirt. He seemed to be the boyfriend.

"Screw you all," she swore back at them.

"I want to see your big tits shaking, baby," said Johnny, performing a merry jig, the words altering the mood in a heartbeat. The men, cowards to his bully, put down their beers, unsure of what to do.

"Look, man, watch what you say."

"Johnny, let's get out of here," said Alistair, getting off his stool. "Devon's going be pissed we took his car."

Johnny shoved him backwards, into the stool, clattering them both to the ground, then turned back to the girl. He advanced on her, lunged, ripped the buttons off the front of her shirt. Her companions leaped to her rescue, one jumping Johnny from behind, the other trying to wedge himself in front of the girl. Johnny, enraged, swatted them away, gripped the front of girl's bra, clawing at her breasts.

The barman scurried around the counter, fumbling with a canister of pepper spray, but Alistair got there first, connecting Johnny across the back of the head with a full bottle of wine. He swayed and tottered, collapsed, one hand still gripping the torn front of the girl's shirt, pulling her down on top of him. Alistair stared at the bottle in his hand, amazed it hadn't shattered, amazed he'd had the balls to use it.

The girl stood up, furiously brushing herself off. She kicked viciously at Johnny's face, screaming hysterically. "You fucking animal!"

"I'm sorry," said Alistair, the air purple with screamed obscenities. The men pulled the girl away, pendulous breasts flapping from her shirt.

Jesus Christ, it's the *Jerry Springer Show*, thought Alistair.

With the barman's help, he dragged Johnny's unconscious form to the car. Alistair slipped him a hundred rand note.

"Don't come back," he said.

Alistair delivered a mock salute, dropped the car keys as he climbed into the driver's seat. The booze had obviously worked on him, too.

▶

A strange sequence of events; he wasn't sure if it were real or a dream. He'd woken up—or had he?—still drunk, with a full bladder and thirst; tiptoed in the inky blackness through to the toilet, sound the only guide to ascertain accuracy. Stumbled through to the kitchen, opened the gas fridge, poured orange juice down his throat, like liquid running onto dry sand. Then a noise. Quietly pushed the fridge closed with his bum. The door of Devon's room opened. Richard stood in the doorway, gas lamp swaying, the dim luminescence highlighting his pale white body and flaccid penis. The words "I love you" drifting toward Alistair. Richard's footsteps creaking across the wooden floor, Alistair motionless, the secret voyeur, afraid to breathe in case he drew attention to his presence. Then back in his bed, asleep.

⊙

Richard was on duty again before the old black metal hob: fried eggs and bacon, orange juice, toast. Alistair moped at the breakfast table on the wide porch, Devon opposite him, quiet. In the eaves above, a swallow darted back and forth from her mud nest. Johnny lumbered outside, a bear with a sore head.

A text beeped on Alistair's phone.

hey jude nanny got ur tung? givn up?

He replied:

Nanny no show. How can I make u smile?

"Who're you texting?" Richard set the table, looked over his shoulder.
"My sister." Alistair deleted the messages.
"What'd you say happened here?" Johnny rubbed the dome of his head.
"You must have had a bottle of tequila. Fell back off your chair and thump. Against the bar counter." Alistair used two hands to credibly illustrate what hadn't happened.
"And here?" Johnny pointed to the cut where the girl's stiletto had sliced him in the face.
"Your glass. Smashed as you hit the ground. You might want to check there's no glass in there."
Johnny lifted his shirt, a morass of grazes and carpet burns. "These?"
"Uh. Well, when we were dragging you to the car..." Stick to the truth, change only what you have to.

"I'm going to go lie down." Johnny's pained face departed, the wounded bear retreating to its cave.

Devon chuckled. "That isn't what really happened, is it?"

"Without a lie." Alistair made a cross on his heart.

"I phoned the bar this morning. The barman said two men drank copiously, fought with the locals, and then one man hit the other over the head with a bottle."

"Isn't that what I said?"

Richard delivered the plates to the table, sat down alongside Devon.

"You skate on thin ice with that fellow, Alesandro."

"Hey, he's the idiot who brought it on himself. He skates on thin ice with me."

Devon stared at Alistair across the rickety table. The color of his eyes appeared grey-blue, the usual charcoal lightened by the morning sun.

"Skating? I love skating," Richard chirped up, mimicking an American accent.

Alistair shoveled a toast/egg/bacon mouthful and peered across at Richard. He wore a little white vest and runner's jogging shorts. Of course. Why hadn't he worked it out before?

⊙

Alistair studied the clip carefully: South Pacific, 1994. Richard controlled the Windows Media Player. The video showed an underwater view of a shark, supposedly docile and predictable, ripping a man's calf muscle.

"This is the best one," said Richard, clicking on another file.

A man in the water swims slowly, stretched on his stomach, a boat on either side, one from which the camera rolls. No further than five meters away. The voices are speaking English. A number of people watch from the other boat, caught in the background of the video. The pitch of a solitary voice is higher, the message inaudible. The swimmer looks about, his legs drop down below him. A dark black shape passes under him, indistinct, but a slight turbulence. The movement of the swimmer changes. A cry: "Shark!" The picture shakes, the cameraman curses, loses the focus, blurry shots of the deck and his feet, the sound of panicked voices.

"I wonder why they were filming him?"

Devon smiled. "And why so many people were watching? I guess we always wonder that now."

"And he's alone in the water while everyone else is on board."

"Go back to the point where the shark appears," instructed Devon.

Richard tracked back and paused.

"That's the money shot," said Devon. "You'd want a close up on his face if you could get it."

"It's classic reality video," remarked Alistair.

"But you see fuck all," said Johnny, still moody. "That guy lost his leg. Right off!"

"You're right, Alesandro. It's the perfect scene," said Devon. "If only the cameraman had held his nerve. Tight shot of the swimmer's face, slow pan back to catch the reaction of the onlookers."

"I think it's more effective this way," said Alistair. "The terror is heightened by the voices, the blurred shots. It's more *Blair Witch Project*. But obviously the cameraman stops filming when he realizes what's happening."

"Stupid fuck," said Johnny.

"Let's get back to business," said Devon. "We're going to have some fun with this one, an opportunity to do some boating, check out False Bay, spend some time in the sun. Maybe something will come along, maybe it won't. We launch the boat from Kalk Bay a couple of times a week, to fish or spear dive in the bay."

"We should probably vary it, don't you think? Maybe find some other launch spots, so we don't look suspicious," Richard said, trying to be helpful.

"Sure. Vary it a bit. We dummy run the course of events and ensure other boats notice our presence, so when—or if—a D-day arrives, no surprises pop out the woodwork. The other boats will say we told you so. Then we'll need to do some chumming when they're not around, find some good spots, see how hard it is to attract the star of the show. Give Seal Island a recce because we're guaranteed to find them there."

"But won't it always be surrounded by tourist boats and cage divers?" Richard again.

"I've called around. There are three licensed operators for False Bay. One guy very rarely makes trips, a handful per year, but the other two go out regularly, whenever conditions are good. But they mostly go in the morning, from the sounds of things, so we might have to check it out later in the day, catch them feeding at dusk."

The others nodded, absorbing all the information. Alistair was unsettled by Devon's research, immaculate as usual. And the planning—nothing left to chance.

"I also want to test the cameras. See what type of clarity we can get, check that the pole mount works..."

"But what's the point without a victim?" Johnny interrupted. "This sounds like a lot of work for no reason. What's the point? Where's the money coming from?"

"Relax, Johnny. Learn some patience. Alistair will find us a terminal patient and use his charms."

I will, thought Alistair. Well, he did know a nurse...

Johnny shook his head. "It'll never work." He prodded a finger into the stiletto wound, a trickle of blood appeared.

"Old dying guy signs up for last payout," laughed Richard. "It's a bit far fetched."

"Alistair thinks it can work, don't you, Alesandro?"

"I do?" Alistair looked quizzically at Devon.

"It's bullshit," said Johnny, his face contorting as he drew on a smoke.

Richard waved his hand in front of his face. "Can't you take that outside?"

"You're in on this now, Morgan?" asked Johnny.

Alistair looked at Devon and shrugged. "Well, I'm keen to see some sharks, so I'll come along for the ride. And if you really insist, Devon, I'll check out a hospice or an old age home, just to prove what a ridiculous idea trying to convince someone to jump into a shark's mouth is. That's it, nothing more."

Johnny nodded, seeming to agree. "The sharks are tame! Cage diving's altered their behavior. They swim up to the boats when they hear the motor. That's why my deal makes sense. We bet Carlos I swim with the lurkies. Even chum up the water. I'm cool with that. How many shark attacks are there, for fuck's sake? What's the chance?"

"They may not deliberately hunt us, but I wouldn't call them tame," said Alistair. "They're curious. They'll give you a bite just to see what you are—and that's your leg gone, thanks for playing."

"Attacks are a mistake!" Johnny replied. "If you know what you're doing, keep your eye on them, you're fine."

"You sure, Johnny?" Richard piped up. "Reckon you'll be thinking that when it's swimming past your nose? I would be crapping in my pants. I almost am just thinking about it."

"You saw those guys free diving in that video? They looked fine to me."

"They're experts! Been around sharks for years!"

"Whatever, little Ritchie, last of the fearless warriors. I feel shit for sharks. Let me get in the water with the shark. I'll bring home the cash.

We can cut through all this waiting shit."

"You been in the sun today, Johnny?" Alistair getting in a dig.

"I'm warning you." Johnny wagged his finger at Alistair. "You keep provoking me, one day I'll take you down. Down to mother ground, my friend."

"Woo," said Alistair with a mock shiver. He smiled at the memory of crashing the wine bottle on Johnny's head.

⊙

Alistair slept on the back seat for the duration of the ride home. Belsen was quiet when he returned, students preparing for the onslaught of a new week of lectures. His room was warm and musky, bed unmade. He fell on it and pressed his head into the pillow.

Project Grey Suit. He felt strangely detached, as if it didn't really matter. What were the chances? In the current, he'd just have to go with the flow.

He checked his watch, ten thirty, wondered what Terri was doing. She had replied to his earlier text:

    if u have 2 ask u will never know

He looked up a solution on the net. "How do you make someone happy?" One: "Walk in the rain."

He texted back, 10:31

    Lets go 4 a walk in the rain?

She replied, 10:32

    its not raining

Two: "Do something that involves sweating." Pass.

Three: "Be nice." Hmm. He tried again, 10:35

    I like the way ur hair shines

He regretted it as the sent message flashed. She replied instantly, 10:35

    yawn

Four: "Be honest." 10:41

> Sorry. Not good at making u :) Glad I met u tho

She replied, 10:42

> sweeter than a boy scout on do good sunday.
> g2g sleep

Devon had slipped him a brown plastic phial of thin blue tablets when they'd dropped him off. He took two and went to sleep.

MANGLE

He'd finally pinned her down. Waited on the grassy mound outside Tugwell, lots of girls waving, asking him what he was up to—"Just chilling"—until he saw her hop off the Jammie Shuttle Bus. Her blonde hair was tucked under a scarf, emphasizing her face. He did a double take. It made him realize how perfect her features were.

"I've been phoning and phoning," he teased. "Every time you ignore me, it's a dagger to the heart."

Terri smiled, wasn't sure what to say.

He threw a cursory look over his shoulder. "You want to come for coffee down the road?"

She swayed her head from side to side, pondering the decision.

"I really have been trying hard to get hold of you."

"I know." She hugged her varsity books to her chest. She wore a fluffy white T-shirt with a light brown skirt, laceless tackies, no socks. "Who did you go away with?"

"Just some guys. No nannies."

She seemed to be assessing him, he thought, evaluating his capacity for honesty.

"Coffee?"

"I don't drink coffee."

"Tea? I want to talk to you."

"About what?"

"Why are you making it so hard for me?"

"Alistair, I told you, I..." She placed her hands on her hips.

"And I told you I understand."

She raised her eyebrows expectantly.

"I can't explain," he mumbled. "Come. Please. Humor me. I'm pleading here."

She sighed and started to walk, beckoning him to follow. He skipped after her.

They wandered down to Main Road, Rondebosch, walking in the shade of the giant oaks. He led her to Bella Vista, a student café above Pick'n 'Pay, knew he wouldn't bump into any of the Gorillas' gang there.

"Do you have Buitenverwachting?" he asked the stout waitress.

"We got white and we got red. By the glass."

Terri undid her scarf and shook out her hair.

"Two glasses of white, please."

"Wine?" said Terri. "No, not for me."

But it was ordered. And it arrived quickly, worked its magic. They chatted about varsity, beaches, happiness, cellphone contracts.

"So. What did you really want to talk to me about?"

"I feel so terrible about what happened to you."

She frowned, sipped at her wine. Her second glass. She shrugged her shoulders. "I really want to put it behind me, Alistair."

He pursed his lips. Two students came through the door, slammed their rucksacks on the counter, ordered beers; they looked happy and relaxed.

"Have you?" he asked.

"I'm trying."

Alistair closed his eyes. Jumpy images flashed back to him. Cars upside down on Hospital Bend, brakes screaming, steamy visions of naked strippers, legs spread, Sasha's vacant expression, her head in her arms, body thudding back and forth....Why were the images stuck in his head? Why wouldn't they just disappear?

"Alistair?"

He opened his eyes and blinked. "You know you said something about a feeling? A premonition?" she said.

"Yes."

"It's strange. I've got a feeling too. I keep wondering about it. And it just won't go away."

"What's the feeling?"

"It's dread."

⊙

"Aren't you hot?" his wife asked. Carlos brushed off the remark, dabbed at the perspiration on his forehead. Beneath his clothes, the sweat streamed down his flanks. But he wasn't about to take off his cardigan or his long trousers. Not with all the hair growing back; the ingrowns and the patches.

He watched his wife at the water's edge, barefoot, such a nimble little fairy, dress hoisted up into her panties, feet kicking off the jetty into the water, holding the kid. Gramps and Gran rocked on the bench, enjoying the view, the day, the family frolic. If only they knew where all the money came from...

He looked back toward the stately mansion, its multilevel garden rolling down toward the water.

This life, he'd created.

A decade before, he'd got together with a partner, a fellow Brit, borrowed £250,000 to buy a few blurry photographs of a princess dying in a tunnel. The bad ones that the tabloids wouldn't even consider. Sold them for double a week later. And they were in business, riding the internet boom.

"That's the thing about shit," his partner had told him. "There's a shitload of it!" And when the heat finally came, the partner couldn't take it—swallowed the barrel of a Walther—so he skipped the UK, ditched the then-wife, a new and anonymous life beckoning in the States. Met a new princess, blonde and fifteen years younger. And respectable, just looking for a prince to lavish her...

He'd been determined to do it right this time. And it had taken some time.

For all their old money and wariness, Gramps and Gran weren't shy to accept the SUV he got them, or the beach cottage, or the European holidays. He'd behaved immaculately, held his temper. Kept the fists down. This new life of his....He wondered if it was worth the effort.

Carlos turned his face up toward the sun. He could feel his pale skin burning. What would the week be like? Two potential new agents to screen: one in Venezuela, another in Japan. And a few more letters to the Department of Justice; the legal video sharing companies were airing some really ugly stuff these days. Appalling. Decent citizens shouldn't stand for the stuff. The Israeli army massacre on Watchit was just terrible...

It wouldn't happen again, that's for sure; he'd seen to the errant Israeli mules. But he'd use that cockup to his advantage.

"And how are your parents, Carl?" They always asked that. Parents-in-law always ask about their counterparts. He didn't answer.

"Carl!" the wife called sharply. "Mom is talking to you."

"Uh, sorry." He forced a weak smile. "They're, uh...fine."

"Oh, I'm pleased to hear that, Carl."

He mentally scanned through his database of clients. He didn't need a printed list; he had that sort of brain. In his head he visualized the typed names, their addresses, their preferences, one hundred and sixty-five active, five new ones last week, each with a unique obsession. He'd need to brief the agents, up the ante.

And then there was the email from Mangle. Bloody Mangle. Who the hell were they? Making strange enquiries, checking him out.

The baby shrieked. He scanned the perimeter of the property. So what if he had the only electric fence in the suburb? And if they got over that, there was the laser. It was impregnable.

"Carl," his wife hissed. "If you're gonna lurk around all day like some dumb English monkey, you may as well go inside."

Fucking bitch, he cursed silently. But he took the gap. The first email he opened elicited more curses: Mangle!

⊙

Richard heard a dull thud. He stood up from his desk—swotting new search algorithms—and opened his door.

"Hello?" He ventured out.

The passages of the house were quiet. Johnny was at rugby practice, Devon probably asleep after a long night. He'd heard murmurs of his voice deep into the morning.

He walked down the passageway to Devon's room, familiar creaks on the wooden floors preceding his intent. A dent in the closed door of the room caught his attention.

"Devon?" He knocked gently.

"Come in."

Devon's room was sanctity. It was always locked. Richard pushed the door open, looked around the room, meticulously ordered.

"What was that noise?"

"My fist. The door."

Richard tried to touch Devon's hand, but he pulled away.

"We've got a big problem."

"What is it?"

"Look at this!"

He showed Richard the email.

```
To:      D.Deacon
Sender:  Dark Video

Subject: What's going on!!!

Devon,
What the bloody hell is going on!??
We picked up this clip from Mangle—the tech boys
reckon it came from Cape Town. Is this the rape
video Johnny tried to vend? It's visual poetry,
did you see her reaction? We could have made
big cash here. We are still tracing but do you
know anything about it!?
```

```
Get back to me urgently.
Carlos
Click on: www.darkvideo.com/priv176.wmv
and password 4255266
```

Devon clicked on the link and entered the password at the prompt on a blank blue screen. A black box appeared with controls beneath. Three minutes forty seconds. The header: "Assjacker. Sasha is a dirty girl."

"Freak!" said Richard, before a grainy black and white copy of the video flickered to light. "It's Johnny's video. How the hell?"

Devon slapped the side of the desktop and killed the video window. He slumped in a chair, one hand on his head.

"I thought you destroyed the copy," said Richard.

"I did."

"You played that video. To Alistair."

"Yes."

"A cached copy on disc?"

"You think I didn't think of that. I deleted it from the Devon directory. And I also checked Johnny's. There were no copies."

Richard logged in from Devon's work station and scanned the network. His fingers flew at the keyboard, his eyes darting at the screens as file names and numbers flashed across.

"It's not here now," he said. A list containing emails sent flashed on the screen. Devon ran the cursor down through the list. "Not sent from here either."

He logged back onto the Dark Video reference and clicked on the video again, as if hoping it would disappear.

"How could Dark Video get it, if it was sent to Mangle?" Devon asked himself aloud.

"And who would have sent it to Mangle?" asked Richard.

"Johnny. Obviously."

"Dark Video could be clients of Mangle," proposed Richard.

"Yes. Good thinking. It's common practice. Know your enemy. What I want to know is how Johnny hooked up with Mangle in the first place?"

"We've spoken about Mangle before," suggested Richard, his eyes flicking, never leaving Devon, watching Devon's hooded eyes, his clenched jaw.

"But not how to contact them."

Richard scanned Carlos's angry words.

"Shit," he said. "Johnny's an asshole. What're we going to do?"

"The question is what's Carlos going to do?" Devon ran his finger across his throat.

"Johnny?" said Richard. "Surely not."

"Carlos is mighty pissed. This is serious."

Richard scanned the message from Carlos. "Visual poetry? I thought you said DV didn't want the video. Why didn't you send them the copy?"

"It's not my style. And it was rape, no two ways about it."

Richard looked away.

"Who helped Johnny?" asked Devon, his eyes narrowing. "He couldn't send a file if he had it in his hand. Someone helped him find and send it."

Richard shrugged.

"What about the girl?" Devon said.

"Sasha? She's not going to send her own video. Is she?"

Devon nodded. "She's a junkie whore. Needs money."

"What about Alistair?"

Devon straightened up and turned to face Richard. A thin smile tickled his mouth and he slapped Richard lightly on the cheek.

"You're still sweating Alistair, aren't you, Ritchie? Relax. There's nothing to worry about."

"I'm not worried. I'm just being prudent." Richard picked unconsciously at his face. "We know he has been seeing Terri."

"Yes. We know. Please don't scratch like that. You're bleeding."

Richard wiped his forehead with his sleeve; Devon grimaced.

"Well, I worry about Alistair. Don't you?"

"I don't."

"Why?"

"Richard, I watch and understand people. You do IT, Alistair law, Johnny phys ed. And I do psychology—among other things. Alistair is the most dependable. Do you know why?"

"Tell me."

Devon reached into his pocket and extracted a tissue, dabbed at Richard's forehead. "Because he has the most to lose...of themselves, who act most ruthlessly to protect their interests."

"What about Terri?"

Devon held an open hand up.

"We'll handle it."

A MILLION BUCKS

Without make up, the nurse appeared demure in her uniform: dark blue trousers and tunic, purple epaulettes on the shoulder. She was surprised to see him; the corridors of Kingsbury Hospital were unusual surrounds for Alistair.

He smiled his cheeriest, friendliest smile.

She dropped out from her group, nurses coming off shift, waited, deliberately making him come to her.

What did you call a group of nurses, he wondered? A gaggle? A harem? No, none of them sounded right. He'd have to think of one.

"Look what the wind blew in." She acknowledged him coolly, knew he'd been avoiding her.

He rubbed his hands together.

"Well, what're you doing here?" she asked.

"I came to see you," said Alistair. Nonchalance without a blink.

"Sure. What happened to you at the dance? All the messages I left? I even came to see you. My friends warned me." She started to walk again and he followed.

"I've got a punishing schedule at the moment, lots on the go. What did your friends say?"

"You're the Cape Doctor—a bad wind. Anyway I'm seeing someone now. He's a real doctor."

"Congratulations. Who's the lucky quack?"

"Charles Walker."

"Chip Wanker? He's not a flipping doctor. He's a med student. He'll probably end up a male nurse. His nickname's Chipolata, Chip for short."

"You're such a bitch, Alistair."

He grabbed her by the arm. She felt the tingle race through her body.

"Can't we be friends?"

"No." She stopped and turned to him.

He leaned in toward her ear, whispered: "You let me lick your belly button."

"I wanted to remind you what you were missing out on."

"And I did. I ran back to my room and wept on my pillow."

A small smile tickled her lips. "Sure you did."

"I did too!"

She pointed to the cafeteria. "You can buy me a coffee."

$\odot$

"I guess you won't be needing the video any more?" said Alistair, sipping a plastic cup of coffee.

"I'll hang on to it. As collateral."

"I'd really rather you didn't. But maybe if you and Chip need to spice things up....So what's it like doing it with such a small, er..."

She grinned and rolled her eyes. "Charles does not have a small penis, Alistair. It's quite big actually."

"But not as big?"

Her grin widened. "No, Alistair. Not as big. But at least it stays in his pants."

"You can say that again. Or in his hand."

"You're a funny thing, you know that. As funny as you are mature."

"I'll take that as a compliment."

The smile dissipated and she stared at him. "You're a bastard, actually. We had a vibe going."

"I know," he lied. He had lost the momentum, his ego getting in the way of his original intentions. "Listen, do you know anyone who works at the Rondebosch Hospice?"

"Why'd you want to know?"

"I have my reasons. They're private."

"Tell me or I won't help you."

"OK." Alistair coughed into his palm. "I've been feeling a bit guilty about my lifestyle. All the money and the material things and girls.... You know. It gets a bit much. You realize you can't just take things for granted. You want to give something back. I felt, maybe, I could spend some time with old people. You know, read to them in the afternoon or something."

His eyes were genuinely misty. To be a good liar you almost had to believe your own story. It occurred to him for an instant that maybe he did.

She eyed him suspiciously, her lip puckering a little. She did that, he remembered, the snarl—scary.

"Give me another one. You? Alistair? This I've got to see."

He narrowed his shoulders piously. "By all means, you could join me."

She stuck out her tongue.

"That is, of course, if Charles consents. I'm not exactly his favorite. He may think I'm trying, you know, to lure you back with my amazing pecker."

"There's more to life than a big cock, Alistair."

"My thoughts exactly."

Why can't I keep my mouth shut, he wondered?

She lifted her cellphone and flicked through the address book.

"Rondebosch Hospice. I'll send you a business card."

His phone beeped.

"You're a darling." He sprang up and blew her a kiss. "I must shoot now. Send Chip my love."

"Wait. Your turn to help me out."

"Anything." He took two steps away from the table.

"My place, over the road, now," she said, looking him directly in the eye. Alistair gulped and took another step. He put his hand on his heart. "What would Charles say?"

"I'll give you back the video."

He paused, gave her a quick once-over. Not quite the tight white outfit of fantasy. Consented. "Lead the way."

Alistair reached into his pocket and produced the brown plastic phial. He extracted two tablets.

⊙

Alistair was sweating profusely, the nurse's naked body an oppressive weight on top of him. He commanded himself to concentrate as her hand completed a cursory reconnaissance to confirm what he already knew.

"What's the matter?"

The apartment was a minute's walk from the hospital; small, shared with a couple of fellow nurses who were now mercifully absent, a poster of Wentworth Miller above a two-seater couch. She'd quickly ushered him into her room, pushed him onto the single bed, undressed in an instant, uniform kicked into a corner.

At least the unflattering tunic and trousers were gone, Alistair had thought as she unsnapped her bra and straddled him. But the sight of her body—the same lithe flesh he'd ogled across the Belsen pool, filmed grinding in his room—had not elicited a positive response. And now, even as she worked her hand under his boxers, there was still no reaction.

"Uh. Nothing. I don't know."

The superhighway was blocked. No messages going through.

Concentrate, he urged himself. Imagine...

He ran his hand over the curve of her bottom, slipped a finger between the crease, pulled her up against him.

This can't be happening.

"I know what to do," she breathed, easing herself down his body. But he stopped her, drew her back up to him.

Take control. He embraced her firmly, one hand behind her head. At least his tongue was working.

OK, think of something else. Think of the best sex you've ever had, think of all the girls you want to do it to, think of Terri's video, her body bobbing up and down on your shoulders. Think of...breakfast...Where did that come from?

What was going on? He'd seemed to be back on track. Return from Arniston with new resolve. Exit Dark Video and focus on studies. Terri in the Rose Garden. She made him feel something. What was it? Like he wanted to give. Not take. And now...

Time for a reboot. He pushed her aside, jumped up out of bed.

"Just need the loo and I'm right back," he explained, adjusting his boxers, covering himself.

"Down the passage."

He slipped into the bathroom, closed the door and dropped down to his haunches on the mat, slumped sideways against the bath.

OK, now what? Viagra would be good.

He stroked his errant companion. Nothing. As though he'd drunk a case of beer.

Come on! Come on!

He rolled onto his stomach and fired off ten quick pushups. The blood swirled around his body—but not where he needed it. He heard a knock on the door.

"Are you OK in there?"

"Aah...I'm not feeling very good."

"What?"

"I think I ate something bad. At lunch. Seafood." He imitated a heavy retch into the toilet, flushed, groaned loudly. A minute's wait, then he flushed again, exited the bathroom, head down, wiping his face.

"I think I better go," he said, hurrying to the bedroom and gathering his clothes. The nurse followed him, arms folded, naked but for a pair of red panties; she stood in the doorway watching him dress. As he pulled on his jeans, he cast his eye around the room.

"Er, I don't suppose..."

"You looking for this?" A silver DVD glinted in her hand. She threw it at his feet. "You're pathetic, Alistair. Get out."

⊙

Twenty gaunt, glum, emotionless faces stared at Alistair. He lowered the script in his hands: *Withnail and I*.

"We should put a jukebox in here," said Alistair to no one.

The patients at the Rondebosch Hospice looked like prisoners in a concentration camp. If ever a place deserved the nickname Belsen it was here, he thought wryly. He doubted any of the inmates could hold a lucid conversation, let alone plunge into False Bay and paddle around.

It was all a joke anyway. To humor Devon. Give it a few weeks and then call it off.

Three days later there were nineteen.

One candidate stood out: the youngest, terminal illness but otherwise in what appeared to be a fairly sound state of mind.

"Rather bad luck, sir," Alistair said, after his second half hour reading session. The old fellow nodded.

"What's your name?"

"Derrick."

"How old are you, Derrick?"

"Fifty."

"Just fifty? You're a spring chicken."

"Soon to be poultry."

"Can you swim?"

His eyes glassed over. "Sure. Who can't? Why do you ask?"

"No reason."

"We had a swimming pool at home. Used to swim every day before the repossession."

Alistair swallowed hard. "Repossession?"

The glassy eyes became misty. "Don't know how my wife will cope when I am gone."

⊙

"What's the status, Alesandro?" Devon asked. "Don't forget we're counting on you."

Alistair looked around the room. The curtains were drawn, all eyes focused on him.

"It's going to be a long process."

"It's a waste of fucking time," said Johnny, bouncing a tennis ball repetitively against the wall.

"Johnny's right, it's a long shot," agreed Richard.

"I have faith in you, Alesandro. Everything you touch..."

Richard stood up and walked through to the kitchen.

"There is this one guy. Derrick Young. Terminal. He can swim. And his wife will be left destitute when he's gone."

"How long's he got?"

"Six months."

"Sounds perfect. You working on him?"

"Sure."

Johnny blew air loudly through his teeth. "Bullshit! I know Morgan. He's got fuck all. He's stalling us."

"If Alistair doesn't want to do the deal, he'd tell us," said Devon. "Wouldn't you, Alistair?"

"Sure," said Alistair again. He rattled the brown plastic phial in his pocket.

"It takes patience, Johnny. Try to learn some," said Devon.

Richard returned with a tray of tea. "I baked banana bread."

Johnny shook a limp wrist effeminately; Richard pulled a finger.

"Why don't we go my route?" Johnny repeated. "It's a dare. If the shark eats me, I get nothing." He grinned at Richard's contorted expression. "Obviously. And if it checks me out, bumps me, I get a million. You film me, direct me, get the expression on my face—very professionally."

Devon feigned disinterest. "Johnny, we're trying to have a meaningful conversation here. Alistair's making progress. Stop speaking shit all your life and listen. You might learn something."

He turned to Alistair. "So he's fifty. He's a swimmer, no problem. Six months left. You think you can persuade him?"

Johnny guffawed. "When you tell him about the shark, please let me be there to film it. Please. It'll be the best piece this summer. We won't even need to get him in the water."

Devon silenced Johnny with a wave of his hand. "Alistair's winning his trust. How much time do you need?"

Alistair shrugged. "I'll go back tomorrow." He hadn't planned to go back. Ever.

"I'll speak to Carlos," said Devon. "Other agents are working on this project so we need to push to close it first. But don't rush. We have the location. I'll buy time."

Johnny shook his head belligerently and hurled the tennis ball at the wall.

"Don't forget the dry run on Saturday," reminded Devon. "I've organized the boat."

⊙

First light. They floated the boat off the trailer into the calm water of Kalk Bay harbor. His uncle hardly ever went out any more, Devon had explained, was happy to let them use it for a while. A twelve-foot ski boat kitted with rented wet suits, rods and reels, bait. Its load delivered,

Richard drove the Mercedes off the slipway, over-revving, and parked it, under Devon's wary orders, in a lot several hundred meters away.

Johnny, waist deep in the harbor water, anchored the boat as Alistair and Devon loaded duffel bags with the camera equipment.

"Beautiful fucking day," Johnny muttered, looking out to sea. A low mist swathed False Bay, reducing visibility and lending an eerie atmosphere to proceedings.

"Perfect conditions," replied Devon. "Calm seas and no wind means we don't get seasick. And this mist will burn off in an hour or so, I reckon."

This was practice session number one—a test flip, part of Devon's grand plan to rehearse every aspect of the script. Today they were getting used to handling the boat; hopefully they could rig up some of the equipment, get some test shots out at sea. The sharks would come later. The early start was designed to avoid attracting too much attention from locals who might take notice of a group of suburban landlubbers struggling to put a boat to sea.

It was a tedious day's work. Up before dawn, out for the whole day in the baking sun, the sound of the engine, the smell of diesel, the salty spray of the ocean, the rocking of the boat as the breeze picked up.

"What are we? Fishermen or divers?"

"Both," laughed Devon.

The extensive video equipment was disguised as extra dive gear. Devon had even purchased a frozen yellowtail the previous evening to demonstrate success on the jetty if their token fishing session didn't deliver any luck.

They didn't get a bite.

But they managed to navigate their way east to Seal Island where they observed the two cage diving operators chumming for sharks a couple of hundred meters off the island's south shore. They didn't hang around, though, giving them a friendly wave before altering course, veering south, in the direction of Cape Point.

A kilometer or so off Smitswinkel Bay, Devon cut the engines for their first equipment check. The underwater camera was attached to the telescoping pole and linked to a small onboard monitor, the feed coming through clearly after a painstaking rigging process. Johnny was ordered to dive in to serve as a test subject, to ascertain what distances they could clearly film to underwater.

But the monitor image only lasted a few seconds before the picture was lost. Johnny spent several minutes treading water as Devon and Richard performed some emergency troubleshooting to no avail.

"Must be water getting in somewhere," muttered Devon, as he checked the connections. Eventually he gave up trying to fix the problem, concerned that there might be a casing leak, which would put the actual camera in jeopardy.

"That's why we do the test runs," he remarked, as Johnny pulled himself into the boat, cursing the entire expedition. "Better not risk the other camera today if we've got a possible leak."

"Fucking waste of time," Johnny muttered, stripping off his wet suit.

Alistair laughed quietly to himself in the front of the boat. At the console, Devon practiced keeping a steady hand on a rocking boat.

When they returned to the slipway in the late afternoon, they made a point of chatting to a couple of harbor locals. Not too conspicuous; not too aloof. *Project Grey Suit* was under way.

⊙

"Derrick, look at this article," Alistair said, holding up a recent issue of the *Sunday Times* magazine. He'd waited until after the reading session, his third, when the other patients had been wheeled off to their rooms.

"Read it for me, won't you?"

Alistair narrated the stories of several prominent Hollywood stunt men, focusing particularly on the large sums of money they earned, proportionate to the risk taken. The article ended with an exposé on stunt men within the South African film and advertising industry.

"Stunt men? As in Evel Knievel?" said Derrick.

"Exactly. And in South Africa too. They can die. They risk their lives for a payout."

"Didn't Evel Knievel die?"

"Uh, yeah. But of natural causes, I think. He was pretty old in the end."

"What are you telling me, lad?"

"Well..." Alistair paused for a moment. Where was he going with this? What exactly was he trying to achieve? "Well, your life is not at risk. Because you know you are going to die either way."

"That I do."

"So perhaps you could do a stunt. Because there's no need to worry about the danger aspect of it."

Derrick Young's body convulsed into a coughing fit. Alistair reached for his glass of water and offered it to him.

"Thanks, lad. You're cheering up my days, at least. What sort of a stunt could an old man in my state do?"

"Oh, I don't know," Alistair replied, taking a large gulp of water for himself. "But just imagine: you could gamble on anything. The most dangerous of stunts."

"Getting down the stairs would be a stunt for me, lad. I don't think anyone's going to pay me for that."

"But maybe there's something else..."

⊙

Boat trip number two. This time they launched from the Buffelsbaai slipway in the Cape Of Good Hope Nature Reserve, thirty kilometers south of Kalk Bay—Devon had wanted to avoid getting into a routine. He had fixed the faulty connection, ensured there wouldn't be any problems this time round.

Once at sea, Devon and Richard rigged the onboard Canon on a tripod at the back of the boat, with automated pivot and zoom functions. The pole camera, fixed and operating properly, was returning good shots of Johnny treading water next to the boat; Alistair operated the pole, while Devon tested the controls, rotating the camera and zooming in on the bottom of the boat, then panning back to Johnny. Both cameras were wired into the central controls, where the monitor allowed them to watch two outputs on a split screen, or flick from one cam to the other in full screen.

"Aren't we going to try lure a beast or two?" asked Johnny, as he hauled himself back into the boat, unzipping his wet suit to the waist.

"In good time, Johnny," replied Devon. He watched the monitor closely as he tested the onboard camera's automatic controls, flicking over the surface of False Bay, zooming in to the dramatic cliffs of Cape Point, then out, panning slowly north along the peninsula.

"Check it out," he said. "They think no one can see them."

The monitor showed two topless sunbathers dropping in and out of view as the boat rose and fell on the swell. They were tucked in between the rocks at Venus Pool, over a kilometer away.

"Jesus, the zoom on these things is crazy," said Alistair, clearly impressed.

Devon smiled and flicked to the underwater view: a sinister blue-green haze, visibility about eight to ten meters.

"The trick is to synchronize. Both cameras must train on the same spot—which gets a bit tricky in the heat of the action. Ritchie, make sure you get the hang of operating this one manually." Devon indicated the onboard camera. "You have to be aware of the swell. And Alistair, if you can control the pole with your left arm, you can film with the handheld in your other hand. Never know, it might be useful."

"Surely we need to get a shark in now," insisted Johnny. "What if we can't attract them?"

"Not yet," repeated Devon. "Let's not get ahead of ourselves. Two weeks from now, we'll head out to the island when the cage divers have gone. If we just start chumming for sharks now, someone will report us."

Two weeks, thought Alistair—where did that come from?

The rigging and derigging of the cameras was painstaking; the equipment disguised in plastic containers and duffel bags to avoid detection, the presence of video equipment on the boat entirely secret.

That evening after docking, Devon told another skipper about a huge great white that had circled the boat while they were snorkeling.

"You getting into that water?" the skipper asked incredulously.

"Sure. Lots of people dive in False Bay."

"Ja," he agreed. "But I'll just stay in my boat, thank you very much." He walked away shaking his head.

⊙

"What's it like to know you are dying?"

Derrick rocked back and forth.

"I have long since accepted it. I'm only fifty, but I feel old. Tired. No energy. I am not afraid. Except for Dorothy. It eats me deeper than the cancer. We have spent our lives together. Now I leave her with nothing."

"But do you think about the...actual death?"

"I suppose so. You just shut down, fade out."

"Do you not think of ending it early?"

Derrick chuckled, a rasping sound coming from deep down. Alistair felt a deep, abiding pity for the man, frail and vulnerable. He wanted to tell him that he was being stitched up, conned. That he should just tell Alistair to leave and get out of his life. Instead, he continued probing, detached, as if his voice were independent of his thoughts.

"I know someone who works for a foreign company that performs mad, crazy stunts. But the risk is great. He asked me if I would do one."

"And what stunt is that?"

"Swim with a great white."

⊙

"You look haggard," Silverman said. "You missed class."

"Are you my mother?" Alistair lay on his bed in Green 212.

"No. But I can be. Mamma wants a hug."

"Buzz off, Silverman. I need to sleep."

Devon had phoned in the morning, urgent for a progress report on Derrick Young at the Hospice. Alistair couldn't understand it; one minute it was a six-month timeline, then suddenly two weeks.

"I came to borrow your opener," said Silverman, holding up Alistair's corkscrew. "But these caught my eye. What, pray, are they?" He pointed to the brown phial of tablets.

"Anxiety pills."

Silverman picked up the phial and twirled it in his hand. "No label?"

"A friend makes them up. They're natural or something."

"Hmm. What's in them?" Silverman popped the lid and sniffed.

"Put them down," said Alistair, sitting up.

Silverman lifted the phial to his mouth and poured in the contents, about a dozen pills.

"No!" Alistair jumped up and grabbed him by the shoulders. "Spit them out, you idiot!"

Silverman opened his mouth, showed him the contents, then crunched his teeth together and swallowed.

"You're insane, Silverman."

"In sin! What's in them?" Silverman turned and headed for the door, corkscrew in hand. "I think I better go lie down."

"Damn it, Silverman!" shouted Alistair, hurling the phial after him.

How am I going to relax now? he thought.

▶

"You look tired," said Terri. Alistair had slept the whole day.

"I'm under work pressure." Khaki shorts hung loosely on his hips.

They lay on their backs on the grass in the Rose Garden, close enough, but not touching. A breeze blew a wisp of her hair across his face and Alistair leant over to tuck it behind her ear. He felt lethargic, as whacked as the students dawdling down the hill.

"You know," she said, "what happened to me changed my life. As terrible as it was, it has defined me. I am a different person."

A shaft of sun filtered through the trees.

"Better or worse?"

"Different."

He waited for her to explain.

"I don't know what it is, but I can talk to you, Alistair." She pushed herself into a sitting position, ran her hand along the sleeve of her T-shirt. He wiggled his toes against hers.

"Do I make you happy?" he fished.

She considered the question for a moment. "You've become a good friend."

He stopped wiggling, not sure if he was satisfied with the answer.

"I met Henri in my very first week at varsity. He was my first boyfriend."

"First?" He sat up too.

She looked away and blushed. "Can you believe that?"

"I think you should be proud of that. I wish I could say the same."

She laughed and kicked him. "I won't tell you what Katie said about you."

"I know! More charming than a bridegroom, sweeter than a boy scout. Does Katie know?"

Terri frowned. "She knows about you helping me."

"No, I mean, about us seeing each other."

"Are we seeing each other?" She giggled.

"Well, you said...you said we were good friends."

Above their heads, the clouds motored across the sky, high winds beating a slave-like tempo to an indefinite location. Inside the Rose Garden, the air seemed to hang breathlessly.

"Do you still have the dread?" he asked.

"It's fading."

"I think I've got it now."

"Do you ever wonder what happened to me?"

"I know what happened," he replied quickly, then paused. "An act of revenge. Henri's ex. It must have been."

"I sometimes wonder."

Alistair fell back and closed his eyes.

"You look so tired," she repeated.

"I think it's these pills I've been taking."

"Pills. For what?"

"Anxiety attacks."

"I can't believe that." She laughed. "You. Anxious. More confident than a..."

He looked away.

"I'm sorry. I didn't mean to make fun of you."

She shuffled over, leaned in. Her hair fell down around his face creating a cocoon. He breathed deeply, her nearness, her scent, the subtle heat in her cheeks, the movement on her lips; he could even sense the warmth of her skin as she lowered her lips above his. She kissed him lightly.

"What was that?"

She threw her head back, blushed. "I always wanted to kiss Jude Law. It's the new me."

"I like the new you." Alistair sat up and pulled her back toward him. "Want to try again?"

She backpedaled, resisted his pull. "No. Once is enough. Been there, done that." Her eyes sparkled.

"Where've you been all my life?" he asked.

"You don't believe for a moment that kind of talk will work with me, surely?"

"I can only try."

"You're not my type," she said, patting his hand.

"I thought your type was someone who made you happy."

"That's the old Terri."

Alistair stared at the sky, the marching procession of white clouds. "What's your type now, Terri?"

"Someone I trust myself with."

Alistair rolled his eyes.

"Counts you out," she laughed.

⊙

"You're going to swim with a great white?" asked Derrick Young, eyes wide. "Must be crazy." The room smelled of disinfectant.

"I am...thinking about it." Alistair placed a marker in the *Withnail* screenplay. Most of the other patients were asleep. "The money is just so tempting."

"Madness, I'm telling you."

"Do you know how much they'll offer?" said Alistair.

"You'd be mad to, boy."

"But if the money was right, it's got be worth it....Have you ever heard of snuff movies, Derrick?"

⊙

"Don't take them too often," said Devon. He produced a new phial, green plastic, with white tablets. Alistair had been complaining of drowsiness.

"You take the blue from the brown when you're anxious; you take the white from the green when you're drowsy."

"Uh huh, doc. What are they?" Alistair sniffed. His nose had started to run; he wiped it with his sleeve.

Devon passed him a tissue. "The pills are my own special recipe. A mixture of concentrated ephedrine and Rescue Remedy formula. Working?"

Alistair rubbed his stomach.

"Lost your appetite?"

"A little."

"Any other effects?"

There was one, thought Alistair. The afternoon with the nurse. Which reminded him: her last text was far from complimentary. He wondered if she had a copy of the video. Imagine if it turned up on Watchit. Or Mangle? Nah, it wasn't much good.

"How's it going with Derrick?"

"Painstaking. He thought snuff was a type of tobacco."

"Take your time."

⊙

Johnny hung his legs over the edge. The boat rocked from side to side.

"It's pointless. You can't see a thing," moaned Johnny. Murky water slapped repetitively beneath the boat.

Third launch, bad weather, Devon fiddling with the cameras, adjusting light levels on the monitor. "Just get in," he snarled.

The wind whipped in from the north. Everyone was in a bad mood. Richard retched again, a dry, painful heave. Alistair kept his eye on land; he'd been told it helped to prevent seasickness.

This is a nightmare, he thought. Why hadn't he walked away from it all yet?

The boat lurched on a big wave. Richard collapsed onto the floor; Johnny gave Devon another imploring look.

"Look, we have to be able to get our setup right in any conditions," Devon said firmly. "We may only get one crack at this. So just get in the goddamned water. Please. I don't care if we can't see a thing."

Johnny pulled down his mask and fell backwards into the water, stroked backwards until he was several meters from the boat. Alistair lowered the pole beneath the chop. A second later the monitor was displaying murky images, visibility no more than a couple of meters.

"What's it look like?"

Devon fiddled with the controls, moving the lever horizontally and vertically. They could make out Johnny's legs treading water rhythmically nearby.

Alistair thought of a scene from *Jaws*. The view from below of legs beating underwater, the unknowing look on the doomed swimmer's face, then the hit...

"Perfect," said Devon.

It was far from a word Alistair would have used. He rubbed his forehead, anticipating the drive from the harbor to the hospice, another chapter from the screenplay, then a conversation with a dying man. He stared back at the land. He needed some more of those relaxation pills.

IN THE WATER

This time, conditions were ideal: clear skies, a faint breeze barely touching the relaxed waters of the bay, gulls circling above Kalk Bay Harbor, soliciting for scraps.

They arrived at three o'clock in the afternoon—in two cars, Devon's Mercedes and Johnny's Cressida, pulling the boat. It was floated in minutes, their practice runs paying off. Alistair was sent to park Devon's car down the road, while the others loaded containers, duffel bags, and cooler boxes into the boat.

The sun was on its downward arc. It was their fourth practice as a group, a quiet Tuesday—a week since their previous outing. In between, Alistair had managed to avoid two excursions to Gansbaai, past Hermanus, along the Cape South Coast, where Devon and Richard had joined cage diving tours to pick up more tips about shark behavior. They'd made a point of not using the False Bay operators—Devon's caution preventing this. Alistair had managed to worm his way out of the trips, using the excuse that he needed more time to make inroads with Derrick—and he quietly hoped this might be the start of his departure from the group.

"I think I'm getting somewhere with Derrick," he said airily, as the boat puttered out of the harbor entrance. "What's with the two cars, by the way?"

"Good, good," said Devon, behind the wheel, ignoring the question. A fine mist sprayed up over the bow as he opened up the engine.

Alistair moved to the stern, where Richard was unpacking gear, preparing the cameras.

"What do you think?" laughed Johnny.

He displayed three pairs of board shorts. "What's their favorite color? Blood red, sea blue, or my personal choice: yummy yellow."

Alistair made circles around his ears with his right index finger. Johnny laughed even louder and lit up a smoke.

Half an hour later, Devon cut the engines. They were a distance from Seal Island, close enough to just make out the two cage diving operators with the naked eye. He rotated the onboard camera automatically, zooming in on the nearest boat, in time to see a shark cage being winched out of the water. The company name was displayed on the side of the boat in green writing: White Shark Adventures. On board, two men gave each other a high-five.

"Good timing. Looks like they're just packing up."

He focused on the island behind the boat, a barren mass of granite, thronged with Cape fur seals staring out to sea as if waiting to be rescued. Gentle waves were breaking on the shore in puffs of white.

"Nice afternoon for a swim," said Johnny.

"Are you getting in?" asked Alistair. "Near the island?"

"You bet."

Alistair turned to Devon. "What's the plan for today?"

"Full dress rehearsal," he said, without looking up from his activity. Alistair frowned and turned to Richard, who shrugged. Johnny, alone in the front of the boat, had his shirt off, yellow trunks on; eyes shut as if in meditation, he sucked in deep breaths.

"Let's get the rods out, for appearances' sake," Devon continued. "We should be good to go in a while, once these guys have left. For now, let's get the equipment out of sight."

Alistair watched Richard lay the camera and tripod down on their sides on the transom, then cover them with towels. Devon rustled about for a rod, cast from the stern into the sea—no bait—then set the rod in a holder. He pulled several beers from the cooler box and handed them around. "I think we could all do with one of these," he said, settling back into the skipper's seat.

Alistair, uncomfortable on a side bench, surveyed the boat, looked out to the island and back. "What the hell's going on?"

"Relax, Alesandro. It's all going to plan."

▶

The sun had dipped in the sky, teetering as it dropped toward the horizon. Theirs was now the only boat in sight, the cage diving operators having disappeared back to shore, their passengers satiated with closeup visions of the oceans' most frightening predator.

Devon cut the engines again, this time as the ski boat assumed a position several hundred meters off the south coast of Seal Island. Johnny, in the front of the boat, released the anchor.

Devon turned to Alistair and Richard. "Alesandro, when it's time, you must keep the pole steady under your left arm, but try to get some decent shots with the handheld, too. And Ritchie, keep checking the monitor to see what the underwater camera is doing. Remember, we must be in sync to get the best shot."

"What shot are you talking about?" asked Alistair. "What are you talking about?" They'd been at sea for two hours and he still didn't know what was going on.

Johnny sat quietly, attaching a length of blue and white cord to his middle. He looked up and grinned widely. "For fuck's sake! Someone tell him."

"Johnny's going to have a swim with the sharks," said Richard.

"What?"

The boat rocked as Johnny mounted the side, ready to tip into the water behind him. He was enjoying watching Alistair's reaction. "I'm dying of cancer, Morgan. They're gonna pay me a bar."

Alistair looked to Devon, still confused. "What's going on?"

"Like Richard said, Johnny's going in. We're going to film him. Now. With a shark."

Alistair raised his hands, appalled. "Here? At the island?"

"That's right," replied Devon calmly. "No point in messing around if we want a shark in the shot."

"You guys are fucking mental." Alistair shook his head in disbelief.

"Alesandro, if I'd told you what we're going to do, you'd never have come."

"Isn't that my choice?"

"No. I don't think it is. Not any more."

"What the hell's that supposed to mean?"

"We're in this together. We've come too far now." Devon busied himself at the monitor, not meeting Alistair's eye.

Johnny hooted with laughter. "I've never seen Morgan like this. Give him some more anxiety tabs, Dev!"

"Sit down," Devon commanded Alistair, turning to him. "Look, the deal's changed. Carlos wants to go with Johnny's idea. It's a wager. But everything's in our favor. If the stupid Americans want to be so thick, then let them be. Turns out Carlos has got some client with a serious *Jaws* fetish. So we drop a body in the water—Johnny—and we chum and attract a shark. The guy's desperate for some decent footage of a great white sizing up a human. It only needs to brush him. But it must be visible, a clear shot."

Alistair couldn't think of anything to say, his mind racing. He stared blankly at Devon, then over to Johnny, grinning on the side of the boat.

"We'll get two hundred and fifty thousand dollars, Alesandro. That's over two million rand at the current exchange. Johnny gets the first mill. After that we split the difference four ways."

Two fifty. The previous deal had been the same for an attack, double for a breach. How desperate had Carlos become?

"You can't be serious?" he said eventually.

It was a trick; it had to be. He regretted taking the tablets that morning. They seemed to be affecting his logic. Next thing they'd all start laughing and slapping him on the back.

"You better believe it, Morgan," shouted Johnny.

It wasn't like Devon, thought Alistair. He was too careful. They were only on their fourth trip. What if the sharks didn't come? They hadn't even seen one yet. What if one came but they screwed up the take? What if it...

It was too horrible to imagine.

"Relax, Alistair. You're looking at earning close on three hundred grand for sitting on a boat and aiming a camera," said Richard. "We'll all be laughing this evening."

"Hey, Morgan!" whooped Johnny. "Get in with me and I'll cut you a deal!"

Alistair ignored him and turned to Devon. "No way, Devon," he implored.

"Look, I can't argue now. Johnny's indemnified us. You can try talking him out of it if you really want. But I promised Carlos a deal. We're lucky he wanted to negotiate." He turned to Johnny. "Hey, where're your car keys?"

"On the dash."

It didn't add up, thought Alistair. It wasn't Devon's style.

"Johnny," said Alistair.

"Fuck off, Morgan. Don't fuck this up now. Where's my mask?"

"No mask," said Devon.

"What the hell?"

"You want the bet or not? If you want it, you comply with their requirements. No wet suit, no goggles. They want to see the shark eat a human, not a frogman."

But there's not supposed to be any eating, thought Alistair. What do we get if...? He couldn't bring himself to ask the question.

"The fucking shark won't eat me," said Johnny, almost reading his mind. Alistair shivered. The heat from the sun had disappeared; dusk was approaching: hunting hour.

Johnny grinned and let go of the side, emerging several meters from the boat. "*Project Grey Suit*, scene one, act one," he declared, floating onto his back, hands sculling at his sides, the blue and white rope an umbilical cord between him and the boat.

"This isn't happening," Alistair muttered to himself. What was this? Silverman was right. Something big had been growing and it wasn't fun any more.

Devon extracted a silver bladder from one of the duffel bags, once a reservoir of box wine. He held it at arm's length over the side and slashed it with a knife, smelly red and brown liquid dripping into the water, an oily slick coating the smooth surface.

"Didn't you wonder what the stink was, Morgan?" Johnny shouted.

Alistair shook his head, watching as the light breeze tugged at the slick, dispersing it downwind. He knew it was no joke. He realized why they'd sent him to park Devon's car.

"Is it cold?" called Richard, nervously scanning the horizon.

"Not too bad." Johnny stroked tentatively, one, two, three meters. "I'll put up with it for a million fat ones."

"Further," instructed Devon. "Let's get some shots of you far out, looking helpless. But we'll need you closer to the boat when the action starts." He checked the underwater camera. Visibility was good, around twelve meters.

Johnny rolled back onto his stomach and rolled his arms over, each smooth movement an extra meter of ocean between him and the boat. "Sixty minutes," he bellowed.

Devon acknowledged his shout by pushing a button on his watch. "Richard, get a shot of him bobbing in the distance. Make him look as far away as possible."

⊙

"You getting tired?" Richard shouted to Johnny. Ten minutes in. He had settled into position now, two-and-half boat lengths to the rear, slightly to starboard, in range of the underwater camera.

"Nah, I'm fine." Johnny treaded water lazily. He had settled on a routine, remaining in one place for a couple of minutes, then swimming around slowly to relieve the monotony and work different muscles. He was fit, a water polo player back at school, played rugby now and studied physical education—an ideal candidate.

Alistair shuddered to think of Derrick Young in the water. How could he have tried to con a dying man?

"One million bucks," Johnny called out.

The boat rocked gently with the swell. Devon scanned the horizon with binoculars, watching for unwelcome attention from passing boats. He checked the monitor, then over to Richard manning the onboard camera and Alistair, with the pole wedged under his arm, gazing into the distance, wishing he was a thousand miles away. "Just hold your nerve, you two," said Devon. "Maybe try some shots with the handheld now, Alesandro."

Alistair looked down at the small camcorder in his right hand, flicked it on for the first time that day. An image appeared on the LCD: his foot, the transom, a patina of chum against the white of the boat.

Devon reached into a cooler for a beer. "Drink, anyone?"

Alistair declined, gazing numbly toward land. Richard wasn't interested either, focusing intently on the camera viewfinder. How could he be handling this, thought Alistair. Richard! But he seemed to be operating on another level, focused, detached from reality.

"What's the sixty minutes got to do with it?"

"It's the agreement I've made with Johnny." Devon volunteered nothing further.

"So if nothing happens after sixty minutes we can get the hell out of here, right?"

Devon put his hand on Alistair's shoulder. "Calm down, Alesandro. Do you know the chances of us pulling a shark?" He made a zero with his fingers. "Next time you don't have to come if you don't want." He turned back to the sea, following the slick to the horizon, scanning intently.

"How about a cold one for me, fellows?" shouted Johnny.

The underwater camera produced a surprisingly clear image of Johnny's feet, gently kicking against the green waters of False Bay.

$\odot$

It arrived from the deeps: silently, alone, unnoticed on the underwater monitor. A ripple of white water five meters off the stern preceded the scythe of its dorsal fin before its massive black torso gently broke the surface.

"Fuck! Fuck! Look!" Richard shrieked, first to spot it.

The great white came at an angle, steering slowly through the water, rolling over slightly to get a view of the boat as it passed on the port side.

Alistair rushed to the edge for a better view, peering over, heart thumping. More than three meters, almost as long as the boat, the shark was much broader than he had anticipated, yet its movements were deliberate and graceful, almost as if in slow motion. He could make out the distinct cuts and abrasions on the dark grey skin as the clear water flowed off its back.

"Fuck me," he whispered, sucking in his breath and aiming the handheld camera at the huge animal as if by instinct.

The shark dropped beneath the surface, a long black shadow now, and veered to its left, a series of S-shaped movements taking it out of sight to the port of the boat.

"Hey! What's happening?" Ten meters away on the opposite side, Johnny strained to see what was going on.

"We've got a visitor," Devon said calmly, his voice carrying clearly across the water. "Everyone, get a grip now and do your job properly. Alistair, make sure the underwater cam is in the water on the right side."

"Come on!" Johnny yelled, eyes wide, adrenaline pumping. "Take one!"

Devon untied the cord connecting Johnny to the boat, fixing a large sack of fish guts and entrails to it. Reeking brown juices ran down his arms and onto the floor.

"What are you doing?" Alistair asked. He felt like an outsider, unrehearsed.

Devon dropped the bag into the water. "Pull," he called to Johnny.

"Devon," said Alistair horrified. "You're crazy!" He scanned the water for the shark. Nothing.

"It has to bump him," Devon replied calmly. "That's the agreement. Otherwise this is all a waste of time."

Alistair stared, speechless. Agreement? What *was* the agreement? What was going on?

Johnny winched in the bait, grim-faced, getting ready for the show. A red soup of stinking entrails filled the distance between him and the boat.

"Keep it as close to you as possible," Devon yelled, as he frantically scooped more brown liquid into the water, reaching into a cooler box and ladling it into the sea with a plastic bailer. The supply depleted, he quickly rinsed his hands in the water, then settled in behind the monitor, flicking to the split screen, trying to locate the shark.

"Look!" Richard spotted it again, turning slowly and deliberately in a wide arc, thirty meters away. It made for the boat in a direct line now, a small bow wave preceding the dorsal fin and a wake streaming from the thrust of its tail, before it slipped beneath the surface. Devon switched his attention to the underwater camera, full screen: the heavy shape emerged from the murk, thick and massive, pectoral fins like wings at its side, the unmoving grin making straight for the camera, filling the screen. The big shark passed underneath, the boat rocking in its wake. The camera swivelled, catching the thrust of its muscular tail.

"Quickly, Alistair!" Devon demanded. "Other side of the boat. I need to focus on Johnny."

Alistair obeyed without thought, edging around in front of the tripod stand and projecting the pole camera toward Johnny, bobbing ten meters away. He looked down and dimly registered that he was still filming with the camcorder.

Through a haze of fish entrails, Johnny's kicking feet came into view on the monitor.

"Come on, baby," Devon urged. "Now be our star."

The shark had looped left, slowing down again, and was now heading back toward the stern of the boat, nosing its way through the oily water.

"I'm losing sight of you," shouted Devon to Johnny. "Swim toward the boat. Splash! Attract attention to yourself!"

A wave of nausea swept over Alistair, as the scene unfolded in front of him. This was sin, big and evil; it would burst through his door and spill down the passage. This can't be happening, he thought. It's a dream. I'm going to wake up soon, warm in my bed, in Green 212.

He lurched for the side, vomited into the water, a further ingredient to the soup of chum.

"Keep steady!" Devon ordered. "I must get the shot!"

"Where is it?" Johnny shouted, trying to raise himself out of the water. He spotted the fin to the stern of the boat, heading away from him, then looping left again back toward him, saw it submerge.

Alistair, Devon, and Richard watched transfixed as the dark shadow made a beeline for Johnny, twenty meters away.

"Johnny, for Christ's sake! The shark! Get out!" Alistair shouted. Johnny was two boat lengths away—fifteen seconds and he could be on board. Fifteen seconds to safety...

But the shark closed the gap with a couple of flicks of its tail.

"Motherfucker, here it comes!" Johnny screamed. He took a deep breath, clenched his fists, pulled his legs up to his chest, careful not to leave any limbs exposed.

"Don't move!" shouted Richard, eye attached to the camera viewfinder.

Johnny lifted almost entirely out of the water and came crashing back down, disappeared as the shark's wake washed over him, then reappeared a second later.

"I kicked it!" he screamed. "I fucking kicked it!"

"Got it!" shouted Richard. "I got the shot."

Alistair, on autopilot, had also got the shot, on the little camcorder, the LCD still returning images from the water: Johnny spinning around frantically, looking for the shark, then running his hands up and down his body checking for injuries.

"Fucker, nicked me!" Johnny called out. "I'm bleeding—grazed my ankle, I think."

"Hurry, Johnny, get the hell out of the water," Alistair shouted, suddenly returning to his senses. "Swim! Get out now!"

Behind him, Devon remained at the console, reviewing the underwater footage, not saying a word.

The great animal surges into view toward Johnny's curled-up form, entering the frame from below right in a flash of bubbles and white water, jaws apart, Johnny riding up on the bow wave, makes contact—then, in an instant, the shark alters course to the right, away from the camera, flicks its tail several times and disappears into the green sea. Only Johnny remains on screen, yellow board shorts, white legs pumping as he stabilizes himself.

"Not interested," said Devon, subdued.

"What? What happened?" asked Richard in a shaky voice, still manning the tripod.

"It's not interested," Devon repeated, louder. "Bumped him. Was just checking him out, friend or foe, seeing what he was."

In the water, Johnny was suspended in a sitting position, back to the boat, legs splayed, paddling only with his hands, peering anxiously below him to his right and left, looking for signs of the shark's return. Even in the fading light, a distinct puff of red hung in the water, emanating from his lower left calf and mingling with the lingering chum cloud. Alistair couldn't watch, dropped his head and stared at the camcorder LCD instead, as if the digitally generated pixels might displace him from the reality of the situation.

"Just get out of the water," he heard himself calling.

Johnny didn't react. He seemed paralyzed but for the sideways movements of his head and the muted paddling motions of his hands.

"Stay where you are," said Devon calmly.

"Is it coming back?" For the first time that day, Johnny's voice was brittle with concern. "Where? What must I do?"

"It's not coming back. It's already gone, bolted out of here," said Devon, matter-of-fact.

"You sure?"

"Positive. It was just checking out the smell, didn't like what it saw. It'll be a rugby pitch away already."

"Well, thank fuck for that then..." Confidence returned to Johnny's voice. "Thank fuck for that!" Then realization; fists pumping above his head. "I won, I won! I'm rich! Yeehaa!"

He extended an arm and stroked back toward the boat, rolling over, several strong strokes and he was there. He reached for the metal ladder on the stern.

"Wait a second, wait a second," Devon stopped him, flustered. "We need to get a shot of the injury while you're out there."

"OK, but hurry up, damn it, I want to get the fuck out of this water."

Johnny extended himself full length on his back, left leg on the surface so that Richard could get a close up of the wound, head glancing about awkwardly. Alistair focused in with his camcorder, too, the LCD revealing a two inch laceration on the front left of his calf. The blood dispersed like ink in the water.

"OK, can I get the hell out now, please?"

"No! Stay where you are." Devon's voice, loud, authoritative—a trace of panic. "Don't you dare move, OK?"

"What's your problem, Devon? I want to get the fuck out, I've just been attacked by a goddamned great white."

"The deal was an hour in the water, you've got eighteen minutes to go..."

"Fuck that for a bad idea. The deal's done."

Johnny swam forward, reached for the ladder with both hands, placed a foot on the bottom rung.

"I'm warning you! Get back in the water!" The boat rocked as Devon lunged forward, taking position above the ladder.

"Jesus, Devon," Alistair whispered as the gun appeared from Devon's pocket. A shot rang out, a resounding crack. Johnny fell back in the water. Alistair watched the body splash on the LCD, arms flailing, as if in a movie. It was a movie—but this wasn't in the script.

Devon held a .38 special above his head. Alistair stared, unable to digest it all.

"Devon!" screamed Richard. "You've shot him!"

"No, I haven't."

Johnny resurfaced, a body length from the boat, face enraged. "What's your fucking problem!" Fury and terror combined.

"A deal's a deal, Johnny. Now stay where you are." Devon stepped back, looking over his shoulder, moved to the console. Alistair watched, not saying a word, panned the camera from Johnny to Devon at the controls, scrutinizing the monitor, back to Johnny, prisoner in the water.

"Devon, please..." Richard, shocked, trembling, tried to intervene.

"Shut up, Ritchie. Shut the fuck up and concentrate on what you're doing." Devon leaned in to the monitor. "Keep the fucking cameras on him. The light's going so watch what you're doing. Sixty minutes. That's the deal. Johnny gets out now, we get fuck all. Understand?"

"Dev, just put down the gun. Let him out," Richard tried again. "We've got the shot."

Devon shook his head.

"Devon," Johnny pleaded.

"Shut the fuck up, all of you!" Devon raised the gun in Johnny's direction, squeezed the trigger, another crack as the bullet hit the water. "You take another stroke and I swear to god I'll shoot you."

"F-f-f...Hey, this...this wasn't the deal!" Johnny stammered, his body convulsing, the adrenaline wearing off—shock, hypothermia, the new threats.

"He wants to get out!" Richard screamed.

"Shut up! Everybody, shut up!"

"Devon, please!" shouted Johnny. "I'm bleeding, I'm not sure how much longer I can last."

Another shot rang out; a small plume exploded in front of Johnny. "Stay where you are!"

"Devon," Alistair said softly. He hadn't moved for several minutes now, the camera pole still wedged under his left armpit, camcorder still rolling, eyes transfixed to the screen, transcending the madness around him. "This isn't...happening."

Johnny trod water in the center of the LCD, struggling now, on his back, his face pale, sickly. Alistair watched, watched, straining on the image— then, for a split second, the color of the murky water below seemed to darken.

"Oh Jesus Christ..."

The great white hits hard from below, striking amidships, a blur in the screen as it hoists Johnny clear of the surface, arms flailing, body enclosed in the gaping pink maw between thigh and chest. The huge shark rises with its prey out of the water, crashes down, away from the boat, plunging Johnny head first into the murk from where it has emerged. A mass of churning white water cascades upwards and rains down onto an empty surface. A flash of pale belly reflects for a moment through the frothing sea water as the creature sinks out of sight, before a dark cloud appears from below, casting a pall across the screen. In moments, the boiling sea surface regains its form, a pink sheen replacing bright scarlet, Johnny's blood dispersing on the swell.

"Johnny!" screamed Richard.

Beneath the surface, the underwater camera catches a shot of the great white, enormous: two meters longer than the previous shark and twice as wide; it circles slowly, eyeing its victim, then turns away nonchalantly and fades from view. The camera tracks back to Johnny's broken body, suspended below the surface, ruptured like a rag doll, slowly sinking, insides trailing in the bloodied gloom.

Alistair huddled in the corner of the boat, hugging his knees. His retching had stopped; remnants caked his T-shirt, nothing left to bring up. Richard, too, sat in silence, staring straight ahead, consumed by shock. Devon held the .38 in one hand as he dismantled the equipment and packed it into the duffel bags.

The sun touched the horizon. A light wind had picked up, dispersing the chum and the remnants of the attack, all physical evidence of the event deleted.

Devon exhaled deeply as he slipped the gun into his jacket pocket, the calm returning. He scanned the horizon, looked at his watch. "Five more minutes then we can head back."

Neither Alistair nor Richard looked at him. Alistair hardly heard the words. His mind's eye was set on action replay: the animal emerging from the sea, Johnny rising out of the water, shocked expression, mouth open, no screams, just surprise. Then the compression of the jaws and violent shake of the head. Had he captured the exact moment of Johnny's death?

Devon wiped his fringe out of his face. "I can't believe it. I thought he was going to ruin it. I never thought..."

Richard started to sob. "You should have let him get out," he cried, almost inaudible.

"What?" Devon slumped back in the captain's chair. "That was just.... That was beyond my control..." He paused for a moment. A pair of seagulls cried out, hovering above the boat. Devon looked up, nodded. "But what's done is done. We've got to hold things together now."

He spoke to neither Alistair nor Richard; neither made any attempt to respond.

"Right, let's get our story straight." Devon got up, unzipped another duffel bag and retrieved three wet suits, fins and masks, and a spear gun. "Fish weren't biting so we thought we'd get in the water and have a go with the guns." He knelt at the stern, dunked the wet suits into the water, then threw them on to the floor of the boat.

"We left here earlier, anchored off Miller's Point. Swam around for half an hour, no luck. The wind picked up and we nearly lost sight of the boat. Johnny was with us but he drifted off. We grouped back at the boat, no Johnny. We saw nothing. No lurking fins. Nothing. Maybe he got cramp or something, swallowed some water. We searched the area until sunset."

Devon rinsed the fins and masks off, then the spear gun, dropped them next to the wet suits.

"Now for us. We've got to get in. It's got to look like we've been diving." He removed his T-shirt, shivered in the breeze, darkness falling. Standing on the top rung of the ladder, he tentatively eyed the water behind him, then grabbed the railing with both hands and hopped in and out in one quick movement.

"Your turn," he indicated to Alistair and Richard, still huddled in their respective corners.

"I'm not getting in," Richard snivelled, fear becoming a reckless anger. "No way! You can shoot me if you want."

Devon looked at him, shaking out his hair.

"Me neither. Not a chance." Alistair, quietly.

"Fine." Devon reached for the empty cooler box, earlier swimming in fish entrails, dipped it in the water and poured it over Richard's head. Alistair, next, had the presence of mind to undress first.

Devon threw them each a towel, then picked up his cellphone from the console. "One more problem to solve."

Devon knew that the expected action in their situation would be to call the emergency services immediately, which would bring NSRI, the National Sea Rescue Institute, to their assistance. They would be dispatched immediately to search for the body, by powerboat and possibly helicopter. But this would place their boat and its contents under scrutiny. He immersed his cellphone in sea water.

"Anyone else brought their phone? No? Good."

Alistair remembered Devon's instructions to leave their cells in the car. "What about the radio?" he asked, as he dried himself.

"Faulty. Conveniently stopped working after we put out to sea. See for yourself if you want."

Devon assumed his position at the console, started the engines, pulled the boat around and headed south, parallel to the shore, in the fading light.

Alistair pulled his soiled T-shirt back over his head; it flapped in the wind. He felt numb. He had to get off this boat.

Lying down on the transom, a pale corpse, Alistair realized that the really hard moments were still to come. A thumping headache couldn't erase the images in his head. It was the blood that had shocked him; how it rose to the surface, how bright it was. That, and the expression on Johnny's face as the life was crushed from him. He glanced at the duffel bags with the camera equipment; the camcorder he'd used was in one of them, his memories stored in digital format.

"Twenty minutes and we're on shore," said Devon, navigating in a wide loop, to approach the harbor from the south rather than the east. He picked up Johnny's Camels off the deck and emptied the packet into the sea.

⊙

Evening in Kalk Bay. On their return to harbor, Richard was ordered to contact the emergency services on his cellphone—in the open, in case anyone was watching. Devon quickly transferred the black duffel bags to the boot of Johnny's Cressida. The rest of the diving kit went in to the back seat, more conspicuous. The boat was loaded onto the trailer.

Within half an hour members of the NSRI and Simon's Town Police and Fire Services were on the scene. Devon repeated their story to three separate officials: arrived in the victim's blue Cressida, cruised around, fished without luck, went for a dive, visibility reduced as the wind picked up, no sign of Johnny on return to the boat.

"No point in sending a team out now," said Captain Burger of the Simon's Town Police Station, looking up at the evening sky. "We'll have an NSRI team out at first light. I hope you understand."

"Certainly, certainly."

Devon gazed out to sea. Waves rolled in to the wall of the harbor, tide coming in. More rescue people arrived, disappointed at how little they could do.

"Bloody kids went out without a working radio," he overheard Burger tell his second-in-command.

The press was soon at the harbor: two reporters, a photographer. Devon intercepted them before they picked out the other two.

"The sea was calm this morning. How could you lose a swimmer in that water? Could he swim well?"

"As far as I know," said Devon. No need to elaborate.

"How long between the time you last saw him and when you realized he wasn't with you?"

"About half an hour or so."

"What were you doing out there?"

"Just snorkeling around. We hadn't had any luck fishing, so we decided to get in. A couple of us had spear guns." He gestured toward the back seat of the Cressida.

"Where exactly were..."

"Could a shark have taken him?" interjected Alistair, huddled inside a towel. The reporters and service personnel spun on him; he felt the blaze of Devon's black eyes.

"The water was quite clear, visibility wasn't too bad. I sensed an explosion, you know, like you feel when you are underwater in a pool and someone heavy jumps in. A displacement of water."

"Was there blood?" asked a police diver skeptically.

"No, nothing," shot in Devon, wresting back control of the story. "We saw a few seals bouncing about, but nothing untoward."

"You weren't near Seal Island?" asked Captain Burger. "That would be crazy at this time of the year."

"Or ever," muttered someone else.

"No way," said Devon. He pointed in a southwesterly direction. "We were miles away."

"Could be a lurky," another voice piped up.

The reporters ears pricked up, pens flicking at pads.

"Let's not jump to conclusions," said Burger. No need to start a press feeding frenzy and scare everyone off the beaches. He leaned against the back of Johnny's Cressida. The door was open, wet suits and spear gun in view.

"Did he have a suit on?"

Devon nodded.

⊙

"I guess you have questions." Devon stood in the Gorillas living room, stone-faced, hands on his hips.

Alistair, slumped against the armrest of the two-seater couch, rubbed his bleary eyes. He had driven Johnny's Cressida back to the house while Devon had doubled back and fetched the Merc, Richard with him.

The Audi stood in the driveway now, where Alistair had left it early that morning, before sunrise. He wanted to jump into the car and drive away forever, never to see this house again. His mind kept replaying events: that great mouth emerging from the sea, the rows of serrated teeth grasping Johnny, the life vanishing from his eyes, blood boiling to the surface...

Silence. No music in the lounge of Gorillas. No thumping bass.

Devon cleared his throat. "It's a tragedy. But it was his choice. We never made him take the bet."

Alistair stared straight ahead; Richard, on a separate chair, cradled his head in his hands. Mugs of tea in front of them remained untouched.

"Is no one going to speak to me?"

Alistair opened his mouth as if to say something. Nothing came out.

"Look, Johnny owed one of the Nigerians a significant amount of cash, through his dealer mate, Jeff. Drugs. Gambling debts, too. He was desperate. After I destroyed his rape video, he looked for other outlets. He was crazy. You guys didn't see it." He paused.

"Richard, maybe you did," he continued. "He begged me. Phoned Carlos himself, started making life very complicated for everyone. The last straw was when he contacted Mangle. We'll settle his debt with his share."

Alistair listened in a dull stupor. He felt neither hungry nor thirsty, nor able to support or dispute Devon's revelations. Johnny owed a drug dealer; no surprises there.

It's a dream, Alistair thought; a nightmare. Any minute he'd wake up and the Gorillas crowd wouldn't exist. No Devon, no Richard, no Johnny.

Except there was no Johnny any more.

Devon's voice droned on in the background of Alistair's awareness. "Funny to think Johnny owed so much money because it was Sasha who caused most of the problems. She's a total junkie. Could never work out why he was such a fool to fund her habit."

Sorry, Johnny, for thinking you were an addict when it was all Sasha's fault. Alistair felt the sarcasm stick in his throat. Didn't even know you liked her. Don't worry, we'll sort out your debts.

"Anyway, they've notified his parents. The NSRI will look for the body again tomorrow. Perhaps they'll find it."

"What?" Alistair blurted out. He shook his head slowly. "What are you talking about?"

"Alistair. Snap out of it. He drowned. We need to keep thinking like that."

Alistair wanted to scream; wanted to race from this room. He remained seated.

"It'll be in the newspapers. Speculation about a shark. Thanks to you."

"Johnny was a very strong swimmer," said Alistair in monotone.

Devon and Richard looked at him.

"Yes," Devon said slowly. "Sure. But people drown. Happens all the time. Johnny gambled and lost."

Devon's expression changed, head cocked, color back in his cheeks. He sat down on the living room floor, alongside the unpacked duffel bags.

"Can you believe it?" he said to no one, genuine amazement in his voice, running his hand along one of the Canons. "Two sharks. What are the odds?"

Alistair looked at him. Given that we were a couple of hundred meters from Seal Island, he thought, the odds were pretty fucking good.

"It's a freak accident," Devon continued, his tone excited. "It wasn't our fault. How could it have been?" He looked to the others. "We did nothing wrong!"

Except that we filmed a man dying, Alistair thought. And you fired at him with a gun.

But he had no desire to argue. The episode had been so sudden, so unlike Devon: the lack of planning, the loss of control, the level of risk. It was compulsive, an act of desperation. What if a boat had seen them? What if there had been no second shark? Devon had three more bullets in the gun.

Richard sobbed softly.

"Calm down, Ritchie. The sooner we all realize just how much of a risk Johnny posed, the better. A risk to all of us. It was only a matter of time before he went to the cops about the forest attack."

Alistair swallowed hard. He stared at the poster of the King Kong.

"We must move on. We've got a five hundred thousand dollar video here," Devon said, indicating the cameras. "I will get started on it tomorrow. A pre-production screening in the afternoon?"

Five hundred thousand? Wasn't it two fifty? Alistair's mind was muddled. He raised both his hands, shook his head. No response from Richard.

"OK. I'll manage it on my own, then. Will get it to Carlos by Monday. We'll be paid before month end. A clean split, once we've sorted out Johnny's debts. We're looking at a million and a half or more. Each."

One million five hundred thousand rand: a generous slice of the pie. Alistair could hardly comprehend the figure.

"The deal with Carlos...Dark Video. Was there ever another plan?" Alistair's voice seemed strange in the room. He wondered what Derrick Young was doing.

Devon looked him in the eye.

"No, Alesandro. There was never another plan."

BE STILL MY HEART

"Damn, Carlos! You owe me big on this one."

Carlos clicked his phone onto loudspeaker and picked up the nail file.

"What have you been doing?" he asked, starting on the nails on his left hand.

"I been looking and I been listening," replied the big hit man, real name Samuel Chester, also known as Chestwound, also known as Warnabrother. He looked out his window. Woodstock. That was the suburb's name. "This place doesn't work for me, man. Shitty job in a shitty town."

"What's the update on the project?"

"Interesting goings-on yesterday: four set out to sea, three came back. Man, Carlos, you got to see the dive I'm staying in. Polyester sheets. You'd love it."

Carlos ignored the small talk, preoccupied with the latest development. "Troublemaker sorted out?"

"Yeah. The rough one. No more problems from him. The movie's shot; he didn't make it off set. Official word is he drowned, but talk of a shark attack in the papers this morning. Sounds promising."

Carlos held up his left hand to the light, admired his handiwork, each nail perfectly rounded. He turned the file over and began pressing back his cuticles.

"Excellent. Can't wait for the review. I have a feeling that Devon will be putting together something quite special for me this time. He didn't care much for Johnny."

"What I seen no one cared much for that motherfucker."

"Right, keep an eye on the other three for the time being. Until I've got their submission. What about the other problem?"

"Man, that's a dead end. If it was Johnny, then the action's gonna stop. Cos he's feeding fish."

"Devon seems to think so. What's the intelligence say?"

"Intelligence? Man, Carlos, you're kidding me, right? Cops here don't have a clue. They got no leads. If polo neck's on the button, it'll go quiet now. But who knows in this place? Murder capital of the world, right?"

"Right. Well, let's hope that's the end of it. We lose a couple more clients and suddenly our second-quarter results aren't looking too good."

Warnabrother cleared his throat. "I hope that don't..."

"Don't worry, my friend. You'll get your cruise. I'll throw in another honey just for you—for all the fine work."

Carlos picked up a hand mirror off his desk. He admired his reflection, ran his hand down along his smooth chest toward the edge of his white thong. Laser hair removal, he marveled. Why hadn't he thought of it before?

⊙

Layabouts basked in the morning sun outside the Belsen mess. Alistair pulled into his parking spot, noticed several heads turning his way; a buzz of curiosity as he slipped up the back stairway to his room.

Did they know what had happened? Could they see the guilt in his face? Or was he being paranoid?

He had fallen asleep on the couch at Gorillas, a frenzied, frantic sleep, dreaming about Johnny, waking up in a panic, dry mouth, wondering about Terri's bra—and when it would all come out. He'd popped several pills, slept again; this time deep and thoughtless. Woke up with a start, not knowing where he was, checked his watch: ten thirty a.m. Felt like he'd slept for a week. No sign of the others, no duffel bags, no camera equipment. Had he dreamed it?

Silverman burst into his room, a copy of the Cape Times held up in his hand. Alistair rubbed his face, bit on his nails.

"Does everyone know?"

"Some. You OK, man?"

Alistair nodded.

Silverman disappeared to his room, returned with a glass of dark liquid and a few pills.

"Take these. Guaranteed to calm you down and help you sleep."

Alistair accepted the pills, sloshed them down with the dark liquid.

Alistair opened the newspaper. Page three, two columns; at least it wasn't headline news. And no photos. Now, if only they had printed the picture inscribed in his head, on the camcorder: the black monster breaking the water with Johnny's body clutched in its mouth.

He read the story:

MAN FEARED DROWNED DURING BOATING TRIP

A 22-year-old University of Cape Town student is presumed drowned after he went missing in False Bay yesterday. The student, John Jackson, had been spear fishing with friends.

Witnesses reported seeing Jackson and three men departing Kalk Bay Harbor in a white ski boat in the early afternoon. The men were identified as Devon Deacon, 25, Richard Walker, 21, and Alistair Morgan, 22. They are all students.

It is believed that Jackson became separated from his companions in moderate swells southeast of Simon's Town. Deacon, who officials confirmed held a registered skipper's license, said that Jackson was last seen approximately one hundred meters from the boat and more than two kilometers from shore.

"We entered the water at around 4pm in fairly good conditions. Half an hour later we returned to the boat but there was no sign of Johnny.

"We waited until 5pm before becoming concerned and we started to look for him."

Captain Pieter Burger from the Simon's Town Police Station told reporters that the ski boat's onboard radio had evidently failed while at sea, and that there were no working cellphones on board.

"If they had been able to contact us at the time we could have got an NSRI boat out there and maybe the Skymed helicopter, with probably an hour of light to search. But it was already dark when the call came in."

He confirmed that a search for the body would be conducted at first light this morning.

One of the swimmers reported sensing an "explosion" under the water. Deacon confirmed that they had spotted several seals, but had not seen a shark.

In June 2005, a man was killed by a great white while spear fishing approximately 150 meters offshore, near to the spot where Jackson went missing.

Lionel Jansen, spokesperson for the Shark Research Center at the Iziko-SA Museum, said Jackson's disappearance could not be linked to increased shark activity in False Bay.

"Sharks can be attracted to a diver's catch, but in this case they appear not to have seen many fish, let alone caught anything.

"There is no proof at all that a shark was involved. There are far more drownings in our waters than shark attacks," he said, citing the fact that there were only four attacks in South African waters in 2007, none of them fatal.

"Was he a good friend?" asked Silverman.

"No. Not really."

Alistair shook his head to clear his thoughts. He reached for his cellphone. He wanted to call Terri but he felt hazy; the room spun.

"Can you phone Terri and tell her what happened?"

Silverman's eyes twinkled as he grabbed the phone. "Should I ask her to bring the video along for us to watch?" he joked.

But Alistair was sound asleep.

$\odot$

"How long have you been sitting there?"

He looked at her through half-opened eyes, sitting on the end of his bed. An unbuttoned white shirt over a black top, denim jeans. A warm sensation filled his chest.

She looked at her watch. "Four hours."

It was dark outside.

"You haven't moved for four hours?"

"Well, I popped to the toilet. Your neighbor, Luke, uh, Silverman, kept guard for me. I've been reading."

"Silverman?" Alistair lifted his head. His door was open. Silverman stood like a sentry, wearing an old pair of army browns and roller skates, no top. He had a bucket on his head.

"The four hours passed very slowly," she said with a laugh, indicating her reading material: *Great Expectations*, English setwork.

"I'm so glad you're here..." For the first time in a very long time, Alistair's principle emotion was not fear or uncertainty.

Silverman rolled into the room, came to a sloppy attention next to the bed. "Silverman reporting, suh," he said, tottering on the wheels. He put himself at ease and produced a clipboard and Alistair's phone. "Your father, suh. Relieved you are OK. You must call him. Sisters. Times three. I asked if they looked like you. They answered negative, so I thought it safe to proposition them. Two of them are married. The unmarried one also said no."

"You have three sisters?" said Terri. She ran her hand along his brow. "Boy, did you get hot."

"Me too," said Silverman, from behind Terri's back, making unsubtle gestures as to the source of his fever. "Then there's been the warden, the matron, Maggie, about five hundred girls, who I sent away."

Terri spun around.

"Joking."

Alistair put his hand on Terri's. "Thanks, Silverman. Now beat it."

"You have to dismiss me."

"Dismissed."

Silverman executed an elaborate about turn, almost losing his balance, before skating out the door.

"Quite a character. He's been teaching me how to..." She raised her hand to her mouth and giggled. "Fart."

"Fart?" Alistair could never imagine Terri farting.

Terri's giggles intensified, her eyes went watery.

"Did you learn anything?"

She couldn't talk. Alistair started to laugh too.

I'm not going to think about it, he told himself. I'm going to shut it out. It's a dream. Laugh. Laugh with Terri.

Eventually she composed herself, tears running down her cheeks. "Apparently, it's a science on Green second. What did he say again? The three Ps. Product, position, pressure."

"He makes you laugh."

A fresh bout of giggles muddled her attempted reply. "I don't know if I want to hear any more from him, though. My manners will be shot."

Alistair reached out to a glass of water on the bedside table—and the accumulation of all his fears burst, the bag of fish entrails, a filthy baggage of lies and deceit. He sobbed.

"What's wrong, Alistair?"

He covered his face with his arm.

"It's OK. It'll all be OK." She put her hand on his arm.

He wiped his eyes with his sleeve. "When I woke, I didn't open my eyes. I knew you were on my bed. I couldn't see you or hear you, but I sensed you. It felt so...comfortable. I didn't want to open my eyes."

"Why not?"

"In case you weren't there. In case it was a dream. My life's been like a dream lately. A bad dream..."

She looked away.

"I'm sorry. I'm emotional."

"Don't be." She turned back to him, her eyes intense. "Remember me? You saved me; maybe I can repay you."

"You can?"

She smiled, leaned forward, kissed him lightly on the cheek. He could feel her breath.

"And that?"

"A little bit of saving."

"Save me here?" He pointed to his lips.

She sighed, smiled again, darted in quickly, the kiss a whispering touch only.

"That all?"

"For now. You need to get your energy back up. Here, I bought you some food."

⊙

Devon arrived ten minutes after Terri's departure. The thumping heart returned. "Nice pad, Alesandro," he said, surveying the room. He bent down and stroked the Persian.

"You said that last time."

"I know." Devon took a seat at Alistair's desk, turning the chair toward the bed, crossed his legs, calf on knee. Alistair sat up in bed, brushed off the covers.

"You're feeling better, I hope? Been eating, at least."

Two empty plates lay on the desk. Terri's delivery, some fruit squirreled away at Tugwell lunch, and a full dinner of roast lamb and vegetables from Mrs. Harrison.

Devon stared at Alistair without saying anything, smiled. Despite the sustenance—and Terri's recent visit—Alistair looked unkempt, gaunt, eyes hollow, five-o'clock shadow. And something missing: the cheeky smile.

Devon rubbed his face and adjusted the neck of his polo shirt. He was freshly showered, clean-shaven, his black hair shiny and slicked back. In his hands he held a grey folder.

"So, how are you...handling things?"

"How'd you think?"

Devon lowered his head. He placed the folder on Alistair's desk, put his hands in his pockets.

"Do you hate me, Alesandro? Richard does. I tricked you."

"Johnny's dead, Devon."

Devon stood up and walked to the window, shifted the blinds. He paced back, leaned against the closed door, fiddled in his pockets.

"Yes. Johnny's dead," he said, nodding slowly. "Do you think I should've let him get out the water?"

Alistair said nothing. He had been hot after finishing supper and had stripped down to his underpants. Now he wished he hadn't; he was uncomfortable and vulnerable sitting on his bed. He wanted to stand up tall and give Devon a piece of his mind.

"Johnny owed a lot of money to people who don't take kindly to being stuffed around."

"You fired at him with a gun, Devon. You threatened us, you made us act against our will. Johnny is dead because of you."

Devon sighed, tapping the back of his head lightly against the door.

"I know. I know." He shook his head from side to side. "But there was no choice, the deal was sixty minutes. We needed a better shot."

"How ironic."

"You do realize that we were Johnny's collateral, don't you, Alistair?" A shift in tone, sterner. "He was about to go down and we were next. The Nigerians were already starting to shake me down. And these are nasty people, my friend. Very nasty. And then the Mangle thing too, possibly even those murders we've read about. Very heavy stuff."

Alistair frowned. What could he believe? Where was the line between truth and fantasy?

"I can't believe you involved me. Why?"

"Sometimes we need to stand up for our convictions, be a man, accept our responsibilities. Johnny was a threat to us all, not only me, and you know it."

Alistair shook his head. It wasn't disagreement; more like despair.

"You participated in the planning," Devon pushed. "You offered input, you came on the dry runs."

Alistair remained silent.

"You tried to get a person to agree to—what? Commit suicide? Be a part of an illegal snuff movie?"

"I went through the motions. To humor you. I knew he'd never do it." Alistair on the defensive.

"You never stopped the boat on Saturday."

"I didn't know you were going to shoot him!"

"I didn't shoot him! I only stopped him from getting back on board for fifteen minutes. Stopped him from ruining everything."

Their eyes met. Devon's gaze was calm and steady, Alistair's nervous.

"I find that hard to believe. You knew!"

"Yes, I knew, Alistair. I cast the second shark. He cued dead on time." Sarcasm now a part of Devon's offensive.

He walked to the fridge, opened it and stared in. Closed it without removing anything.

"You have to get rid of the video," Alistair said quietly. His eyes felt heavy; he wanted to close them, roll over, disappear to another reality.

Devon sat down again, looked at him. "I don't think I can do that, I'm afraid."

Alistair's jaw tightened. "Devon. If that film comes out...we'll be up for murder. Worse. It's the sickest thing I've ever heard of."

"It'll never come out. Dark Video's business is private."

"You've got to get rid of it."

"I can't do that. We have a deal."

"Fuck the deal!"

"We owe a lot of money because of Johnny. We've got commitments to Carlos. We're in more trouble if we pull out than if we go through with it. What's done is done, Alesandro. I can't change it. No more than I can change what happened to Terri in the forest."

Alistair shot Devon a look.

"Yes. I know she's been here."

Alistair's expression hardened.

Devon was quicker. "Alesandro. Be rational now. If you panic, everything will fall apart. I'll tell you how it is, how it'll be. First thing, accept that Johnny had to go. He had to! As much for you as for anyone else. What type of person wants to get in the water with a shark? With a great white!"

What type of person is prepared to film it? thought Alistair. But he was quiet now, resigned to Devon's bullying.

"Johnny was crazy. I've been intercepting his correspondence for the past few days. You might be interested."

Devon produced a small key from his pocket and held it up. "I found this on his desk. I also found a message to Sasha on his cellphone: if anything happens to him, she must fetch the key and retrieve the contents of a safety deposit box at the Rondebosch Post Office."

Devon walked to Alistair's desk, lifted the grey folder and produced three letters. He flipped through them, reciting the intended recipients: "Sasha; Chief of Police, Rondebosch Police Station; Warden of Kopano."

He handed Alistair the last envelope; the writing was Johnny's.

"Can I get a beer?" Devon pointed to the fridge.

Alistair didn't respond, fiddled absentmindedly with the envelope.

Devon picked out a beer, twisted off the top and sat down at the desk.

"Johnny wanted the gamble, needed the money desperately. He begged me for it, eventually wore me down. And Carlos wanted the action. So Johnny played the great wheel of fortune..."

Devon sipped slowly on his beer, his eyes trained on Alistair.

"And after all his cockups in the last few months, fate really did have it in for him. Can you believe there was a second shark?" Devon shook his head.

"I couldn't believe the first one didn't go for him. I thought of Johnny's deceptions, him lording it over us, compelling us to pay him out and something snapped."

Snapped? It didn't look like anything had just snapped, Alistair thought. And what about the gun? Where did that come from?

Devon stood up, placed his half-finished beer on the desk. "Anyway, it looks like we won't be seeing one another for a while. It's in our best interest. And I'm sure that will please you. But, Alistair, I need to know whether you're going to be a problem?"

Alistair shook his head feebly, wiped his nose with the back of his hand.

"I'm not so sure," said Devon.

Alistair looked him defiantly in the eye.

"Not deliberately," Devon continued. "But look at you. You look like shit."

"My friend just drowned. I'm expected to look like shit."

"I don't think you're acting." Devon took out his car keys and swiveled them around his index finger. He looked intently into Alistair's eyes.

"Alistair, you and I are very similar. You may not think so, but we are. Now you need to suck it up and be a man. Just relax. Johnny can no longer threaten us. His debts will soon be paid off and everything will be fine, no liabilities. But Terri Phillips…"

"What about her?"

"Don't get sweet on her, Alistair. You're already in breach of our agreement. If she ever works out how you actually met, it threatens us all. Just fuck her, if you must. And get it over with. But do it quickly."

Devon put his keys back in his pocket, picked up the unfinished beer, and drained it in two large gulps. His words seemed to have sucked the air out of Alistair's lungs. "Why's she a problem?" he managed. "I thought the forest video was a dud."

"Not a dud. Just not as explicit as Carlos would have wanted. But it turns out he's got a client interested. The video's been reserved. When a video is reserved, no one else can see it. It becomes private property."

Alistair stomach lurched; he felt ill. The thought of some sick freak watching Terri…

"Where's Terri's bra?"

"What?"

"Terri's bra? Johnny took it. You said you'd get it. It's a loose end."

Devon frowned. "I'll find it. And I'll get rid of it. Like you must get rid of her."

He twirled the empty beer bottle in between both hands, as if molding pottery, contemplating the situation.

"Alesandro. We're in the clear." He deposited the bottle into the wastepaper basket. "I sent Carlos a rough cut of the attack. Unedited. He is frothing at the mouth. Says it's the most sensational clip he's ever seen. Sure, I have some ethical issues, but it was kill or be killed. And now we have created something unique—and acquired a lot of cash in the process."

Alistair felt a shiver run through his body. "I'm not interested in the money," he said. "I don't want anything to do with what happened out there. Keep it."

"I thought you might say that," said Devon, extracting an envelope out of his pocket. "So I thought I'd bring you a little advance payment."

He opened a drawer in the desk and carefully placed the envelope inside.

"Twenty K. Cash. You deserve it, Alesandro. For your troubles. And when the money from Carlos comes through I'll keep your cut aside for a while. I think you'll change your mind."

Alistair looked away from the drawer, arms folded, not saying anything.

"But it never was about the money for you, was it, Alesandro?"

Still no response.

"Well, if in a year's time you're looking for kicks again, then give me a shout. Otherwise, I think it's time to say *hasta la vista*, my friend."

Devon picked up the grey folder. A curious look descended over his face: disappointment, perhaps. Or sadness. He waited a moment for Alistair to say something.

"OK then, I've got to run." He leaned in and grasped Alistair's hand, warm and clammy, pumped it once, then withdrew. He pointed to the brown phial on Alistair's bedside table. "Best to take it easy with those for a while."

The door closed. Alistair rolled over, head in his pillow. His face burned.

⊙

Silverman woke Alistair in time for dinner.

"Another day's sleep. You really have been out of it."

"Has Terri been here?"

"She stayed an hour. Left a note." Silverman reached for the note on the desk, but Alistair snatched it away. "Chill, I've already read it. Hope you feel better. Wah wah wah. Kiss kiss."

Alistair scanned the note: "Hope you're feeling better x x x."

"Supper? Lamb chops."

"No appetite," said Alistair. He placed Terri's note on top of the unopened letter addressed to the Warden of Kopano.

How could anything ever be the same? Alistair thought. He wanted to rewind. To last week, before the attack. But which attack? Before the forest. Before he'd ever met Devon. He was trapped.

A message buzzed through on his cell. His father:

Thinking of you, son. Hope you're feeling better

He put down the phone on his desk, lifted the brown phial, twirled it in his hand. Time to stop being anxious, he thought, replacing it on the desk. Time to get back into the swing of things.

Tomorrow he'd ask Silverman to fetch his outstanding tutorials from campus.

⊙

The brown phial of anxiety pills remained untouched on Alistair's desk.

"Babotie and yellow rice?"

"Ew."

"Another note." Silverman handed it over. He'd inserted his own additions: "I want to fuck your brains out" and a doodle of fornicating stick people.

"She's coming back later."

Silverman cupped his hand in a whisper. "I caught her checking you out. Your one leg was out the sheets. Like this."

Silverman tried to pull Alistair's leg out from under the sheets but he kicked him away.

"And she was also looking under like this..." Silverman lifted up the sheet at the bottom.

"Get out of here, Silverman."

"I'll secure your daily sustenance. Oh, by the way, I collected all your tutorials. They're on your desk."

Alistair shot upright, eyes wide.

"On top of the letter addressed to the Warden of Kopano."

Silverman looked nonplussed; smelled his armpit.

"Look like you've just seen a ghost, Morgan. Time to get your shit on a stick."

Alistair exhaled deeply, rubbed a hand down his stubbly cheek. "Right. I'm coming to dinner." He got out of bed, pulled on clothes.

"Meet you down there." Silverman farted as he turned on his heels.

Alistair's phone rang. He didn't answer, waited for the beep of the voice mail, dialed 121.

"Alistair. This is Derrick Young. I need to speak to you. Please get in touch as soon as you can."

AWESOME

"Awesome! No other word to describe it." Carlos was pleased. He'd watched the final cut of *Grey Suit*.

"Really glad you like it."

"Like it! I'm bloody ecstatic over here. A tranquil scene erupts in an orgy of gore and horror. It's visceral, it's appalling, it's your worst nightmare. It's sweet fucking cinema genius! Down to the look on the faces of the deck hands. I'm thinking of starting my own Oscar party. You're nominated. How are you coping?"

"A little shell shocked, I guess."

"No surprises. But you're surviving, I take it?"

"I'm managing. After what Johnny got up to, I can't say I'm particularly upset about his loss."

"I warned you about him. Only a lunatic would agree to such a bet."

"Yes, a lunatic is without doubt what he was."

Silence for a moment. Carlos ran a hand down his hairless chest. "You still convinced he was involved in the murders?" he asked.

"Absolutely. After what you've told me before, about Johnny having contacts at Mangle, both of them Mangle clients, both with recent rape video downloads, his erratic behavior here—absolutely. I checked through his computer last night, internet history, emails, and I suspect he's been in touch with them for a while, may even have sent them videos previously."

"Right, right. That could make sense. He sends in a twisted home production, a merry rape scene or similar, discovers who's been watching his videos in his vicinity, then makes a house call..."

"That sick cunt deserved what he got."

"Fair enough," Carlos agreed. He was slightly surprised at the vehemence in Devon's voice; satisfied, though, that Devon's discoveries backed up his suspicions.

"Well, let's monitor that situation, shall we? Keep me posted if you find out anything else."

"Certainly. And I'd appreciate it if you let me know what you find out about Mangle. They worry me somewhat."

"We're working on it. Trust me. They won't be around for too much longer. Now, what about the other loose ends?"

"Loose ends?"

"The girl in Johnny's video, for one."

"Sasha. We discussed her. I don't think she's a risk."

"I do."

"With all respect, Carlos, she's a drug addict. She likely has no recollection of what happened to her. Probably just latched on to some other loser to keep her supplied."

"No chances, Devon. I think it's time our man in Cape Town, your good friend, comes into play and earns his salary."

"Carlos, really..."

"The stakes are high, boy. We need to mitigate risk. If Johnny was involved with Mangle, there's a good chance Sasha is too. I am comfortable you say your other two, Richard and Alistair, are on side. But the two girls..."

"Two girls?"

"The other one. In the forest."

"We've got no connection to her."

"None? Pity. She's gorgeous. Alistair not getting misled there?"

"I was concerned briefly. But it's not a problem any more. He hasn't seen her."

"Well, as long as there's no link. But the Sasha situation must be.... resolved. It's not your responsibility, though. I'll leave it to—what do you call him? It's Warnabrother, isn't it?"

⊙

Devon stood in the doorway to Richard's room, Richard sitting on the bed in a pair of white underpants, laptop balanced on his folded legs. The windows were closed and the room was neat, but stuffy. A video camera above the computer on his desk blinked as Devon's motion was detected.

Devon smiled without emotion, waved at the camera.

"Hi Ritchie."

He sat down alongside Richard, running a hand along his arm to his shoulder, his neck. "A masterly performance," he said, clapping his hands together. "You're in the wrong profession."

He tossed a selection of snapshots onto Richard's keyboard: images ripped from Alistair's *Grey Suit* camcorder showed Richard looking shocked, sniveling in the corner of the boat, retching over the side.

Richard shrugged, gathering the photos and setting them aside, then continued tapping on the keyboard. "We did what we had to do. But the vomiting was no accident, I can tell you that much."

He stopped typing, shook his head briefly as if exorcising a thought.

"We did what we had to do," echoed Devon.

"And made a million and a half out of it."

"Each!" Devon leaned in, checked the screen of Richard's laptop. "You've checked everywhere for any last messages from Johnny?"

Richard nodded.

"Facebook, MySpace....What about Sasha's profiles?"

"Don't worry, Dev. When I check, I check. Johnny's left no electronic messages. The slate's clean. Sasha's clean too. Weird woman. Who hangs out with a guy like that?"

Devon rubbed his hands together. Richard hibernated the computer and placed it on his bedside table, stretched.

"How's the rich kid doing? Ego holding up?"

"He's fine."

Richard shifted on the bed. "You've seen him?"

"Yes."

"When?"

"I checked in yesterday, at his residence."

Richard turned away, stared at the wall, then retrieved his laptop and restored power. "Why should we carry him, Devon?" he asked, angrily punching keys, navigating through a series of passwords. "We've done all the work and he gets a freaking fortune. More than a million rand! For doing nothing. For being traumatized!"

"Calm down, Richard. Look at me. I have a loyalty to Alistair, as he has to us. From the outset we agreed never to cross the line. And we have crossed the line..."

"We had no choice. Dark Video..."

"He has a right to feel betrayed."

"Yes, but..."

"No. We crossed the line. I didn't want to. But if we didn't get rid of Johnny, we'd have had Dark Video at our throats."

"You don't have to moralize with me, Devon. Johnny was a rapist. He got what he deserved. Our profit is poetic justice. But Alistair..."

Devon held up his hands. "Relax, Richard. He's refusing his cut anyway. It's not the point, but that's what he says."

"What? What's that fool's problem?"

"Who cares? But I figured he might make this call. So I gave him a little something anyway. Insurance policy in case he develops a spine to accompany his newfound morals."

Richard smiled, calmer, enjoying Devon's barb. He fiddled with the brightness on his screen, flicked between several open windows.

"It's not the money, Dev," he said softly. "It's about getting what we deserve. The effort, the time. I've worked so hard on this, for months now, since we first...started out. Alistair's a coaster; he's just ridden on our hard work. We deserve more than that spoiled brat. I deserve more."

Devon put his arm around Richard, pulled him close. "Of course you do. Of course you do." He ran his fingers through Richard's hair. "You just need someone to recognize your talents. And that person's me."

Devon's soothing tones disguised no lie in that moment: he was truly grateful to have access to Richard's skills. Best computer brain in the land, he'd said and meant before. Richard had even located Carlos's residence recently, pinpointing it in Yarrow Point, zooming in with Google Earth and marveling at his sprawling mansion.

It had been a painstaking process, more than a year's work, analyzing every communication with Carlos, technical dead ends, the hops traced back to some site in Puerto Rico. The breakthrough had come by analyzing conversations with Carlos, combining logic with Richard's tech knowledge, narrowing it down to the States, reviewing the time of Skype calls, subtle questions, asking about the weather, comparing reports, working out the time zone, then tracing through every internet service provider in the area. Everything pointed to Washington. After that a simple matter of elimination using the power of Google. Carlos regularly discussed his obsession with security, had mentioned the laser activated security alarm, the electric fence, the problems being on the lake....Turned out his house was the only property in Yarrow Point with electric fencing and access to the water. He wondered what Carlos would say if he knew.

Devon flicked back to reality. "What are you doing?"

"Some more investigation."

Richard was tapping away at the keyboard again. "I've been thinking about Mangle. How they contacted Johnny. I still find it hard to believe Johnny knocked off two clients. I mean, Johnny's a freaking asshole, but a murderer? What's the motive?"

"Blackmail? Anything for cash—he was desperate, remember? Carlos thinks Johnny was doing a deal with Mangle, might have been trying to force their arm into accepting his clips."

Devon rubbed his hand along Richard's upper arm.

"I don't know. The timing's funny. Did Johnny even know about Mangle when that first murder happened?"

"I don't know." Devon looked confused. "Maybe he was cleverer than we realized. Could have broken into our communications maybe?"

"Not into my computer, he couldn't."

"Why the interest in Mangle?"

Richard pursed his lips. "Knowledge is power. Who helped Johnny get a copy of the video to send to Mangle?"

"It was obviously Sasha."

"Obviously?"

"Who else could it be?"

"Alistair?"

Richard"s lip curled as Devon laughed at the idea of Alistair the computer geek.

"Ritchie," Devon said soothingly, stroking the side of his face, still a boy's face, fluffy stubble, dotted with red irritations. "Get off Alistair's case. I assure you my interest in him is purely platonic."

"I'm not jealous of him! I'm the one who's upfront and honest about our relationship. I don't go rushing off to soothe his anxieties. He texted me, too, you know." Richard held up his phone.

"It's my job to keep tabs on everyone, Ritchie. Just doing my job." Devon grinned and stroked Richard's arm again—to little effect.

Richard looked down and resumed his laptop tapping. "I'm going to find Mangle," he declared. "I don't believe Johnny killed their clients. I think Dark Video was involved."

"They were Dark Video clients as well," Devon reminded him.

"Whatever. How did Mangle find Johnny?"

"Perhaps he found them?"

"And why would Mangle buy Johnny's disgusting video when Dark Video said it was shit?"

Devon gripped Richard by the wrist. He continued to type. Devon tightened the grip.

"Ow!" A little twist and Devon knew he could snap the wrist as easily as twisting off a beer cap.

"Cool it! Remember who you are and what your role is."

Richard stopped typing, clutched his hand to his chest.

"Johnny was a gambler," Devon stated, rising from the bed. "He gambled with us and he gambled with his life. He had to go. Mangle is irrelevant."

He walked to the door.

"Don't think you own me, Devon."

"Wind your neck in, Ritchie."

⊙

Green Block, Alistair's room.

Alistair had spent the day at lectures, battling to pick up the pace of the work, needing to catch up, his mind not able to cope. He couldn't afford to miss any more work.

He sat at his desk now. Derrick Young had phoned again. Probably wanted to know when he'd be around to complete the reading of the *Withnail* screenplay. Or could it be about something else? Alistair deleted the message.

In front of him lay the envelope intended for the Warden of Belsen, care of Johnny's druggie ex-girlfriend Sasha. He picked it up. It was handwritten.

```
To whom it may concern

If you get this, I will be dead, killed by a group
of people, one of which, Alistair Morgan, is a
resident at Kopano. I suspect they are plotting
to kill me. I suspect they will drug me and throw
me overboard in False Bay and then film me being
attacked by a shark. They are involved with a
company called Dark Video who have infiltrated
a website called watchit.com. Dark Video trades
in illegal videos, snuff, pornography. Please
ensure that my death is investigated thoroughly.

Yours, Johnny Jackson, 24 April 2008
```

Alistair couldn't contain a burst of unintentional laughter. What a ridiculous letter, he thought, tearing it up, shaking his head. Another piece of evidence erased.

But the nightmare refused to disappear. He opened his desk drawer and looked at the envelope, fat with debt, still where Devon had placed it.

Had Johnny really done all the things? Blackmailing Dark Video, working with Mangle, even murder?

He was in the clear, though. Time to get over it, move on. Extract himself from the hell that had become his life.

He thought about the money. Perhaps he should take up Devon's offer and take it all. He had the twenty thousand rand now anyway—what was the moral difference between that and the full payout? Nothing. Unless he gave it back...

Even by Alistair's standards, a million rand or more was a lot of money. Take a year off. Cut to Europe. With Terri.

Terri.

What should he do?

She had phoned twice. Each time he'd let the phone ring, waited for the voice mail, immediately listened to it, hanging on to her every word.

"It's Terri. Just phoning to see how you are."

"Thought you might need some rescuing. My hands are cold. Please call me."

I can't do this, Alistair thought. I can't. Why would Devon warn him about seeing her? "Just fuck her and get it over with." As if he accepted that Alistair would do the inevitable, then bail—problem solved.

He locked his door and walked down the hill. At Tugwell the reception-ist announced his arrival: "Terri Phillips, gentleman to see you."

"Send him up."

BRER RABBIT

"Just the two of you?" Katie gasped.

"Uh-huh." Terri swapped the phone to her left ear, a sliver of hair flicking over her face. She blew it away. Sting on the Audi's sound system underscored the conversation. *Every little thing you do is magic.*

"Terri! What did your folks say?"

"They don't know."

"Terri!"

"Katie, I'm a big girl."

"Yeah, right. You haven't even kissed him. Weekend away with a stranger?"

Terri giggled. Alistair rubbed his arm; he felt goose bumps. *Everything you do just turns me on.*

"He's right here. Want to talk to him?"

"Listen here, Alistair Morgan," Katie said as Terri held the phone to his ear. The car raced along the N2 toward Arniston. "You hurt her, you're dead."

"She says I'm not her type. Got any tips for me?"

Terri wrenched the phone back, said goodbye, kicked her feet rebelliously onto the dashboard, scrolled through Alistair's iPod: *Cassie, Me & You.*

"I love this song!"

"I never thought you'd say yes," Alistair said, glancing at her, an airy cotton shirt, the length of her slim brown legs enhanced by the shortness of her khaki shorts, toes making imprints on the front windscreen.

"You look like you needed a friend. What did she say to you? Katie?"

"She said I should give you the treatment."

"Oh yeah?"

Alistair laughed. "Only joking."

"Well, be careful." She poked him playfully. "I may just give it to you."

"I'm not your type."

"You're right. You're not my type."

Alistair shifted from fifth to fourth; the sun slipped lower. He wanted to get to Morganhouse to show Terri the sunset.

⊙

"What's the plan for tonight?" she enquired.

They sat on the couch in the lounge of Morganhouse; Alistair in board shorts and a T-shirt, Terri plopped in his lap. A faded collage of family photos smiled back at them from the walls.

They had arrived too late for a swim. Alistair had unpacked Terri's bags into Shelley's room, his own to the Anchor Room. He was going to do this properly.

"Date night."

"Date night?"

He ran his hand along her neck, drew her closer and kissed her neck.

"Is this the date?" she asked, fluttering her eyes innocently.

"No, silly. Arniston Hotel."

"Dress up?"

"I'm going as I am."

She slipped a hand under his T-shirt, rubbed her fingers along his six pack.

"You're still not my type."

▷

"You're different to how I imagined," Terri said, placing her knife and fork together and staring across the table. The candlelight flickered, her face shone, hair curly from the sea air.

"Could it be, after all you have said, the cruel jibes and hurtful remarks, that I am your type after all?" he teased and wiped his mouth with a serviette.

"If you were, it may not be good for you."

"Oh yes. I remember. Your type is someone you trust yourself with."

The waiter brought a second bottle of wine, white. Arniston Bay. Buitenverwachting not on the menu. They'd both ordered the line fish, Cape salmon, and shared a Greek salad. He removed the empty plates.

"Katie said you were—her exact words—a lady slayer. I asked her why and she said someone else told her."

"And someone else told *her* and someone else told *her*..."

"What's it like to be famous, Jude?"

"Infamous? Does it matter to you?"

"The old Terri would've been mortified."

"The new one?"

"Thinks you are different in real life."

"Real life? What does that mean?"

"You're nicer."

"You haven't seen me get going yet," he said, picking up a knife and waving it around.

Breakfast served: two-egg omelettes, parsley and cheese.

"You can cook," said Terri.

They sat down to eat.

He had led her home after dinner the night before, tiptoed barefoot over the stone road and thorny grass, knew she'd drunk too much, lowered her onto her bed, covered her with the duvet, her hands reaching out to him—"No, not yet"—lain on his back in the Anchor Room, the words "Hurt her, you're dead" repeated over and over again. For a day she'd held him in her spell, a new reality, the nightmare temporarily dispersed; Devon, Richard, Warnabrother, Carlos—and Johnny, the mouth, the teeth, the blood...

"Wow, very impressive," Terri declared, omelette judgment passed. They cleared the plates to the sink.

"What's that sign on the door?" she asked, propping herself up on the kitchen counter.

Alistair told her about the crumbling foundations, the house that would one day slip down the cliff and into the sea.

"Can I have a look?"

He searched for the key in the kitchen drawers.

"No luck. My mother's hidden it again, hates us going out. I'm terrified of heights, ever since my father played a trick on me when I was a kid. There's a hidden ledge on the edge of the cliff. You don't see it from the land. I was watching him; he walked backwards and toppled over the edge. I thought he'd fallen over into the sea. Next thing he popped up again."

"That's terrible. Your father? How could he do that?"

"It's one of those things," he said, moving toward the counter where she sat. "Good idea at the time. He was very sorry afterwards, though. Especially when I had to sleep in his bed!"

"How old were you?"

"Eight."

She leaned over and drew his head against her chest. "You poor thing! No wonder you're scared of heights."

He felt the softness of her breasts against his cheek, an instant message throughout his body. He clapped his hands and pulled back.

"We're going for a swim."

He grabbed a couple of towels from his room, checked his messages quickly: nothing. Maybe he was in the clear.

⊙

A morning of sun and swimming. Alistair had noticed how every man on the beach turned to catch a better view of Terri in her pale green bikini.

"I'm amazed at you. After what happened..." he said. He lay on his bed in the Anchor Room, Terri sitting alongside, sharing sliced fruit from a bowl that she had prepared.

"Coming away with me, taking such a chance."

"It's because of what happened," she replied. "I completely trust you."

She scooped from the bowl, offered him a spoonful. Alistair propped himself up and rubbed his hands across his face.

"So I'm your type now, am I? Trouble is, if you trust yourself with me, nothing exciting happens."

"What's exciting?" She poked his nose with her index finger.

She noticed the expression on his face change.

"What is it?"

He looked down at the bowl, slivers of strawberry, banana, mango, peach. "Nice salad."

She peered intensely at him, searching his face for emotions, for truths. "Who were those people on the boat, Alistair? Were they friends?"

"I suppose. Friends..." he started.

"Where do you know them from?"

"Terri, I want to tell you something..."

She sensed the tension in his arms, the broken voice, his eyes clouded, murky.

"I have made some mistakes. I want to..."

"Shhh," she said. "I don't need to know. Not now."

She lifted the bowl and placed it on a side table, lay down on the pillow alongside him, the bed squeaking with their weight. He felt her body warm against his, her skin salty—"You're so flawless..." They slept side by side, until the late afternoon sun filtered in from the curtains.

⊙

Saturday night, faces glowing with the sun's color, refreshed from the afternoon sleep. A fragrance of thatch from the roof pervaded the house like incense.

Terri busied herself in her room. "Same again?" Alistair suggested, tapping on the door. Five field lengths from Morganhouse to the Arniston Hotel.

He would be honest with her tonight, he thought, tell her everything over dinner—then see if she would still have him.

"No more wine for me, thanks," she called. "I think it may be a better idea to stay in tonight."

Alistair stood with his back to the door, looking out through the glass-fronted living room, a wide panorama stretching from the full moon blazing red to his left, rising opposite the dying sunset in the west.

"A bad moon," he declared. "Don't go round tonight. We can stay at home and I'll cook a pasta."

She laughed. "I have a surprise for you. Come on in."

The lights were dimmed when he entered the room, the door to Terri's en suite bathroom closed. He sat down on the edge of the bed, hands on his thighs.

"You ready for me?" she said through the door.

"Sure. What's going on?"

Terri emerged wearing a flimsy red dress, framed by the light behind her. She twirled around extravagantly, posed for him.

He gulped.

"You like?"

"God. You are so beautiful." His hand came to his mouth.

"I have something to show you."

"Terri, I..."

In a fluid movement she pulled the dress over her head, dropped it to the floor, no bra, black G-string. The sight of her sucked the air from Alistair's lungs.

"See anything here you like?"

"Terri," Alistair whispered. "You don't have to do this."

His vision swam. Devon's charcoal eyes stared at him. Get it over with. Katie's accusing voice. Hurt her, you're dead.

He blinked. There she was in front of him, tangible, real, sensational. Face exquisite, eyes flashing at him, her blonde hair settled midway down her neck. His gaze caressed her body: small breasts, round and perfect, petite shoulders into ribs and narrow waist, long, toned legs, barefoot. She put her hands on her hips, shook her hair wildly.

"This is the new me."

"I love the new you," he managed. "But I don't want you to..." He was looking for the word "rush."

She looked at him, determined, intense, hooked her thumbs into the elastic of her panties and wiggled them provocatively down the extent of her legs, to her feet, over her toes, kicking upwards suddenly, laughing. The G-string landed at his feet. He stared at it for an instant, flimsy black lace, almost unbelieving. This was Terri Phillips, as pure as a fresh mountain stream. No longer a scared little girl in the woods.

"Terri."

"No talking! Undress!"

"We..."

She advanced on him and attacked the buttons on his shirt, pushed it over his shoulders, thrusting him backwards, her breasts in front of his eyes.

"We..."

"What?" she interrupted, laying her hands on his bare shoulders, staring into his eyes.

"We haven't even kissed properly yet," he said softly.

She brought a knee up on to the edge of the bed, straddled him, slipped her tongue into his mouth.

"Mmm." It sounded like she was humming.

She withdrew, for assessment, looking at him, as if checking a gauge. His eyes dropped from hers, down her body, he could see the goose flesh on her skin; breasts, stomach, he couldn't bring himself to look any lower.

He laughed.

"Why are you laughing?"

"I'm just thinking. I mean..." One week ago, it seemed his life was over. Now it was dreamlike. Dark Video was gone; Devon said they were in the clear. "I don't know. I don't know."

She pulled his hands around to her bottom, the taut flesh cool in his hands. She dug the nails of her left hand into his back and started to work on his pants with the right.

"No. Wait." He pulled back.

"What's the problem?"

"I want to look at you," he replied, holding her at arm's length.

She retreated, climbed off him and stepped back from the bed, held her shoulders, crossed a leg, suddenly self-conscious under his scrutiny.

"Is this a test?"

"Terri, before I can go on, I have to tell you something about me first. I have to. If you still want to make love to me after..."

He reached for her hand, guided her to a sitting position on the bed next to him. He turned his body to face her, looking rattled, shirt gone, pants half off.

"I don't trust myself with you," he said. He noticed the G-string on the floor, reached down to retrieve it and passed it to her.

"I'm not your type?" She was nervous, confused, the confidence of earlier gone.

"You're so my type, Terri, I can't tell you. But I am the most selfish person you know. I give nothing; I get everything. I have everything."

She leaned forward and pinched him lightly on the leg. "You seem OK to me."

"Pinch me again."

She did, left her hand on his knee.

"I met you. And I..." Alistair didn't know where he was going with this. "But in the Rose Garden. I thought about what happened to you. How terrible it was. It churns me up inside..."

Terri retracted her arm and dropped her face into her hands; her elbows covering her breasts. She shook her head, breathing in deeply through her fingers.

"What's the matter?" he asked.

"Here I am trying to perform the great seduction with the lady slayer, Prince Charming, Mr. Handsome. Trying something new and different. And now he's giving me reasons not to....It's a bit of a blow." She threw her arms apart. "What wrong with this?"

He looked at her, open arms, the way her breasts moved as she spoke, her slender legs tapering over the edge of the bed, her feet bouncing nervously up and down on the carpet.

"I'm trying to tell you something, Terri. Something you must know."

"I know. I make you happy. Do something for me now, for heaven's sake!"

Alistair's racing thoughts dissipated in an instant, a moment of clarity as he gazed at Terri, the warm sensation returning to his chest. He instinctively reached for her, gathered her in his arms, kissed her on the mouth, long and wet, rolled on to her. Hand in the small of her back, he lifted her body, slid her backwards up the bed, the hand slipping under her buttock, along her inner thigh, spreading her legs, slipping downwards on her body, his face into her, feathery hair tickling against his lips. He softly split her with his tongue, probing inside, then out and against the nub of her clitoris in a slow arcing movement.

"Mmm." A gentle hum from her lips.

She smelled clean, peaches and talcum powder, unlike any smell of sex he knew. Up and down he traced with his tongue, arms around her waist, raising her up, pressing deeper into her. The pitch of her humming lifted, steady gyrations pulsing through her body, the rhythm of her approaching climax. Her hand grasped his hair, willing him deeper. The humming struck a crescendo, then an exhalation of air as a deep moan enveloped her, a long shiver, rolling to her side, hands at her groin grasping for the pleasure.

"My god!" she whispered, flopping her arms back above her head, warm skin glowing with perspiration. She lay still for a minute, chest heaving.

Alistair rested his head on her stomach, drew lines on her thigh with a languid finger.

"What just happened there?" she breathed in amazement, her query rising up to the thatched ceiling. She propped herself up on her elbows, looked at him, mouth open, shaking her head, half laughing. Then she grabbed his face in her hands, hooked her legs up behind his buttocks, dragged his body onto hers. In a moment he had slipped inside her, wet, his back tensing and arching. Her free hands cupped his face, as their bodies ground together.

"Alistair, look at me."

He opened his eyes.

"Look at me."

"You're so beautiful, Terri."

Alistair supported his weight on his arms, eyes not leaving hers, felt the intensity spread, euphoria to be inside her, a feeling he had never experienced.

$$\odot$$

They lay together under a cotton sheet, skin on skin in tight embrace, Alistair behind Terri.

"My god, Alistair," she repeated. "I've never..."

He squeezed her, arm across her chest; she hummed.

Neither have I, thought Alistair. It felt like the windows of a stuffy room had been forced open, clean air circulating inside, gentle music, the aphrodisiac scent of love.

"Terri."

"What?" She turned her face.

"I don't want to move. I want to stay like this forever."

"Well, we can't." She wiggled her bottom.

"Why not?"

"For one, I need the loo. And for two, my phone is ringing."

"Leave it."

"I would, but number one can't wait," she said, slipping off the bed. "And now that I'm up, I may as well answer!"

She picked up the cellphone from the dressing table, turned to him and winked. "Hello."

He watched her movement, not bothering to cover herself, easy with her body, relaxed with his eyes on her, the object of his obsession. She stepped into the bathroom, closing the door behind her.

"Hello?" he heard her repeat.

"Who was it?" he asked a minute later.

"No idea. Number withheld."

She deposited the phone back on the dresser table and leaped back onto the bed, laughing.

⊙

Alistair sat on his bed in the Anchor Room, alone, Terri sleeping soundly in her room. He held his cellphone in his hand.

Three missed calls. Devon. Devon. Devon.

The warmth was gone.

He walked to the kitchen in his boxers, poured a glass of milk from the fridge. Checked his phone again.

Devon. Devon. Devon. Heart beats.

What happened to *hasta la vista*?

The key to the back door poked out from under the plastic cutlery tray. He reached for it, unlocked the door, stepped outside, not thinking. Light from the full moon, dropping from the sky, illuminated the cliff top, disappeared behind swirling, dark clouds.

A bad moon?

The Arniston lighthouse cued to the west, emitted three sharp pulses. Alistair blinked his eyes, waited. The lighthouse pulsed again. The phone rang in his hand.

Devon.

Alistair's heart thumped. He muted the phone.

What did he want at four in the morning?

He watched the light of the phone pulsing in his hand, Devon's silent name reaching into his soul, the terrible images returning to his head. Forest, Sasha, Johnny, shark, Devon.

The pulsing stopped. One missed call.

Alistair turned off the phone and walked back inside, locked the back door, replaced the key. He checked on Terri, lying naked on the bed like Snow White, sheet cast off her body. He removed his boxers and fed her legs through the openings, drew them up to her waist, pulled the sheet over her.

Hurt her, you're dead.

He ran his hand across her forehead, buried his face in her hair, her neck, drew in her scent.

"I'm sorry," he whispered.

Back in the Anchor Room, he turned his phone back on, scrolled down, hit CALL.

"Shelley?"

"Alistair?" The croaky voice of his youngest sister. "What the hell? It's the middle of the night."

"I'm at Arniston."

"Yes?"

"I just wanted to tell you I was thinking of you."

Silence.

"Are you drunk?"

"Wildly." Then a pause. "Drunk with love, I suppose."

"Love? Alistair, what's going on?"

"Shelley, you were right about me. You should know that. But I'm going to change, I swear."

"What are you talking about?"

"I'm going to make it right."

"OK, Alistair. I've got to sleep now."

Phone turned off again, he returned to Terri's room, wrapped a towel around his waist and pulled up a chair close to the bed. He settled in, watching her sleep, morning approaching.

⊙

Terri lay on a sofa in the living area, her legs tucked under her, wearing only Alistair's shirt, loosely buttoned. He slumped down next to her. She lowered her book.

"You look terrible," she said.

"Thanks."

"After last night, you should be on cloud nine—like me!"

He laughed a tired laugh, kissed her leg.

"I think it's the medication you've been taking. You better get off those anxiety tablets."

"I am. Have sworn off them. A good thing, otherwise..." He remembered the embarrassment of his last encounter with the nurse.

"Otherwise?"

"Never mind. What's that book?"

"Oh this. *Brer Rabbit*. I found it in the guest room. Look here."

She turned to the cover page. An inscription in child's handwriting read, "Alistair Morgan age 8."

"I loved this story," she said. "My mother used to read it to me." Her voice morphed into a *Brer Rabbit* impersonation. "Lippity clippity, clippity lippity. Please Brer Fox. Anything. Anything. But don't throw me in the briar patch."

"Oh yeah," Alistair remembered. "I used to read this all the time. Brer Rabbit and Brer Fox—mortal enemies. Rabbit looks doomed when the fox catches him but tricks the stupid fox into throwing him into the briar patch, where all his burrows are. Sneaky bugger."

"I'm sure you learned a lot of valuable lessons from this book," teased Terri. "Do you know the moral?"

"Know your enemy?"

"Uh-uh. Know where your holes are." She giggled.

"You're naughty. You ever played the Brer Rabbit game?" he asked.

"There's no Brer Rabbit game, you moron."

"There is," he insisted.

She slammed the book shut.

"You're Brer Terri, I'm Brer Alistair," he continued.

She giggled again. "Am I the fox or the rabbit?"

"You're the fox," he said. "Quite clearly."

"OK, I'm going to drown your ass in the waterhole, Brer Alistair."

"Brer Fox does not say ass!"

"Well, I'm Brer Terri."

"It's scratch out my eyeballs. Or tear my ears out by the roots."

"I want to drown your ass."

"Whose game is this?"

"OK, OK. Brer Alistair, I'm gonna scratch out your eyeballs and tear out your ears by the roots."

"Anything. Anything, Brer Terri. But don't take me to the Anchor Room and ravage me like last night."

He ducked as the pillows came flying.

⊙

Sunday afternoon, Alistair dropped Terri at Tugwell. He watched her skip away, turned to wave, then was gone. The air suddenly felt stale again, murky. Devon.

He phoned him from his room, nosy Silverman mercifully absent.

"Where've you been, Alistair? Christ, I've been trying to get hold of you for a day."

"I've been away."

"Where?"

"Away."

"We have to talk."

"About what? I thought we were done."

Hasta la vista.

"We were. Some issues have come up."

Alistair fumbled in his drawer. The envelope, still there, untouched, some lecture notes. There: the phial. He popped it open. Two tablets.

"I don't know if I can deal with this, Devon."

"They want us to sort out Sasha."

"What do you mean, sort her out. We agreed..."

"Carlos doesn't agree. He's putting pressure on me. Alistair, are you there..."

"He can't force us to do anything. We..."

"There's more, Alistair. Terri. I warned you about seeing her. Now listen to me. If you continue to see her, you'll place her life, and ours, in danger."

"What? Why?" Alistair was sweating; he wiped his brow, ran a hand through his hair.

"The client who reserved her video...Carlos is paranoid about Terri finding out about the video. Cut ties, Alistair. Now. Today. Stop seeing her or there will be consequences."

"I want no part of this, Devon. I told you, I'm out."

"I realize that and wish I could just let you go. Richard feels the same. But what's done is done and we've got to face the consequences. We're in over our heads here."

"How can Dark Video threaten us?" Alistair asked, suddenly incensed. "If they expose us, they're finished as well."

"Alesandro, we're in trouble here, OK. Carlos is insistent. We're too far in to back out. But if we do what they say, we'll be cool."

Alistair could feel his pulse thumping, blood racing through his body, his world collapsing around him. Terri....He'd go to the authorities, there was no other way, he'd get his father involved.

"No, Devon, listen to me! This was never part of the deal. If we don't make a stand now, they'll never leave us alone."

"Carlos is a businessman, Alesandro. And he's ruthless. If he's threatened, he'll make business decisions. Sasha is a risk. Johnny made her a risk, which means she's our responsibility. But I can take care of it."

"What does that mean? Take care of her? Kill her?"

"Christ, Alistair. Who do you think I am?"

Alistair didn't reply. He lifted the cuff of his shirt, held it to his face. It smelled of Terri. He slid the sleeve across his face, the scent of her everywhere. His throat constricted.

"I'll handle it," Devon continued. "But promise me. You can't continue seeing her."

"Never see her again?"

"That's about it."

"Just like that?"

"Just like fucking that! Jesus, Alistair, women throw themselves at you. There are oceans of pussy out there. Find someone else to fuck. Get rid of her!"

Alistair couldn't speak. It didn't seem real. Nothing was real.

"If he thinks she's a problem, Carlos will send Warnabrother and he'll tear her to pieces," Devon said calmly, rationally.

"I can't believe they're so worried about her, though. It doesn't make sense, Devon..."

"Whatever, I don't care. I'm not going to fuck with Dark Video. You'll do as I say, Alesandro. For our own good. For Terri. Never again, you hear?"

Never again.

Alistair put his hand in front of his mouth; sank to his haunches, his veins burning as if filled with acid. He wanted to scream out.

"Are you there?" asked Devon.

"What's going to happen to Sasha?" he said quietly.

"I told you. I'll make a plan. I'll get her out of town. Tell DV that we've dealt with her. Just promise me, Alistair. No more Terri. If this thing blows, we'll either be dead or in jail. Do you want that?"

Alistair rolled another two tablets from the brown phial. "I don't want that."

BIG BLACK GUY IN THE ROOM

The first thing Alistair noticed about the big black guy in his room was the pale blue shirt he wore. It seemed strangely incongruous, given its owner's occupation.

"Nice pad," said the hit man. He sat on the counter at the edge of the window, the furthermost point from the door. He raised a bottle of wine in his right hand, Alistair's prized Buiternverwachting, and gestured to him to come in. The cork and the wrapper paper from the neck of the bottle lay on the Persian.

"I believe you know me as Warnabrother."

For a moment, Alistair contemplated making a dash for it. Surely Warnabrother wouldn't try anything here in res? He decided against it.

"How did you get in?"

Warnabrother held the bottle up to the light, took a swig and scrunched his nose; set the bottle down on the desk; dug in his top pocket, found a match, started picking at his teeth.

"How did you get in?" Alistair repeated.

"The door was open."

The high pitched voice was also out of place; it didn't suit his massive frame. But it didn't make him any less frightening. "It wasn't."

"I'm in, ain't I?" Warnabrother flashed a mouthful of teeth.

Alistair closed the door behind him slowly. "What's your name, actually?" he said.

"You don't know who I am?"

"I know who you are. I just don't know your real name."

"You know Carlos?"

Alistair shook his head.

"You know of him?"

Alistair nodded. He edged along the wall, stopped with his back to the cupboard.

"Well, that's enough then. Nice watch you got there."

Alistair glanced down at his TAG, then quickly back to the hit man sitting in his window.

"You a bit edgy there, golden boy?"

"Should I be?"

"No need, no need. You should be very happy, right?"

"Oh? How's that?"

Alistair was trying to play it cool, struggling. The notion that this could

---

be the person who ends his life flashed to the front of his mind. Shouldn't he be whistling a tune?

"That video you done," said Warnabrother, snapping his two hands together from the wrists, like the mouth of a shark. "Carlos is very happy. Maybe he organize a cruise and get you some dollies."

"What?"

"Never mind."

Warnabrother swallowed a mouthful of wine. He offered the bottle to Alistair.

"No, er, thank you."

"On the contrary, thank you." Warnabrother lifted the bottle slowly to his mouth, his eyes not leaving Alistair's. He brought it down and wiped his sleeve across his mouth. "This is a woman's drink, Alistair. Do you mind if I call you Alistair? Or would you prefer golden boy?"

Alistair shrugged his shoulders, shook his head.

"Got anything stronger?"

"No. That's all."

"Guess you can't pick up chicks with whiskey, huh?"

Alistair smiled thinly, without mirth. This was preposterous, he thought. Here he was, a top third year law student, talking in his bedroom to a professional killer, the business end of a long chain of sick and twisted perverts.

"OK, OK, no problem," Warnabrother continued. "We stick with the wine. So whatcha studying?"

"Law."

"Law." Warnabrother confirmed, face breaking into a wide grin. "Heh, heh. Now that's what I think they call irony."

The smile vanished. He emptied the bottle with another gulp, banged it down on the counter.

"Course I knew that already, golden boy. There's lots I know about you. Few things I don't, though. So here I am making my acquaintance."

Alistair wondered if a man could sense his own impending doom; a primal instinct, perhaps. He didn't feel too nervous, but why was his leg jumping? A couple of pills would do the trick right now, he thought. He felt the phial in his pocket, wished he could get it out right there, tried to push the thought out of his mind.

Warnabrother dropped his head and rubbed his hands together, as if preparing for a presentation.

"Now it sounds to me that you're not so sure about where you stand with this whole thing...so I wanna tell you a little story. It's a fable. No, it's a parable. Or something. Anyway. Once upon a time there was this fairy princess. She was beautiful. Let's call her Goldie. And then, naturally, there was this prince. We'll call him Prince. Some would say he was very good-looking, but it's not for me to tell. You know, I like dollies so I can't discern. Discern? Is that the word?"

Alistair didn't know what to say, stared in silence, waiting for Warnabrother to go on.

"Now you know where this is going. Prince has everything. He got cash, he got gash, he got style. Everything just A-OK. The only thing he not allowed is Goldie. They say to him—wait, lemme see—Big King says to him he must leave Goldie alone. 'Cos Goldie belongs to the king, you see. And the king is the boss. But it's a cruel world, you see, 'cos Prince may have all these things, but what he really wants is Goldie. Don't ask me why. Maybe when you got everything, but you can't have this one small thing"—he imitated a pair of tweezers with his fingers—"then you want it. You may not even like it, but you want it."

Warnabrother brought the tweezers up to his eye, looked through them at Alistair.

"Does that make sense? I'm not sure. But anyways, Prince wants the girl. Bad! But Big King say uh-uh, you go for Goldie and you die. No, wait a minute, I got it wrong—she dies. It's tragic. Now anyone who knows about these fairy tales knows that the prince is gonna try and go for the girl. 'Cos it's a fairy tale, right? You know what's coming. But if he does..."

Warnabrother stood up. His strange shape seemed to disguise his height. He tapered downwards from his shoulders to a narrow waist tucked into a tight pair of stovepipe Levi's.

"You got any more of this wine?" he asked.

Alistair shook his head.

The hit man sat back down, disappointed, shrugged.

"Where was I? Yeah. Prince kisses Goldie, he loses everything. I mean everything. But he's got Goldie, right. It's worth it, right? Wrong. Goldie is possessed by an evil witch. He got nothing."

Alistair feigned disinterest. He felt detached, as though he was watching a movie, not part of the body that inhabited this room.

"I thought you said she dies?"

"I'm not good at this storytelling, man. Bottom line, the prince is fucked."

Warnabrother waited for a response.

"You've been sent here to threaten me, right?"

"Me? No, no. We just worried 'bout you. All us friends: you, me, Devon,

Carlos. We just wanna make sure you OK. That no wicked witch casts her spell on you. Oh wait, I nearly forgot. The moral. You wanna hear the moral?"

Alistair shrugged.

"I gotta tell you. This is a fairy tale, or fable, whatever. You know what the prince is gonna do before he does. He can't help himself. It's a motherfucking fairy tale. These things happen. Yes?"

Alistair gave no acknowledgement, stared blankly at Warnabrother. Imagined himself dashing across the room and tipping him out onto the concrete below.

"But this..." Warnabrother pointed to Alistair, then back to himself, then to the bed, the desk, the wine bottle. "This is real life. We got choices."

"Choices."

"Choices, golden boy. Now you a clever fellow. Do I gotta go spelling this out to you?"

"No, I'm OK," said Alistair quietly.

"You said what?"

"I said I'm OK. I'm a clever fellow." Alistair's focus had snapped back.

Warnabrother nodded. "You OK, then I'm OK," he said, as he hopped off the ledge. "This is a dangerous motherfucking place. You know where they put me? Woodstock! I'm thinking of hiring a bodyguard while I'm here. Whatcha think?"

Alistair snorted and ran a hand through his hair. The focus drifted again: he thought of Terri, the way her eyes shone, the little lines when she smiled, the way she felt against him, as if he'd known her all his life. He found himself staring intently at the wine bottle on the table.

"You sure you OK?" repeated Warnabrother.

"How did you open that bottle?" Alistair asked blankly, a distant memory of Silverman disappearing with his corkscrew.

"It was open."

Alistair opened his mouth to continue, stopped.

"Now you're getting it," grinned Warnabrother. He stood up and walked to the door.

"Oh. By the way. You wouldn't know where I can find Johnny's skinny girlfriend, do you now?"

⊙

"You're avoiding me." Terri caught him jumping into the A3, about to head up to campus to pick up some tutorials. He was two weeks behind

---

classes, wondered if he could make it up.

Three phone calls from her had gone unanswered.

"I...uh, I'm late for an appointment."

"Alistair," she put her hands on her hips. "What's going on?"

She looked confused, her face was filled with questions—sadness lurking. She looked through the window into his blue eyes; they were cloudy, rimmed, dark. He lowered his Police sunglasses from his hair, covering himself up.

"Look, I can't talk to you right now, Terri."

Alistair revved the engine, pulled away. He drove fast, one hand on the wheel, cellphone in the other. He called the nurse.

"I need a favor."

"I'm fresh out."

"No, you'll like this one."

"Try me."

"There a sweet little first year who's keen on me."

"Do I give a shit?"

"I want her to know what I'm really like."

"Right..."

"Don't suppose you made a copy of our video by any chance?"

"Sure I did. For the lonely times."

"Why don't you send it on over to her?"

"Ha! It'll be my pleasure. Should I attach a note?"

"A note—good idea. 'I made a mistake. I thought I had feelings for you, but I was wrong. There's someone else now.' Something like that. Name's Terri Phillips. She's in Tugwell."

"Got it. You coming around?"

"You send the video first and I'll see."

"I'll deliver it personally. We need to make another video, don't you think?"

⊙

"You, Terri Phillips?"

"Yes," said Terri. She'd walked into the foyer at Tugwell, checked her pigeonhole for messages, found an envelope and a DVD.

The thin girl in front of her reached into her bag, delved around, came up with a white sports bra scrunched in her hand.

"This is yours."

Terri recoiled, horrified.

"It's got your name on." The girl turned the bra inside out and showed

---

her the thin, printed label. "Terri Phillips. Tugwell 515."

"My boyfriend gave it to me. I don't think he saw the label. Here."

Terri took the bra, stared at it. She didn't know what to say. Eventually: "How did he get it?"

She shrugged. "He gave it to me as a birthday present, can you credit that? Were you fucking him?"

Terri reddened, other girls nearby turned.

"No! Who is he?"

"Johnny."

"I don't know anyone called Johnny."

"Sure you don't. Don't worry. It doesn't matter. He's dead."

"He's dead!"

"You probably read about it. He drowned."

⊙

He found her standing near the flower sellers on the corner of Main and Belmont. "Sasha!"

The thin girl swiveled, narrowed her eyes to identify him.

"You? You're Alistair, aren't you?" Fear washed across her face. "Get the fuck away from me!"

"Sasha. We need to talk. You're in danger."

She laughed at him. "If you think I'm getting into your car..."

Alistair parked on the double line and hopped out. The street looked grimy, in need of a wash. Two hobos washed clothing in the Liesbeek canal over the road.

She was walking away.

"Sasha. I must talk to you."

She swung around, sudden fury in her face. "Did you have fun? Did you enjoy sticking it up my ass, Alistair? Is that what nice boys like you do?"

"What are you talking about?"

"Johnny showed me the video, you fucking creep."

"The video? You mean....That wasn't me, Sasha. I had nothing to do with it, I swear. It was Johnny, he drugged you. And Jeff. I swear I wasn't involved.'

"You're a liar! Johnny showed it to me. He made it for me. He loved me. Then you slipped in for your fun. Fuck you!"

"Sasha, I had nothing to do with it! It was Jeff, I swear to god."

"You're a fucking liar. A liar and a rapist!" She said it loudly, for people to hear. A man packing groceries into his car hurriedly shut the boot and jumped in behind the wheel.

"Johnny's the liar. He was trying to make money off it....But that's not why I'm here, OK. I came to warn you."

"Warn me? About what, you creep?"

"You're in danger."

Two teenagers walked by, one brushed his shoulder against Alistair, looked back to check his reaction.

Sasha snorted. "Yeah right. I'm always in fucking danger. Behind every corner is a piece of rubbish like you."

"Sasha. I'm serious. That video has caused big trouble. There are some nasty people after you."

"What?" She shook her head, a sarcastic grin of disbelief, discolored teeth, an incisor missing. "I don't know what you're talking about. Anyhow, everybody's after me." She reached behind, under the rim of her short denim skirt, grabbed the cheeks of her ass. "They all want a piece of this. You included. Tell you what, I'll take a swing by Gorillas if you want and we can watch the video again. I hope you smiled when you stuck it in, Alistair."

Alistair gripped her by the arm.

"Sasha. Please do one thing for me. Take down my phone number."

"You want me to call you when I'm feeling horny, hey?" she spat, wrenching back her arm. But she didn't run; stood defiantly, looking him up and down, gritting her teeth.

"Please, Sasha. I only want to help you. You're in danger. You need to go to Gorillas to see Devon. He can help you. But take down my number and phone me if you can't find him."

She dug out her cell from her bag and punched in the number as he dictated it. "I've loaded it under Creep." A car hooted and she spun around.

"Sasha!"

A passing car slowed and she jumped into the back seat. Alistair recognized Jeff at the wheel.

FREAK OUT

Devon's appearance shocked him, his perfect hair unkempt, face blackened with stubble; slumped in the lounge, camera equipment strewn around the room. It looked like he hadn't slept in two days.

"What is it?"

Devon wouldn't say on the phone, only that something terrible had happened. Alistair had panicked, tight chest, thought the worst—Terri—raced to Gorillas.

"Devon, what happened?"

Devon's clothes were creased, the cuffs of his long sleeve shirt hung loose. He looked up slowly, his eyes hooded, black balls hidden deep in sunken sockets.

"Richard didn't come home last night."

The relief was intense; Terri was OK. Alistair could breathe again...

"Is that strange? Where do you think he went?"

Devon stared blankly into the space behind Alistair.

"It's not unusual. I always said to him...I told him he must come home. But he'd stay out all night—playing computer games—at party houses."

Each word seemed labored, drawn out.

"*Grand Theft Auto, Everquest, Manhunt...*" He stopped, put his head in his hands.

"Devon, what the hell is going on? Where is he?"

"Jeff called. About an hour ago. He says Richard's at this place..." Devon's voice trailed off, he mumbled, deep breath as if preparing to dive underwater.

"And what?"

"He's dead." Devon dropped his face onto his forearm.

"Dead!" The color drained from Alistair's face. "Jesus!"

Alistair felt the sensation again: his body separate from his consciousness, reality cleaving apart from his mind. He was outside, hearing a boy called Alistair listening to his friend Devon telling him that their friend Richard was dead. He wanted to run to Richard's room, find him typing on his laptop, shake him, feel that he was alive. He couldn't be dead.

"What the hell? What happened?"

Devon raised his head, his eyes red, dark, drooping with despair. "An overdose."

"An overdose? Richard? No!"

"I knew there was something wrong, I could sense it..."

"No, no, no," Alistair repeated. He slumped on the couch.

Devon related the story slowly, his voice a monotone, as if in a trance. Richard had been clubbing in town, ended up at a notorious Party and Play gig with Jeff.

Jeff. Sasha's dealer. Johnny's accomplice.

Richard had taken a concoction of recreational drugs. Coke, tik, tranquilizers. Speedballs. Jeff the supplier.

Alistair grimaced. "You believe his story?"

Devon ignored the question, continued: "Richard left with Jeff so they could go..." The look of a wild animal passed momentarily over Devon's face—then composure: "They found a place to fuck each other."

"Jesus Christ."

Alistair's face contorted. Another revelation: Richard popping speed-balls and having one-night stands. He was astonished. He scrutinized Devon's face for a sign. Nothing.

"When Jeff woke up this morning—a couple of hours ago—Ritchie was comatose. He thought he was asleep. But then he noticed he couldn't hear breathing, so he rolled him over and his eyes were open, just staring. Shit coming out his mouth. Overdosed."

"What the...? I just can't believe this. Not Richard. I didn't think he'd ever tried a drug in his life."

Devon wiped his brow, looked at Alistair. "He had a little habit."

"A habit? You're kidding me?"

"How d'you think his skin got so bad? He had a habit. So did Johnny. So did Sasha. Fuck's sake, Alistair, open your eyes."

A thought struck Alistair. Did Richard just fuck up? Or was it intentional? He'd last seen him on the day of Johnny's death, distraught, inconsolable. In shock. Like Alistair was now, the nightmare refusing to disappear, the panic rising. The police would investigate, link Richard to Johnny's drowning, maybe the press would start to speculate. When would it end? Derrick Young suddenly popped into his head; he'd left another message that morning.

"What did the police say?" he asked, fiddling with his keys.

"Nothing."

"Nothing? They can't be that useless."

Devon's eyes flicked over the array of video equipment. "I don't think they've been yet."

"What?"

"The flat's rented by the night. It's in Salt River. Crack whore hang out. Someone knocks someone off there every second weekend. And Jeff sure as hell isn't going to be inviting the cops over for a visit. I'm lucky that piece of shit even called me. If I ever....I'll fucking kill him with my bare hands."

Devon picked up a video camera and absentmindedly inspected the equipment. Cables, lighting stands, silver screens were scattered around the room.

The silence embarrassed Alistair. As with so much of his recent life, he wanted to get up and just walk away. He stayed.

"Was Richard addicted?"

Richard, the computer geek: shrill voice, clear eyes—how little he knew of him, thought Alistair. What had his sister Shelley said? "You know nothing about me. You know nothing about my life."

Devon wiped his eyes, tried to regain some composure. "No. Maybe? To computer games, yes. But I always thought he had the drugs under control."

"And now he's dead." Alistair could hardly comprehend it. He tried to picture Richard's dead body, foam dribbling from a grotesque mouth. The image in his mind morphed into the open jaws of a great white shark.... He shook his head rapidly to clear the thought, blinked several times.

Devon was talking.

"I got the address of the place off Jeff. I have to go over there now. I can't just leave him there for someone to find. But I can't do it alone. I need you to come with me, Alistair. Will you come with me? Please."

"I saw Jeff," said Alistair, confused, his mind making disparate connections. "He picked up Sasha yesterday."

"Fuck. Sasha." Devon's thoughts were equally incoherent. "Warnabrother. He was here. I need to find her. Before they do..."

"I spoke to her, tried to warn her. Devon, do you think...?"

"What?"

"Dark Video?"

"What about them?" Devon's eyes were awash with unpredictable emotion.

"Could they have had something to do with Richard?"

Devon rubbed his hand across his forehead. "I don't know, I don't know...This is out of control. I can't handle it."

"But why would...?"

"Richard pinpointed Carlos's location. He was also close to finding out about Mangle. Who knows what they found out about him? But..."

"You need to speak to Carlos."

Alistair stared at Devon, his hair untidy, tear stained face. Everything was falling to pieces, he thought, sin spilling down the corridor, down the steps, sticking to everything.

⊙

The room reeked of booze and vomit. Richard lay crumpled on his stomach, a skinny white carcass on a disheveled bed, grubby sheet bunched at his feet.

Alistair had never seen a dead person before, let alone one he knew, and he stared now, struggling to comprehend the sight before him. The body looked like a wax figurine; it hardly seemed real. Nothing seemed real any more.

Drugs? Reckless sex? Someone stuck a cock in that ass last night, thought Alistair. An image of Richard and Devon flashed in his mind, touching, holding hands, laughing.

He looked around the room. Spartan. Just the bed and sheet, a bedside table and a pile of Richard's clothes on the floor. No rubbish bin, no curtains, no carpet, no lamp. Who'd come to a place like this? Surely not Richard, the fussy little geek?

Alistair noticed Richard's glasses abandoned on the floor, near his clothes. He picked them up, placed them on the table. He looked at Richard again. In that head was a hard drive of information: RAM, but with no power. In death, he was just a fragile, bony child.

Devon sat on his haunches next to the bed, hands in prayer before him, heaving, choking.

Alistair put a hand on his shoulder. "Come, let's go wait in the kitchen."

A police van arrived; two expressionless cops. Then an ambulance. Alistair remained in the kitchen while the police questioned Devon. Words filtered down the passage: a close friend...drug addiction... personal effects.

⊙

"Fucking Jeff!" Devon ranted, in the Audi, on the return trip to Gorillas.

Alistair had never seen this side of Devon; never seen him lose control. He tried to restore focus.

"What about the press? They may be interested in two varsity boys dying, one in a shark attack, one an overdose."

"You see the guy who took my statement? Did he even ask you anything? I doubt he'd recognize a clue if it were hanging out his nose. He wrote down overdose as cause of death. Not suicide."

"Suicide?" said Alistair.

Devon stared blankly ahead.

They headed past Tugwell and Leo Marquad, paused at the traffic lights, into Rondebosch. Alistair noticed the neon sign for Bella Vista wine bar. Less than a week ago he had been in Arniston with Terri. He'd thought the nightmare over. *Hasta la vista.* Now it was back in his face, spilling everywhere.

"It could have been suicide. Richard was depressed. About..." He paused.

"No." Devon shook his head. "Richard overdosed."

Another set of traffic lights, Alistair stopped abruptly. He tapped on the steering wheel, looked over at Devon. "We're in deep trouble, aren't we?"

Devon shrugged his shoulders, said nothing.

"It won't just fade away," Alistair pushed.

"Why not? We haven't done anything."

Alistair stared ahead. Haven't done anything?

The lights turned green, Alistair slotted into gear and sped off. "Will they do an autopsy?"

"Doubt it."

"Why not?"

"For what? He fucking overdosed. What will they do? Arrest Jeff? They don't need the extra work."

"Jeff's got Sasha," said Alistair.

Alistair swung through the gates of Gorillas. He killed the engine. They sat together in silence.

"Look, Alesandro. Let's think rationally. We mustn't go to pieces here."

"I can't think at all. Jesus, Devon. My mind's all over the place. Everywhere I look I see Dark Video."

"Relax. I don't think they're a problem. Carlos wired the money to an offshore account yesterday. Five hundred thousand dollars is a lot money. It wouldn't make sense for him to betray us now."

"They've paid up?" Alistair said, incredulous. He tried to remember an earlier conversation. His memory was fuzzy. He couldn't trust himself. Five hundred thousand dollars. A lot of money. And he already had a down payment in his room at Belsen...

"Did you say something about Sasha?" Devon asked.

"She's with Jeff."

"He's a dead man," Devon stared up with slit eyes. "I swear to god..."

"Where the hell does Jeff fit in, Dev? Think about it. He makes the Assjacker video with Johnny. He's fucking Richard when he overdoses. He's Johnny's dealer. Now he's got Sasha."

Devon shook his head.

"He's a nobody. Richard's just a paying client to him." He patted Alistair's shoulder. "Trust me. I know."

An acorn fell from an oak tree above the car, bounced off the bonnet with a bang. Alistair was startled. "Where's Warnabrother?" he asked.

"I don't know. He's around. You just sit tight now. Don't do anything stupid. I'll sort out Sasha and get her away from here, wait for things to cool down."

Alistair fiddled with the keys in the ignition. "Speak to Carlos, Devon. Find out what the hell's going on."

Devon nodded in agreement, made to open the door, and stopped. "Look, Alesandro, Richard was due a large payout. Now he's gone. I think you should reconsider your share."

Alistair shook his head, waved his hand. "I don't want it."

"But you've already taken a payment, you may as well..."

Alistair thought about Terri. She would have seen the video of him and the nurse by now, got the note. What was she thinking? She must hate him, wish she'd never gone to Arniston, feel ashamed of how she'd given herself to him. He closed his eyes, opened them quickly. Shut it out. Bite off the arm if necessary.

"I don't trust Dark Video, Devon. I don't want their money. Give it back." He paused, his jaw set. "Give mine back. Or use it to sort out Sasha."

"Calm down, Alesandro. You're blowing this out of proportion. Yes, Johnny and Richard are gone. It's massive. But we won't achieve anything if we lose control. We need to quietly shut things down. No risks."

"Devon. I'm flipping freaked out."

"I am too. But I need you now. We need each other. Let's think clearly." Devon reached across and put his arm on Alistair's shoulder.

Alistair looked down, into the foot well. "Just make sure Sasha's OK."

Devon opened the passenger door, climbed out, and walked around to the driver's window. He leaned in to the window, his face close.

"What about Terri? Have you sorted her out?"

Alistair nodded. "You were right. I fucked her and got it out of my system. No big deal."

"Shame," said Devon, pulling back, straightening up.

"She'll get over it."

Devon breathed out, put his hand on Alistair's cheek through the window, composed again. "It was the right thing to do." He smiled at Alistair. "Stay cool, OK? We get Sasha out of town tonight and everything will be fine." He squeezed his hand. "I promise."

YOU CAN RUN BUT YOU CAN'T HIDE

In Alistair's mind, the normality of his life had unraveled like a dropped glass: one slip and the shattered pieces were everywhere, irreparable. In one memory his life was perfect; the next, a broken mess.

But that wasn't right, he realized, thinking about it as he made his way down the hill from campus. He'd missed the Jammie Shuttle, opted for the walk in the heat, perspiration pooling under his arms and sliding down his flanks. He picked at a loose thread on his shirt, unravelled it, realized there was a hole forming.

Weeks of lectures skipped, he was struggling to catch up, a mountain of assignments pending, two surprise tests; he hadn't even attended the classes, let alone studied.

He pushed open his door, a message on a slip of pink paper lay on the floor: "Alistair. I know who you are. I know how you feel. Phone me. Terri."

He scrunched it up angrily, wrenched his cellphone out of his pocket, and thumbed rapidly:

```
U dont know me. I feel nthin 4 u. U wre a conquest
only. 2 times. Leav me alone Terri
```

Send.

His phone rang; he answered instinctively. The hospice. Derrick Young's gravelly voice on the line.

"I've been trying to contact you, Alistair."

"I know, Derrick. I'm really sorry. I have been so busy."

"I read the article in the newspaper. The one about the boy who drowned..."

"Derrick, I can't talk now." His voice was breaking. He cut him off, heart pounding.

The next call flashed his father's name. He let it ring, found the phial, two pills, lay down on the bed, staring at the ceiling, afraid to shut his eyes in case the mouth appeared. Up again, scrabbling through his desk, the envelope of money still there, stationery, a pen.

He sat down at his desk and wrote quickly. Two letters. He folded both and inserted them into their envelopes. One he marked Terri.

```
Terri,
```

I've been on a journey I never should have taken.
I can no longer go back.
But in meeting you, I know I cannot go forward.
I tried to explain the night we made love in
Arniston but my desire was stronger than my resolve.
My life is a total sham.
You were right about me, I can never be your type.
I cannot make you happy and your happiness is all
that matters to me now.
You're the first girl I have ever loved.
I am sorry.

Alistair

The other letter he marked "To whom it may concern."
He dialed his sister, Shelley: engaged. Then he packed a bag.

⏵

Devon closed the door and walked down the corridor toward his room. Gorillas was silent, no boom of music from Johnny's room, no clickety click from Richard's. He traced his hand across Richard's door as he passed, reached into his pocket, and extracted his keys.

In his room, he dimmed the lights and removed his shirt, closed his eyes and ran his hand across his stomach; the familiar feeling of the scars, raised and contorted skin, strangely comforting. He'd seen Dr. Adams that morning: "Satisfactory progress, see you in three months' time."

He thought about Alistair; would he want to move in to Gorillas? He tried to envisage a scene of normality: two friends eating breakfast in the sun....But the images never lasted. In the silence, a man's loud voice intruded—and the smell of burning flesh.

A scraping sound outside the window interrupted his nightmare. Devon stopped, moved quickly to the light switch and shut it off. Someone was outside. He reached into his drawer and felt for the .38, flicked on the monitor on his desk for the exterior surveillance cameras. The message from Carlos was at the front of his mind—and he knew Warnabrother was in Cape Town.

Relief as he identified the figure in the murky darkness of the alley outside Gorillas, then a grin. He put the gun back in the drawer, alongside its twin—he kept two revolvers in there. Then he turned on his bedside lamp and booted his laptop.

The window to Johnny's bedroom was slightly ajar. Sasha pulled it open and hoisted herself onto the ledge, climbed through the window and landed with a light thud. She froze, immobilized, waiting for a noise, a door closing or opening, but none came. She breathed deeply and slipped onto the bed, rolling over, face in the pillow.

The familiar smell washed over her, a hint of menthol, Johnny's shampoo, impossible to forget. Sasha closed her eyes, opened them briefly, closed them again. She felt an overwhelming desire to sleep; the warmth of the bed, the smell, curtains flapping lightly in the breeze.

When she opened her eyes again, there was a figure seated on a chair by the bedside. She sat up, suddenly frightened, unsure of herself.

"Don't panic," Devon reassured her. He wore a jet black polo neck and black jeans, his hair slicked back in dark lines, olive skin shining. "I don't believe we've officially met," he said, rising, approaching her, extending his hand. "You must be Johnny's girlfriend."

"Sasha," she replied. Her hand was limp, nervous; he held it without shaking.

"Oh yes. Sasha." Devon looked directly at her, held eye contact. He'd had plenty of time to scan her while she slept. Now to gauge her thoughts.

"How sad about Johnny," he said. No reply. He released her hand and returned to the chair by the desk, sat, crossed his leg, calf on knee. Sasha fidgeted, twirling the bangles on her arm as if twisting off the lid from a tin.

"A great friend," he continued. "You must be very cut up."

She didn't know where to look. Johnny had told her once that Devon was the devil. He seemed so nice.

"Did Alistair speak to you about the video? The one with you and Johnny..." Devon's voice was gentle, soothing.

"Yes," she said softly. "He lied to me. He said he wasn't in the video."

Devon frowned. "Alistair. In your video?" Then a laugh.

"Johnny said..."

"Johnny said!" He cut her off, rising quickly from the chair. Then, calmer: "Johnny said lots of things, Sasha. He used you."

Devon sat down on the bed next to her, took both her hands in his and looked into her eyes. Intense.

"I know how you feel. I can feel the pain, because I..." His grip tightened; she pulled her hands away.

"Let me go! Johnny would never lie to me. He loved me. He did it for me!"

Devon put a finger to his lip. He waved a silver disc in front of her.

"I believe this will clear up any misunderstanding you have."

He stood up and inserted the disc into Johnny's DVD player, gathered the remote and sat next to her on the bed, his thigh touching hers. She shifted up, but the wall prevented her breaking his contact. He flicked the remote.

The image showed an empty room, dimly lit, the duvet—the room they were in, the duvet they were sitting on. The door opened and in walked Johnny. With her. Devon froze the frame: her face, ashen, wild, rolling eyes.

"Johnny called it 'Assjackers.' That's so crude." He turned to her. "Don't you think?"

Sasha said nothing, eyes blinking repetitively.

"Should I stop it? You don't want to watch this? Do you?"

She saw herself as another person, a foreign object, as if someone else had appropriated her body for that night. Johnny's glistening shaft rose and fell. He lifted her and carried her limp body to the window. The camera changed hands. The grimacing face of the accomplice filled the screen—paused—Jeff.

Devon felt her shudder as an agonized sob took hold of her body.

"Such a shock?" Devon advanced the video frame by frame. "Your friend Jeff. Your friend Jeff, who raped you."

Tears ran down Sasha's cheeks; she buried her face in her hands. Her words were almost inaudible: "Johnny said it was Alistair."

"Johnny was such a liar! Alistair would never lower himself like that." The anger in Devon's voice bubbled to the surface. He grabbed her hand, pulled it roughly from her face. "Now watch it. Watch the rest of it."

He pressed play, continued the suffering in real time, forcing the reality of what had happened into the maelstrom of Sasha's mind. Through the tears, she could sense Devon watching her, not the television, and the fear in her rose, overwhelming the shock.

The screen went black. She wanted to vomit.

"I need to go to the bathroom."

He escorted her like an invalid to the toilet in the hallway, one hand on her shoulder, the other at her waist. She closed the door and rushed to the bowl, falling to her knees, the retching dry and unproductive.

She looked up at the little window above the bath. Could she climb through it? Why had she come here? What was Alistair trying to warn her about? Sasha, I only want to help you.

She pulled out her cellphone from her pocket—what name had she used to store his number?—put it back, opened the bathroom cabinet above the sink; it contained an array of prescription medicines. She pulled out a plastic container and examined the label, Xantrexil, emptied the contents into her mouth. The door burst open and Devon marched toward her, snatched the container away, laughing, reached into his pocket.

"This is more your style, I think."

In the palm of his hand he revealed four plastic straws, melted and sealed at each end. Crystal methamphetamine. Street name: tik.

Sasha stared at the straws, lower jaw instinctively dropping, paralyzed by what she saw. Devon grabbed her roughly by the sleeve and marched her back to Johnny's room. He placed the straws on the desk.

"They're yours. And a copy of the video."

He ejected the disc with the remote. Sasha moved toward the desk, her gaze trained on the plastic phials in front of her. Redemption, escape.

"Wait." Devon held an open palm toward her, shook his head. "Not so fast. You're going to have to give me something."

"What do you want?" she said, unbuttoning her pants. Underneath she was naked, a thin shaved strip of black hair jutted out toward him.

"Do it up, you stupid whore! Is that all you know?"

He grabbed her roughly by the shoulders and flung her onto the bed.

"I need some information. Johnny had an item of clothing. A white sports bra. He used to keep it in his room, but it seems to have disappeared. Do you know where it is?"

She looked at him, shook her head.

"What a pity. It has suddenly become quite valuable to a client. I could help you out if you knew where it was." He indicated the straws with a nod of his head. "They're absolutely pure. Not the cut shit you normally mess about with. A hundred and fifty a pop, ten times what you normally pay. But for you"—he blew through his fist—"free. That is if you're able to recall..."

Her nose twitched, she bit down on her lip, shook her head.

"Are you sure, Sasha? You don't know what I'm talking about? You druggies always seem to have a tell. A little giveaway." Devon twitched his nose, bit his lip. "It would be a shame to waste such high-quality narcotics..."

Violence would be Devon's next resort if need be. It was not a problem for him; he'd grown up with it. He put a hand in his pocket and fingered a photograph he'd taken earlier that day: Jeff with a metal cord around his neck. He smiled grimly and imagined smashing a fist into the skinny girl's face. But he knew it wouldn't be necessary.

He picked up a straw and broke it open with a snap, then slowly started pouring its content of finely ground crystals onto the floor, grinding them into the floorboards with his foot.

"Stop!" She stared at his foot, eyes flaring. "Please. Stop."

"Do you have it?"

She shook her head.

"Did you have it?"

Her nose twitched.

"Where is it now?"

"How do I know they're...OK?"

Devon smiled. "OK? You mean not poisoned? Like Ritchie's?"

Sasha stared, not comprehending.

"Didn't Jeff tell you? Ritchie's booty bump went awry. But then Jeff's not talking much these days either." He flicked her the picture of the dead dealer with the cord around his neck.

She pulled her hand away from the photograph as if it were a hot plate, clutched her knees under her chin, rocked back and forth. Devon leaned forward and patted her on the shoulder.

"Don't worry. I'll be your dealer now. Before he died Jeff cut these to my recipe. Pure amphetamines."

Devon picked up the straws and dropped them in front of Sasha; they fell randomly on the duvet. Sasha inhaled sharply, reached out her hand, then checked herself.

"Eeny, meeny, miny, mo." Devon twirled an index finger over the drugs, settling on a straw. He picked it up, cut the end with a pair of scissors off the desk and poured a small amount of the contents onto his tongue. Sasha darted forward, kissed him, her tongue snaking into his mouth. He pushed her away, repulsed.

"Do you have silver paper?" she asked desperately, rubbing her finger against her gums, eyeing the cut straw in his hand.

Devon swallowed and pointed to the light bulb hanging from the ceiling. "Use that," he said. "But you need to give me an answer first."

"She's got it," Sasha whispered quickly. "She's got it."

"What! Who? Terri?" Devon exploded. "Fuck sake! How's that possible?"

Sasha cowered, eyes on the crystals. "I gave it to her."

Devon balled his fists with rage. He felt like smashing her head against the wall. "Fuck!"

"What's the problem?"

"You've just signed her death warrant, that's the problem!" He walked to the window and slammed it shut, panes rattling violently.

"Do you have any paper?" Sasha repeated.

"If you ask me again, I'll blow it up your fucking ass." He made for the door.

"Where are you going?" she asked.

Devon stopped and looked around at her. "I was once like you, Sasha. Never again!" He reached up, unscrewed the light bulb and tossed it onto the bed. Then he spun on his heels and walked out the door.

When she left, he knew it wouldn't be on her own two feet. He'd marked the clean straw with a tiny red dot. The others were cut with strychnine and antifreeze. She'd never have noticed.

GENTLEMAN TO SEE YOU

"You're a coward, Alistair," his sister Shelley said.

His cellphone was pinned to his ear, the Audi flying down the highway, knuckles white on the wheel, slipping back and forth across the solid line, cat's eyes thumping on the tires.

"Instead of facing your demons, you've run away. Come clean!"

"But the consequences?"

He glanced at his face in the rearview mirror, his face gaunt and grey, dark rings beneath his eyes. The tires grated on the gravel; he jerked at the steering wheel.

"Just own up. What you've actually done is far less than what you're attempting to cover up. You weren't responsible for anyone's death. But no, you can't admit that you're less than perfect to the rest of the world! That you've failed to meet expectations. What would Daddy think?"

"Shelley, please, it's not like that."

"That poor girl…"

"Her life's in danger. I did it for her."

"Bullshit. You did it for *you*. You're a windup soldier. Dad has had you going since day one, and now this Devon character. You're weak, Alistair, you've never stood for anything. Stand for something now."

"It's not Devon, Shelley. It's Dark Video. They're hunting us both."

"Alistair. Can't you see? This guy has you tripping between uppers and downers. *He* killed Johnny, it's *his* fault Johnny's dead, not Dark Video's."

"Johnny would've killed us."

"Where are you driving?"

"Please, Shelley, can't you talk to Father?"

"No. You're going to have to sort this out yourself."

⊙

Arniston beach was deserted. Alistair gathered a clump of sand in his right hand and let the grains run through his fist. Fitting to be here now, he thought, a place of so much joy, so many good memories—or was it ironic?

He stared at the ocean, his clothes and shoes sodden. He had walked into the sea, sunk to his knees in the shallow water, felt the water rush against him and allowed the surf to rock him back and forth. Perhaps it could take him away…

The setting sun disappeared behind a bank of clouds, a giant pink dragon smothering the impact of its setting. In the failing light, a gang of seagulls worked a square of water a few hundred meters from the beach.

Alistair took another swig from the bottle of Jack Daniel's he'd found at the house. He removed his cellphone from his jacket pocket, shook it. Tried to call Devon again. Had he got Sasha out of town? The phone was wet; its hazy screen flickered and died. Even without a working phone, though, he couldn't blot out the imaginary calls that were springing into his head.

His thoughts spun round and round, always returning to the first one. Like the carriages on a big wheel. He fumbled in his pocket for the phials. Which was which? He poured two from each into his hand, peered at them through blurry eyes. Up? Down? Which way did he want to go? Something sparked in his muddled head. Stop the cycle—he knew he had to stop the cycle.

An image of Derrick Young from the hospice in the first carriage.

"I've been calling you, Alistair. Why did you never come back? I want to know how the story ends."

Alistair tossed the pills into the sand; flung the phials into the sea as hard as he could. He tried to halt the motion of the wheel, grab the power stick and shove it down: emergency stop.

He gulped down a mouthful of whiskey. Whoosh. His stomach lurched.

The wheel continued the rotation, another carriage, this time Henri, Terri's ex-boyfriend, charging below a high ball, crashing toward him.

"I'll race you for the girl, Morgan."

He felt Silverman's hand on his shoulder.

"My money's on Morgan. He's on speed."

The metal cranked as another carriage appeared. He lifted the bottle to his mouth and took a swig. The light was fading, wind coming in, no moon yet to ease the darkness.

"You're a great disappointment to me." John Morgan's eyes bore into him, his hands curled into fists. "A great disappointment."

He held the bottle to his mouth, over-poured, whiskey sloshing down his front. Enraged. An extravagant wipe of his shirt front, angry, the clasp on his watch broke, it dropped to the sand.

Creak, creak, crank.

Johnny.

"Fucking asshole!" Johnny hollered.

"Let's go for a bite some time," Alistair yelled back. The great mouth emerged from the dark behind Johnny, consumed him whole.

Then Richard, his face red and blotchy, yellow-green jelly pouring down his chest.

"Ritchie! What did they do to you?"

"Whee!" Richard's head swung back as the carriage tilted and hoisted upwards.

Alistair stood up unsteadily.

"I have to get a grip," he said to himself. "I must speak to Devon. We can sort this out. We can."

"You took all the love," Shelley had said earlier. "If only you weren't so greedy. I could have got some as well."

Alistair imagined the Morgan children queuing up for affection, Shelley at the back of the bus.

The tide was rising; a large wave surged up the beach and circled him, water filtering into the softer white sand. The water level in the Waenhuiskranz cave would be at least halfway up, he thought. What if I went to the cave and waited for full tide? Roll a giant boulder against the exit. Only way out to swim into the sea. At high tide it wouldn't be possible. The strength of the incoming water would push him back into the cave. Drowning must be a terrible way to die, he thought. Would his body surrender and allow the life to slip away, or would he involuntarily fight for life, desperate gasps for sweet oxygen, water rushing into his lungs, frantic adrenaline released to escape the entrapment? Someone told him once that you start to think you're breathing again when you drown; the water is air, peaceful.

His head spun, the carriages of guilt kept turning.

"Mrs. Hamilton?"

"I kept a steak, egg, and chips for you, Alistair. It's Friday night. You're our golden boy."

"I don't think I'll be making it back."

"Ever?"

"I'm not sure."

"Yeehaa!" Maggie's hands were above her head, her corpulent body filling the entire carriage.

"Maggie, baby."

"Allie Morgan. 212. A visitor. Gentleman visitor."

Alistair rubbed his face; it was coated in sand and vomit.

Whoosh. The nurse, naked, sailed by in a carriage. Strange what speed did to breasts, he contemplated, even the best ones. They seemed to have their insides sucked out. He'd seen pictures of naked girls falling from aeroplanes. Where did the middle bit go?

"I gave her the video. Every thrust of my pelvis was a stab to your own heart, Alistair. You were just a conquest to me. But you loved her."

His heart jumped.

An apparition appeared before him, a face directly before his: his own.

Alistair took a last swig of whiskey, dropped the bottle in the sand. He stumbled forward, face down, struggled to lift his head; someone held him down, pushed his face into the sand, suffocating. He broke free.

He stood up and staggered in the direction of Waenhuiskranz.

If you sprinkle thoughts here, they are preserved forever...

His cellphone beeped in his pocket. Somehow it was working again. He pulled it out and squinted at the screen.

The text was from Sasha:

```
Alistair. Beware. Terri has the bra
```

Then a single face appeared in his fuzzy thoughts: the first carriage, John Morgan, tanned, clean-shaven, scent of aftershave, cool, soft hands and deep, piercing eyes.

"Alistair. What in god's name have you done?"

He stopped.

"We can still sort this out."

He turned around.

⊙

"Terri Phillips," the receptionist called from the base of Tugwell Hall. "Gentleman to see you."

NO WAY OUT

"A masterstroke," **said Devon with a broad grin**, reclining on a couch in the Morganhouse living room. His dark hair shone, a single black hue, as if recently polished. He rolled up his sleeves carefully, even folds uniformly below the elbow.

Alistair brought him a cup of tea, placed it on the table in front of him. A female figure lay prostrate on the couch, arms bound behind her back, eyes and mouth covered. Terri. Outside, Devon's gun-metal Mercedes stood parked beside the Audi.

Alistair sat down with his back to the window. Behind him nighttime; dark clouds swirling beneath the stars.

"Lovely place you've got here," Devon said. He glanced around, taking in his surroundings. Alistair watched as he idly removed the .38 from his pants pocket, smoothed the revolver with his hand, tucked it into his pants front. "Been in the family for some time?"

"A while, yes. Three generations."

"Ah." Devon reached for his cup.

"Is she OK?" Alistair asked, indicating Terri's limp body with his eyes.

"She's out for the moment. She'll come around soon."

"How did...?"

Devon raised his hand. He sipped his tea and beamed at Alistair. "We're two of a kind, Alesandro. We think alike. I mean—what a great idea. Carlos will be delighted!"

"Action stems from necessity," said Alistair coldly. "I realized I was going to go down if I didn't sort this out now. And I can't let that happen. So I don't see any other way out."

"Of course. You had me worried for a while, I have to say. I knew I'd have to act. Once Terri got the bra, she'd blow everything. But this idea of yours—it's genius."

Alistair changed the subject: "Where's Sasha?"

"She's sorted out."

Alistair stared out the window. Even in the blackness, he could visualize the shape of the bay, and the concrete deck off the harbor straining with each wave as if reaching for the shore—an eternal struggle. He remembered the times he and Shelley swam out to it on the low tide. His mother had panicked once, watching them from the front lawn.

"It was unfortunate—but it needed to be done," Devon continued. He placed his cup and saucer back on the table, looked at the sleeping girl.

She wore a grey tracksuit, bare feet.

"Your call was perfectly timed, Alesandro. I'd just picked her up. Had a different plan for her, I must admit. But this—this is so much more fitting.

"You got all the equipment?"

"In the car. Now, let's take a look at the set."

Alistair found a big Maglite torch in a kitchen cupboard, located the key, unlocked the back door. He and Devon walked out onto the crumbling limestone promontory together, surveyed the setting in the ambient night light. A brisk wind whipped at them from the south; the sea surged on the rocks below.

"This is perfect," marveled Devon, rubbing his arms to ward off the cold. "Jagged rocks, crashing waves, a brewing storm. A frightened girl cornered, nowhere to go. So much drama."

"Can you make it work?" asked Alistair, as they made their way back toward the warmth of the house.

Devon patted him on the shoulder. "Of course I can. I'll need to throw out some serious wattage, but I've got both the Quartz light stands. It'll work."

Alistair closed the door behind them; they took stock in the kitchen.

"We'll have to watch the weather," said Alistair.

"The wilder the better. I'll set up the cameras and light stands, then we get her out there and do this as soon as she comes around."

Alistair nodded, glanced up at the No Entry sign above the back door.

Devon smoothed out his ruffled hair. A thought occurred to him. "Shall we film her naked?"

"I didn't think of that."

"It'd be interesting. Especially for her private client—imagine the camera following her naked ass out into a blizzard." Devon laughed at the thought.

"I suppose that's an option. But let's not get ahead of ourselves here. Rather we strip her down while filming so we don't give away the excitement too soon. You know, when you see her tits that's climax time for the viewer. We need to keep up the anticipation."

"Yes, yes," Devon nodded. "No need to get ahead of ourselves. And it will help us keep her under control if she's dressed. We let her believe we're doing an action replay of *Forest Frolic*. She's got a fan, we have to do this. Same script then she's free to go."

The wind rattled the doors, a draft slipping through the swollen gaps in the windows.

"It's going to be difficult working out there," said Devon. "You're going to have to keep her calm. Keep reassuring her that we're not going to harm her. It's just a modeling job, nude girl on a windy night, same as before with a different setting."

Alistair's eyes flicked back and forth. "You're going to have to handle all the camera work."

"You sure, Alesandro? And you'll…take the final shot?"

Devon stared into Alistair's eyes, made a gun with his thumb and forefinger. "Bang bang?"

Alistair nodded.

Devon looked him up and down for a second, broke into a smile. "Come on, Alesandro. You're telling me you can go through with this—you can shoot the girl? Dead?"

Alistair's face hardened. "What choice do I have, Devon? Our lives are in the balance. If this all comes out, I'm finished. I'll lose everything. Implicated in murder, abduction. Jail time." He grabbed Devon's collar, eyes wild with aggression. "What chance have I got in jail?"

"Hey, cool it. Just cool it," said Devon. He dropped his hands over Alistair's, slowly removed them.

"I'm not cool, Devon! I'm fucking terrified."

Devon patted him on the cheek, nodded, Alistair's motives approved. He turned away, continued with the plan.

"Surprise is what we're looking for." Devon closed his eyes and envisaged the scene. "I give all the instructions, you lead her to the location. She strips like before. Counts. Then she takes off the mask, sees you pointing the gun at her face. Right in her face. The moment of surprise. It's crucial. That's the money shot. Then bang."

Alistair nodded. "You haven't spoken to Carlos yet, have you? About this?"

"It'll be a surprise," confirmed Devon. "I'd like to see Carlos's face. Or the client's."

Alistair looked him in eye. "There had better be good money for this, Devon. I want my pay and then I want out. And I think it's reasonable to say I want my cut for the shark vid now, too."

"Of course you do."

Alistair gripped Devon by the collar again. "Devon. This is it! Once Terri's gone, it's over. We get our money from Dark Video and walk. It's a condition of the sale, you hear me?"

"We're two of a kind!" chuckled Devon, easing him off to arm's length, brushing off his shirt. "Don't worry, Alesandro. We're out after this."

In the living room, they found Terri on her back, slowly waking. She shook her head, struggled lethargically to free her hands.

"Right on time," announced Devon, looking down at her on the carpet. He turned to Alistair. "Now, Mr. Scriptwriter, I'm going to get the set ready. Why don't you wake up our young star and get her ready for the show?"

Alistair nodded consent, squatted down to Terri's prostrate form.

"Try find something a little....more appealing than this," Devon continued, indicating Terri's grey tracksuit. He grinned. "I don't think we'll be needing a bra."

▷

Alistair lifted Terri off the floor and carried her through to the Anchor Room. He placed her on the bed, loosened her bonds without untying her, propped up some pillows against the headboard and leaned her against it.

"Quiet," he whispered. "Just stay calm, Terri. It's me, Alistair." He dabbed her forehead with some water from a glass, gently patted her cheek. She coughed and he held his hand over the gag that covered her mouth.

"Shhh!"

He sat down alongside her, one hand stroking her arm.

"Terri, can you hear me? Listen closely. Just be calm and don't scream or make a noise, you understand?"

She nodded. He removed the blindfold and gag.

"Where am I?" Her face was puffy and red, her eyes swollen.

"Arniston." Fear flashed in her eyes. Alistair held a glass of water to her lips. She hesitated.

"Alistair?" Her eyes were pleading, desperate.

"Trust me, Terri. You have to trust me."

She sipped from the glass, her eyes locked on his. "What's happening? Alistair. What..."

He pressed his hand over her mouth. "Shhh. You're in the Anchor Room."

He removed his hand.

"I got your letter," she said.

Alistair's heart iced over, he sucked in his breath. "Which letter?"

"Silverman brought it to me. Alistair, I....I was so worried. I thought you were going to hurt yourself."

"Shhh."

She coughed again and he raised his hand quickly to her mouth. He took it away and hugged her. She felt limp in his arms.

"How did I get....There was a man—Devon! I thought Silverman had come back. But it wasn't him. He said you'd had an accident. That he'd take me to you. I don't remember..."

"He drugged you and brought you here."

They heard the kitchen door slam, a shout: "Alesandro, action time! Get her out here!"

"Listen, Terri," Alistair whispered. "We're both in great danger. Just follow my lead and do as I say, OK?"

TO THE EDGE

"Hey, Alesandro, what's taking so long? Let's get this thing going."

"Coming, coming. We're almost ready."

Alistair walked Terri from the Anchor Room into the corridor. The blindfold and gag were back in place. He had let her hair down and brushed it out; raided Shelley's cupboard, found a pair of jeans to go with a little white tank top, stomach exposed.

"Not bad. You weren't thinking of seconds, were you?" Devon winked at him from the kitchen doorway, the .38 held loosely at his side.

"Nah. Had my fill." Alistair puffed out his chest, macho, calm. Heart racing underneath.

"Come on through."

In the kitchen, Devon addressed the blindfolded girl. "I know you're scared, Terri. But nothing's going to happen to you as long as you do what I say."

Terri's body shook. Alistair could make out her nipples pressed like buttons against the thin fabric of the tank top. His mind flashed back to that first morning; the car ride from the police station. It seemed like yesterday—and a lifetime ago.

"Remember the morning in the forest?" Devon continued, paralleling his thought. "Well, it seems you're in demand now. So we're doing the sequel tonight. A quick film shoot for a high paying client. Then we'll let you go, just like last time. You understand?"

Terri nodded.

Devon tested her bindings and blindfold, untied the gag and dropped it on the table. "No more need for that."

Terri sucked in two deep breaths through her mouth, shaking even more. Her legs buckled and Alistair caught her at the elbows, lifted her up. He wished he could wrap her up in his embrace.

"Relax, Terri. Relax," said Devon, stepping forward, putting a hand on her shoulder. "Everything's going to work out just fine. Now, we're going to take a little walk outside. The weather's pretty nasty but that just adds to the atmosphere, makes the film a bit more exciting. When we stop, we'll untie your hands. You may not remove your blindfold yet, understood? But I'm afraid the clothes are going to have to come off."

Devon ran the barrel of the gun from Terri's neck, down her breastbone, between her cleavage. "Once your clothes are off, count to one hundred. Then it's over. Like last time."

The gun continued to trace a path down her clothing, stopped briefly at her exposed navel, then further, under her jeans, prying them forward. Devon leaned forward, looked down. "Let's see if you're wearing some.... alluring underwear."

Terri gasped, jolted back, twisting and squirming. Devon responded with a vicious slap across her cheek with his free hand, clutched her hair, pulled her head forward.

"Don't fuck it up!" he hissed, mouth to ear. "You understand?"

Her head bobbed in nervous acknowledgement, tears streaming from beneath the blindfold.

Devon released his grip, softened his voice: "Just remember last time. Follow my instructions and you'll be safe. Here we go."

He swiveled quickly and wrenched open the back door. A clamor of wind and sea air whipped into the kitchen. Turning and indicating for Alistair to follow, he stepped out into the night. Alistair picked up the heavy black Maglite from the kitchen counter and led out Terri with his free hand.

The three tunneled into the inky blackness, the wind buffeting their progress. They edged cautiously along the path, beyond the walls of the house where it opened onto the exposed promontory. Alistair narrowed his eyes and lowered his head, his shirt flapping wildly like a restrained kite, Terri's hair streaming behind.

No way back except along the path.

They came to two lighting units and a camera on a tripod. They swayed in the wind, held fast by large rocks propped at their bases, filming ready to begin at the flick of a couple of switches.

Devon stopped, pulled Alistair aside and thrust the revolver into his hand. He jabbed a finger to his lips and stepped back.

"You want me to shine the torch for you?" he asked.

"No, I'll keep it," said Alistair, pushing the gun into the belt of his jeans. He steered Terri further along the path, continuing slowly across the rocky terrain. They stopped alongside the cairn of white stones. Behind them, a burst of light appeared, then another, illuminating the ground around them: patches of sand between ominous rocks. Exposed to the gusting wind, clumps of dry yellow grass whipped against their legs.

"Perfect!" said Devon, peering into the viewfinder. Terri and Alistair were centered in the frame.

Alistair knelt behind Terri and loosened the cord binding her hands. She wriggled her hands free, held them in front of her chest, massaging her wrists.

"Terri," Alistair whispered softly as he rose behind her. "Remember, don't look into the light. Look down."

"Camera rolling!" Devon shouted, from his vantage point, his words coming at them with the wind, blasting them like a sheet of sand. "Scene one, take one. Alistair, out the way."

Alistair took two steps back, directly behind Terri.

"Take off your clothes!" shouted Devon.

Terri reached up and lowered the blindfold, blinking, keeping her head down.

"No!" shouted Devon. "Not yet!"

Alistair thrust the Maglite into Terri's hand, stepped forward in front of her, hand covering his eyes, dominating the shot.

"What the fuck! You're ruining..."

"Come out, Devon," called Alistair, as he raised the .38 with his right hand. Behind him, Terri shone the torch directly at the camera stand. They squinted into the lights.

Devon stepped forward, shielding his eyes from the torchlight.

"It's over, Devon!" shouted Alistair into the wind.

Devon dropped to his knees. "I can't believe it, I can't believe it! This is brilliant!" He clutched dramatically at his chest.

"Devon, stand up."

"Alesandro, you are truly a master. What an absolutely brilliant piece of thinking!"

"I said, get up!"

Devon stood up slowly, raised his hands, a manic grin spread across his face. "It's over! I love that! Was it planned? It's over! Classic. Carlos will love this. We'll call it the Double Cross!"

"You're delusional, Devon! It's finished."

A fresh burst of wind raged across the promontory, harder than before. One of the lighting stands crashed to the ground in a flurry of sparks, halving the brightness.

"Shit!" said Devon loudly, looking around. They could make him out more clearly now, the remaining light stand illuminating the scene from an angle. "But one should do."

He reached into his pocket and removed a remote control, waved it in the air. "Action from both sides," he called, gesturing to his left. Alistair turned, spotted a red light peering out from the darkness, the profile shot.

"Cut it, Devon," he said. "Just cut the cameras, cut everything."

"Are you crazy, Alesandro? Scene one's just begun. I can't wait to discover what's next."

Alistair took one step forward, gun held firmly, pointed at Devon's chest. They were five meters apart. Behind Alistair, Terri kept the powerful torch shining into Devon's eyes.

"This isn't a movie, Devon."

Devon roared with laughter, stamping his feet. "Brilliant! This movie, this movie...is not a movie!"

Alistair took another step forward, gun before him, brought his left hand up to the handle.

"What is it, Alesandro? What magic script have you dreamed up?" Devon opened and closed his eyes, adjusting to the beam of Terri's Maglite. "You would've loved my last. Richard. I wish you'd been there. A simple script. Richard takes a tainted speedball and we document his downfall—after a little horseplay, of course. Quite disturbing. Agonizing. I couldn't watch. But some people like that kind of thing. I'm calling it 'Brain Drain.' Not exactly consensual, but it's time we waive that proviso now, don't you think?"

Alistair stared at him, the information flowing through his numbed mind, a revelation. Another one. Of course. But nothing surprised him now: the shark, the body, the drugs, the guns.

A collection of tumbling grass swept past Alistair, out of the light and down to the depths below. Devon laughed again, wild hand gestures swirling in the wind.

"It's showbiz, Alesandro. Ritchie was a good boy. Innocent to start. We had a...thing. But he was too clever for his own good. Came close to discovering a few home truths."

Alistair's mind raced. Richard, murdered. And Johnny, dead. It suddenly occurred to him that Devon had never lost control on the boat; one way or another, Johnny was never coming back from that trip. And what else? What other horrors was he involved in?

The gun shook violently in his hand—the horror of realization consuming his fear, masking the cold that beat at him. Was there a way to resolve this without pulling the trigger? Devon deserved it, he knew that now—deserved to die in agony for what he had done. But could he end a human life? He was always a negotiator, a manipulator even; he had a way with words.

"Devon, we must stand up to Dark Video. If we don't, we'll never be free."

"Dark Video?" Devon laughed. "It's not about Dark Video. It's about me! Finally, I'm meting out justice in return for suffering."

Alistair rubbed his streaming eyes on the sleeve of his free hand.

What was he talking about? "You're crazy, Devon. You're sick..."

"Oh yes, Alesandro? Crazy, sick? And what about you? Terri, has he explained everything to you? Your rescuer, your savior—has he told you about his role in the forest the day he met you?"

Terri stepped forward, holding onto Alistair's waist with one hand, pressing against him, the light beam from the torch shaking.

"And you rush to him now, your savior—when he was one of your attackers in the first place. When he spent weeks coaxing a dying man into being eaten by a shark. Who's sick now, Terri? Or hasn't he told you that one yet either?"

"Don't believe him, Terri. He's insane, he's fucking insane."

"Rich coming from you, Alesandro. How do you explain your actions? At least I have an excuse. Look, I'm the burned boy." He lifted his shirt front, letting the wind gust under, blowing it higher. A pox of welts and burn scars tattooed his skin. He spun around to display his back.

"My uncle. The man with the boat. The Karoo farm. You never asked about him, Alesandro. He liked to use young boys for his fun. I was his favorite. I learned a lot from him. Funny thing about youth, they say you always bounce back. Not me, though. It became a recursive loop. I'd think about what happened and, halfway through, the same scene would start again and again. An endless rerun. Every time he did it to me, another scene was added. I couldn't stop the playback."

Devon paused, a moment of bitter reflection as the wind continued its assault. Then another burst of laughter, mocking, manic. "But he died. A violent death. The start of my therapy."

"OK, Devon, OK." Alistair held his hands out in front of him, palms up, gun pointing off at an angle. He was hoarse, shattered. "I understand. I understand why you've done it. Let's just all calm down. We're going to go get the police around, explain everything. You need help."

"Police? Did you say call the police?" Devon cupped his ear with a hand. "How boring! And I thought you had some scriptwriting talent. No one will buy it! I'm deeply disappointed."

"Devon," Alistair shouted. "There's a letter..."

"A letter?" Devon knelt quickly, picked up a rock, hurled it toward Alistair in a burst of rage. Alistair ducked, turned his head, shielding Terri.

"What the fuck, Devon!" shouted Alistair, pointing the gun. "No more! It ends now."

Devon put his fist to his forehead. "I have an alternative to your police ending. Either you shoot me or I'll kill you both. Choices, Alesandro, you have to offer choices. Don't think I made you read *Dice Man* for nothing."

Alistair gestured again with the gun. "Don't be insane, Devon. Nobody's killing anybody. Let's just go back into the house."

Devon picked up another rock, took more careful aim and threw it hard. Alistair recoiled as it struck him flush on the thigh.

"I'm not afraid to die!" Devon shouted. "Life's not been exactly golden for me. Perhaps you'll put me out my misery. Be brave, Alesandro. You know you want to do it."

Alistair turned to Terri, gripped her by the shoulders, looked into her face. She trembled uncontrollably, face streaked with tears. He felt a hardness well through him. Could he pull the trigger to save her? He felt the steel of the gun in his hand, looked down at it. Was the safety catch on?

Behind them, Devon took a step forward. "OK. No choices. You shoot me. Bang bang! A sure thing. But with a catch..." He knelt down and picked up a large rock of limestone, lifted it above his head. His shirt flapped up, the scars on his body an obscene sight in the flickering torchlight. "I'm coming for you. If you don't hit me, I'll kill you both with my bare hands."

"Devon!" Alistair's body was rigid, his call a plea and a warning in one, the gun swaying in his hand.

"I've done it before and I'll do it again!" Devon roared. "My uncle, my lover, my housemate, other perverts, assholes, druggies. It's no loss to the world. I was doing everyone a favor!" He took a step forward. "But the star and the princess—that wouldn't be nice, would it? You must shoot me. You have no option."

Another step, then a loud crack as Alistair raised the gun above his head, firing into the darkness, the sound quickly lost in the chaos of the elements. He lowered the gun, aimed it at Devon's chest. "One more step and I swear..."

The rock hung in the air above Devon, his eyes wide and wild, the manic grin unmoving. He advanced.

"Shoot him, Alistair!" screamed Terri. "He's crazy. Shoot him!"

"Shoot me! Shoot me!"

Alistair aimed and fired. Devon halted in his tracks, dropped one hand, held the rock above his head with the other.

"Oh dear," said Devon. "You missed. Take another shot. Aim carefully this time."

Alistair fired again. Devon didn't flinch.

"Not a very good shot, Alesandro," Devon laughed, patting his body for bullet wounds. "Three more..."

Alistair and Terri took a step backwards. One step closer to the edge. The gun sunk down to Alistair's side, resigned. Devon had stitched him up.

"And now?" laughed Devon. "Giving up?" Devon hurled the boulder sideways; it pitched and rolled over the edge, disappeared into the void below, lost in the sound of the roaring sea.

"Devon," said Alistair, voice barely audible. "Don't do this."

"Isn't this what you planned? You and that little bitch. Fuck, Alesandro. The first girl you've ever loved. Surprise! I read your little note. I knew she was going to be trouble,"

You're the first girl I have ever loved. He'd meant it. He could feel it now course through him as she clung to him in fear, emotion bursting from him. Anger? Fear? Or the realization that he might never fulfill that love?

The moment of impact, as the cameras rolled.

"Your faces!" Devon shouted. "Priceless! Let me guess what you're thinking now, lover boy. If I placed the letter under the door then, yes, I read the other letter. A sorry little confession. For attention, the authorities. Who're the fucking authorities? They never helped me."

Alistair felt a sudden fury overwhelm. He raised the gun again and fired the remaining blanks into the air, venting his rage. The sound vanished into the night, Devon laughing hysterically as Alistair tossed the impotent gun to the ground.

"The look in your eyes, it's beautiful...The anger, the helplessness. What's going on? Why can't you think straight? You think I'd give you a gun with live bullets? You've been taking too many pills, my friend. They've distorted your reality." Devon's voice dripped with glee. "And that, my stars, is the end of scene one."

Devon reached behind him, pulled out the second .38 Special from the back of his pants. He was calmer now, more subdued. "Now for scene two. Either of you ever seen someone shot before? A real shooting? Watched a bullet hit a body in slow motion? There's no blood spurting. Not like the movies. You see nothing. But if you watch the face...I'm shot! People pay millions for that. I'm going to show you, Terri. This gun's got real bullets. You can have the honor of watching me shoot your boyfriend. You can see the expression on his face."

Terri's hand searched for Alistair's as she clung to him.

Devon released the gun barrel, popped out a bullet and held it up before them, then tossed it at their feet. "Take a look if you want, Terri. Picture the bullet ripping into Alistair's flesh, tearing at his body..."

"No!" Terri screamed. "Please don't hurt him. Don't hurt us."

"That's more like it, girl. Bring out the drama. Now, Alesandro, you got any final wishes? Perhaps a confession—or regrets for your actions? Don't worry, I'll edit it."

Terri threw her arms around Alistair, her head buried into his chest. "We must get away," she whispered.

"There's no way out. There are cliffs on both sides."

"Just jump then..."

"What are you two whispering about?" Devon shouted. "Thinking up a good line? Thinking of an apology?"

Alistair heard the voice of his father.

Oh Allie...

No, Dad. No. Don't go so close to the edge.

Nonsense, it's fine!

"Say something, Alistair! Say you're sorry!" The glee from Devon's interrogation had suddenly vanished, replaced with rage, sadness. "We could have been such a good team. I've watched you closely. I know you so well—I've loved you..."

"Jesus, Devon."

"Not my first, but a love. You would never have known. Too oblivious, too self centered. All the little things I've done for you have had meaning..."

Alistair wasn't sure of what he was hearing. Devon's voice had quietened, the wind stealing his words into the night. Could this be true? Was this final confirmation of his madness, of his fracture from reality? Perhaps he wasn't here; this wasn't happening to him, the ultimate bad dream.

Dad, no please. You're too close.

Too close? I'm miles away!

The cocking of the gun barrel snapped him back.

"Surely you two want to know the script, what happens next? It's the *Dice Man*. A roll of the dice to decide. Let's see. One, I shoot Alistair while Terri watches. Two, I shoot Terri while Alistair watches. Three, I shoot you both simultaneously. Four, I crush your heads with this rock. Five, can't think of anything..."

Alistair shook his head.

Concentrate, he implored, delving into his confused mind. Keep thinking.

"Devon, we can work something out, speak to Carlos. We must let Terri go. I'll buy back the video. No matter what the cost."

Devon laughed.

"You're a real operator, Alesandro. Now the chips are down, you negotiate. How about Five, I let you both go. It's a one-in-six chance. Russian Roulette."

"You're fucking insane, Devon."

"Such language. Not like you, Alesandro. You'll be sorry you said that. No more negotiations, then. Six, I push you off the cliff."

Don't step back. Dad! Please!

Oh, oh. No!

"Not the cliff!" screamed Alistair. "Please, Devon. Anything but the cliff."

Devon's face lit up. Alistair touched Terri's hand.

"Of course," Devon cried, his face lighting up. "You're scared of heights, Alesandro. An incident in the past. Funny how our past haunts us, isn't it? OK. Scrap the cliff. I'll think of something."

"You're crazy," screamed Terri.

"Crazy? I'll show you crazy. Six, push both of you off." Devon shook his head from side to side, spread his arms wide. "Can a crazy person weave such an intricate plot as this? Can he achieve what I've achieved in the last year? Do you know who put Johnny onto Mangle?"

Mangle, Dark Video, thought Alistair. What was real?

"Me!" Devon continued. "Because I'm fucking Mangle. Now, you didn't know that, did you, Alesandro? I've been playing everyone! Carlos, Johnny, Richard, you..."

The whipping wind dropped suddenly, a cloud shifted and a sliver of moon sliced through the darkness.

"I am Mangle," Devon repeated. "And soon I'll be Dark Video."

"Carlos will get you," Alistair said softly, trying to distract Devon, trying to keep the conversation going.

Devon sneered. "Carlos is the shit on my shoes and I'm going to take him down."

"But no one knows where he lives..."

"That's what he thinks, too! But we found him. In Seattle. And when I'm done here, I'm going to pay him a visit and introduce him to my friend here." Devon waved the gun in the air. "And then I'm going after his clients. A crusade, if you will."

"How much, Devon? How much is it worth, Dark Video?"

"Money. You think I did it for the money?" Devon seemed to relax. "It doesn't hurt though. Dollars! Five hundred for *Grey Suit*, fifty for *Brain Drain*, fifty or a hundred for this one. Maybe something extra from Terri's private client?"

Dad!

You should have seen your face, Alistair! You should have seen the expression on your face when you thought I'd gone over. Alistair?

"Devon. You can't do this. I want to get off this cliff now."

The wind had returned, sand stinging their legs, Alistair and Terri braced against its force.

Devon wiped his fringe from his face and checked his watch.

"Four minutes and counting. A bestseller is less than five minutes long. Just enough tension....Otherwise the client's interest wanes. They fast-forward."

"You'll be caught, Devon. People know we're here."

"Who cares?" He reached into his pocket and flashed an air ticket. "Cape Town to Seattle via London, leaving this morning. Then a hired car to Yarrow Point. I'll be Dark Video in no time. I'll have the list of every sick fucking person in the world."

"You're the sick one!"

Devon's grin disappeared again. "*I'm* sick? Don't antagonize me, Alesandro. There's always the cliff. Let me tell you something. Sick is a man who burns a boy with a cigar, who films it, who shows it to his friends. The guy who runs Dark Video is sick. Dark Video's clients are sick..."

"But you want to take over from Carlos?"

"You stupid fool. Haven't you worked it out yet? I've been making videos to fund my crusade. The irony is glorious: Dark Video's clients are paying for their own deaths. Two gone so far—their mistake to sign with Mangle as well. And when I own Dark Video, I'll have all the names. No one will be safe."

"It's not true," said Terri, her voice strong. "You're continuing the cycle. You're doing to others what has been done to you."

Devon's smile returned. "Isn't that the scripture? Do unto others... No matter. I've come to enjoy seeing my own expression on the face of others. Their moment of terror is my moment shared. The man who burnt me with a cigar and showed the world; he is everywhere. I'll find him. I'll find them all."

"Devon. Let us help you," pleaded Terri.

"Let us? Us? You're a couple now? But you can't help yourselves. It could've been different, Alesandro. It could've been..."

"Please don't hurt us," she continued.

"Alesandro, you and I had something..."

"You disgust me!" Alistair shouted.

"Please, Devon, please!" Terri begged.

"Oh. I like that. I like pleading. You don't need a script in this business. It's perfect. I disgust you? Alistair, you're so brave..." Devon paused, closed his eyes. "You had everything. Now you'll find out what it feels like to be the burned boy."

"No, please. Not the cliff, Devon, please." Alistair fell down on his knees.

"Get up. For god's sake, Alistair, get up," said Terri, pulling at his arm. She looked down at him; his blue eyes were clear and sparkling.

"Shut the fuck up!" shouted Devon. He raised the gun, took a step forward.

"You're disgusting, Devon! You're insane, you killed your own lover, you're a murderer." Alistair scrambled back a pace, looked nervously behind him, clutching Terri's arm.

Devon stopped, laughed out aloud. "Brilliant. You've given me the title of the video: *Fear of Heights*. Keep going!"

"No, Devon. Not the cliff!"

"Please, Devon. He's pulling me," Terri screamed. "Not the cliff! He's terrified of heights."

"Keep going!" Devon gestured with the gun. "Keep going. I love it!"

How did you know where it was, Dad? How did you know without look-ing? If you'd missed it by a meter, you would have been over the edge."

Easy, son. You line up the cairn of stones with the beacon. The center is the ledge.

"No!" screamed Alistair. The silhouette of the beacon threw a diagonal line toward the cairn.

"Beautiful! Beautiful! This is fear, this is Hollywood. Farewell, lovers." Devon banged on his chest.

Alistair and Terri reached the edge of the precipice.

"Go! Jump!"

They stepped back, tottered, and fell backwards.

$\odot$

The wind whipping over the edge of the cliff roared with a life of its own, pummeling them in the darkness. Below them, the sea raged, thundering against the rocks. Terri and Alistair sat holding each other tightly, not wanting to let go, never wanting to let go.

Then a scream nearby, wild and incoherent, and an object plummeted over the sandy ledge, flailing into the night, the terror in their ears for an instant—before the sound was lost in the wind.

"What was that?" Terri whispered.

"Shhh!"

They heard a high pitched whistle, a sea shanty. "What can we do with a drunken sailor? What can we do with a drunken sailor..."

Terri and Alistair pressed flush against the cliff. Alistair's thoughts swam

---

with images of the raging sea below. Would he look over the edge?

⊙

"Eh, Carlos?"

The voice crackled over the line: "Yes."

"It's the Chestwound here, man."

Warnabrother had to shout into the cellphone to be heard above the buffeting wind.

"Samuel. Not the best time to be calling..." He'd just watched the wife hightailing it out the drive, baby in tow. Turned out she didn't have the fortitude of the first wife. First time she'd taken a fist and she was running off to her folks. "This better be good."

"Don't worry, you'll 'preciate this call."

"Where are you anyway? What's that noise?"

"It's the sea, man. And the wind. You wouldn't believe it if I told you but it's fucking *Wuthering Heights* here. I been sweeping up."

"And?" This had better be good, thought Carlos as he ran a hand down his bare chest. Goddamned ingrown hairs everywhere.

"Your boy, with the polo neck—I been following him. He led me to the golden boy, you know? And I must say the little golden girl, in person, she's very tidy too. If she weren't so pale..."

"The news, Samuel, the news."

"So anyway. As I see it. Polo neck boy is all set to do the sweeping himself. He's got a gun. And he's got the goldies backed against the cliff, right. Then he starts to give 'em a little confession."

"Confession?" Carlos looked at himself in the full length mirror. Thousands on laser already and the fucking hair was everywhere.

"Yeah. Turns out he's the sick motherfucker that's been taking out our clients. If you know what I mean."

"Go on..."

"And then he says..." Warnabrother broke into a dry laugh. "He's freaking Mangle and he's gonna get on a plane to Seattle and come see you personally, like. You know. As in, see you."

"My, my..." Carlos wiggled his limp member in his hand. He checked himself again in the mirror, felt the organ move. I like the hair, he told himself.

"So here's the funny bit. After he's seen goldies over the hill and into the sea, he steps forward to like admire his handiwork. I see my window of opportunity and I grab him from behind. PUSH. SHOVE. Oops, over you go, polo neck boy."

"So there are three cracked eggs, I take it." Carlos felt himself growing, slipped his hand down.

"Right. But you shoulda seen his surprise. It was beautiful, man. I spun him around, let him work it out for a second. If I coulda taken a picture of his face, I tell you."

"Good work, Samuel. And the bodies?"

"Man, you gotta see this place. Down below there's a pool more wicked than a witch's cauldron. It's a fucking blender down there."

"I like it. I like it." Carlos increased the tempo.

"And here's for the very good part..."

"There's more?"

"You betcha. And this part's so good, you're gonna want to put me on that Caribbean cruise with ten of them pretty girls I been telling you about."

"I can't wait." Carlos had a rhythm going.

"The little beauty, polo neck boy, he filmed the whole fucking thing! *Fear of Heights*!"

"Beautiful. Bring it to me when you return. I've got to go."

The call cut off. Carlos looked down. He didn't need that bitch anyway.

$\odot$

Terri shivered on the ledge. Alistair pulled her head against his chest, rocking her.

"Shhh."

Above their heads, the whistling started up again, before disappearing into the wind. "Shave his belly with a rusty razor, shave his belly with a rusty razor..."

THE VOYEUR

John Morgan checked through his diary. Two board meetings, a golf day, a day trip to Durban, family dinner, lunch with colleagues. A busy week ahead—as per usual.

He pushed his chair back and rubbed his hand across his face, surveying his office domain: plush leather chairs, dark mahogany bookcase, thick oak door, closed, heavy burgundy drapes, drawn.

The flickering screen on his computer monitor showed a young girl naked in a forest; she was trying to retrieve her shorts from the branch of a tree. Morgan licked his lips, looked away, and closed his eyes. He'd watched the clip a hundred times. Her beautiful, anguished face was imprinted in his desire; perfect little body, taut ass as she strained on her tiptoes. He wondered who she was, where she was from. She could be on the other side of the world, for all he knew, or the girl next door—Carlos never gave away his operational details, no matter how much he pried. But he had promised him a keepsake, a piece of her clothing for his collection.

Beyond the room he could hear music filtering down the corridor— Glenda playing music in the living room. Her eyes would no doubt be closed, lips moving slowly with the words, lost in another world, years gone by, little children's voices tinkling, clinging onto the hem of her skirt. His precious Glenda.

He reached down to open a drawer, extracted a Cuban cigar from a wooden box. Clipped and lit, he sucked quickly to ignite the draw. His eye had caught an overturned photo frame in the drawer. He lifted it out, placed it on the desk: a color picture of him with Alistair, no older than eight, side by side; a contrast between the dark tanned features of the father and the golden sunshine hue of the only son. Alistair would be arriving soon from Cape Town, a welcome last-minute visit. Something important to discuss with him in person. Cloak and dagger stuff clearly...

John Morgan smiled at the thought. He sat inhaling the cigar's blend, deep thoughtful draws, eyes reflecting on the photograph, his own muscled body, and then Alistair, distinctly his child, but with a lightness, a gentleness. Alistair's sunshine came from his mother; she'd given him that aura of purity.

He put the photo frame back in the drawer, tapped his fingers on the desk. The white light from the desk lamp struggled through a cloud of smoke. Time to make a call.

He clipped on the encryption device and lifted the handset to his ear.

Thirty seconds later, on the other side of the world, a reciprocal device linked to a home computer registered the call, identifying "MorganJ-SAfrica."

"John. Been a while," said a voice.

"Hello, Carlos. How are you keeping?"

"Never been better, my friend. Business is booming."

"Good to hear it. No more trouble from"—Morgan searched for an appropriate word—"the authorities?"

Carlos snorted with disdain. "All clear for the time being. They're about a year behind us."

"When are they going to learn?"

"Oh, I think they're learning. They're learning that they'll never be able to close us down."

John Morgan laughed in admiration. He loved the small talk and Carlos was happy to oblige.

"We don't exist. Physically, that is. Anywhere in the world there's a computer, we're there. There's no way to erase us. And if they do, someone else will just step in to fill the gap. The market demands it!"

"Of course we do!" Morgan leaned back in his chair, drew heavily on his cigar. The internet was truly a marvel, he mused, a neverending source of opportunity and entertainment.

"And how is life down in Africa, John?"

That was the difference between Carlos and the other operators out there. The net was home to so many amateurs, anonymous and ethereal, but Carlos had never forgotten his customers. That's why he was king. The personal touch.

"I need something good, Carlos. Something real good." John Morgan stroked the receiver against his cheek.

"Great timing, John, I've got just the thing for you. Took a while getting here and I've just finished touching it up, but I think you'll find it was worth the wait. You're going to love this one."

"OK, don't keep me hanging—what is it?"

"It's a thriller. Your favorite actress in a starring role."

"The forest girl! You're kidding?"

"Not a bit. And it's good, John. It's exceptional. No holding back this time. I've got a few clients who would love to get their hands on it..."

"No! This one's mine. I'm online right now, let me have it."

"It's going to cost you."

"Has that ever been an issue?"

"Two hundred."

"Steep....It had better be good. And it's my exclusive, you hear?"

"Absolutely. The code's on its way, low res and full download."

John Morgan replaced the receiver, sat up. His hands shook with excitement. On his desk, his cellphone beeped: two sets of numbers appeared. He couldn't wait for the high res download; he had to see the video right away. He quickly typed in the first code. Enter.

The request fired down the telephone line at the speed of light, disappeared into the computer ether, a digital key to an intangible lock. From deep in the bowels of a computer somewhere, an instruction fired off to another computer, then another and another, until it reached a target, delved into the quagmire to retrieve the demon, free it, unleashed a constant stream of information, ones and zeroes, slipped them onto the network like a curling viper, slithering from hop to hop until it reached its destination.

Within seconds, the Windows Media Player on John Morgan's monitor materialized. Morgan pursed his lips and swallowed. The heat came to his cheeks, to his loins, flowed through his veins.

A message appeared: "Buffering 50%."

He took a deep breath.

Another: "Buffering 90%."

The play button appeared below a black screen. He pointed the cursor and jabbed.

On screen, images appeared of a windy precipice swept by a bright light. He could make out the sound of waves crashing onto rocks.

Inaudible words in the background, then a man's voice. "Take your clothes off!" The camera pans to two figures huddled together at the edge of a cliff. In front, the girl—his girl—blindfolded. Beautiful, fragile. Terrified.

John Morgan felt a shiver of pleasure run down his spine.

The girl raises her hands to her face, removes the cloth across her eyes. Another cry: "No! Not yet!" Then the figure in the rear comes into focus, a young man's face.

"My god!" shouted John Morgan. "Alistair!"

There was a knock on the study door.

Morgan killed the video, wiped the perspiration from his face, his mind racing, heart a jackhammer.

"Yes?"

"John," said his wife, pushing the door open. "Alistair's here. He's brought his new girlfriend Terri to meet us."

⊙

ALSO BY PETER CHURCH

Available in North America
and South Africa in 2019
by Catalyst Press

CRACKERJACK

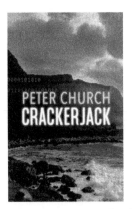

Young, bright and sexy, Carla Vitale has been handpicked to run Supertech, Africa's leading independent Engineering firm. Then one Friday afternoon in Cape Town, her dream is shattered. Her boss and mentor, Nial Townley, disappears, his luxury vehicle is found in a crevice at the bottom of Chapman's Peak and 20 million US dollars are missing from the Supertech's overseas accounts. Three months later and the police are no closer to solving the riddle.

No job, no car, no phone, Carla turns to the one person she believes can help: software hacker turned day trader, Daniel Le Fleur. But Le Fleur's maintaining a low profile in Bantry Bay and he's in no mood to ruin the serendipity.

"Crackerjack is a smart, cleverly plotted thriller that takes readers into the darker corners of the digital world. South African novelist Peter Church has created a great protagonist in hacker/day trader Daniel Le Fleur."
  - JAMES LILLIEFORS, author of *THE LEVIATHAN EFFECT* and *THE PSALMIST*

"All the more impressive when considering that Crackerjack is author Peter Church's debut as crime novelist to an American readership, this impressively original and deftly crafted paperback will prove to be an immediate and enduringly popular addition to community library collections and the personal reading list."
  - MIDWEST BOOK REVIEW

ALSO BY PETER CHURCH

Available in North America and South Africa in 2019 by Catalyst Press

BITTER PILL

Inside the heaving party hub that is Cape Town's student playground, someone is preying on the young and unwary. As allegations of drink spiking and illicit sex hit the local papers, university authorities move quickly to limit the damage.

A world away in Seattle, Carlos De Palma, the shadowy operator behind Dark Video, is plotting his survival strategy in the ever changing Internet landscape. With his precious clients clamoring for heightened thrills, Carlos begins tapping into a new service that blurs the boundaries between the real and virtual worlds.

Enter Robbie Cullen, nice guy and average student, dumped by his girlfriend and struggling with grades. But when it comes to the crunch, Robbie doesn't know the meaning of stepping back. Once he encounters the beautiful and mysterious Fallon, his small town bravado is set to make him some powerful enemies.

Bitter Pill is a gripping thriller that sweeps through the intoxicating haunts of Cape Town's nightlife and lingers on the sugary sand of Plettenberg Bay —before exploding on the streets of the Mother City's exclusive southern suburbs.

Past Praise for Peter Church

"Extraordinary characters thrive in the dark world of drugs, blackmail, violence and sex... Church is a master storyteller."
- DIES BRUNT, *CITIZEN*

peterchurch.bookslive.co.za/bitter-pill

PETER CHURCH

Peter Church is a Cape Town-based writer.

After a successful career in Information Technology, Church's first novel *Dark Video* (2008) was published by Random-Struik in South Africa and New Holland Publishers in Australia. Reviewed as 'one of the best debuts in a long time' by Lindsay Slogrove of *The Natal Mercury*, *Dark Video* was a Sunday Times "Book of the Week."

In 2011, Church followed up with the "drink spiking" book *Bitter Pill*. *Cosmopolitan* magazine's "Hot Read of the Month," the plot was described by Gillian Hurst of The Drum as "adrenalin-laced, [the] gritty (plot) will keep you furiously turning pages long after your bedtime." *Bitter Pill* was nominated for the 2012 Sunday Times fiction prize.

In 2015 Two Dogs published *Blue Cow Sky*, a novella of sexual proportions.

Peter Church is a member of SA Pen and the Kimberley Club. His acclaimed sporting articles are featured on M&G's *Sports Leader* site.

A short story, *The One*, about compulsive love, appeared in a compilation of South African crime fiction called *Bad Company*. Another shortie, *My Side*, was selected for the annual Short Sharp Story collection *Bloody Satisfied*, edited by Joanne Hichens.

Peter lives in Cape Town with his wife Paula and three children Christopher, Megan, and Ross.

CPSIA information can be obtained
at www.ICGtesting.com
Printed in the USA
FSHW010912300919

2 370000 668219